The Flight Across Europe

High Crimes Against the Crown Book II

Patrick DeVaney

Contents

DEDICATION

Deacon Elliott A Shaw

This book is dedicated to the loving memory of Elliot Allen Shaw. Some knew him as Ell. Others called him Dad, Grandpa, Shawzee, or Poppy. Many more referred to him as Deacon.

The Lord called Elliott home in December of 2022. His bags were packed, and it was time for him to join his wife and son along with many family and friends he loved so much.

He was my brother-in-law, my second father, my buddy, my teammate, my golf and fishing buddy, and most of all, my friend. He truly was one of a kind. After marrying my sister Peggy, he joined the army. The newlyweds moved to the site of his first posting, Niagara Falls, NY.

Over the years and six kids later, he was a mechanic, a tax assessor, our Little League coach, and a deacon. He started his faith journey in 1983. Well into his studies, Peg and Ell lost their son Jeffrey, a dark and tragic time. Despite the gloom, Ell and Peggy believed what is written, "The people living in darkness will see a great light" and continued walking towards the light of God and his Church.

He was a giver. Whether it was a baptism, a funeral, an accident, standing with families in their time of need, or being present for anyone needing some words of wisdom, you could always count on Deacon Elliott.

As Elliott moved deeper into the formation of his faith, I brought him into my decision making. When forced with a tough decision, I would say, "What would Elliott do?" Throughout the years, "WWED" helped our family as well as the thousands of lives he touched.

Elliott, my brother, until we meet again.

Slainte!

CHAPTER ONE

The sun kept rising and the little fishing vessel chugged east. The rank smell of diesel exhaust made me wonder about the survival chances of the poor guy in charge of the engines. Striped dolphins raced alongside the fishing boat. Might have been a beautiful day if my life weren't so fouled up.

I felt the same way I had the first day of junior high: alone...and stupid. I sped-read the highlights of last few months:

- Curb stomped by an escaped felon.

- Indefinite leave from the Fort Henry (New York) Police Department.

- Trip to Ireland with my best friend Alec.

- Led into a band of Irish freedom fighters by instincts south of my belt.

- Charged with the murder of a British soldier. (I didn't do it, but doesn't everyone claim innocence?)

- Hiding in plain sight on the Camino de Santiago.

- Treachery...deceit...a narrow escape...and now...

Lucky licked my hand. I quit staring at the endless horizon and knelt. His brown eyes looked at me with a mixture of compassion and concern.

"I'm okay, buddy," I said. "I'm okay."

He cocked his head.

"You don't give a crap about me right now, do you?" I asked. "You're hungry, aren't you?"

Damn! My inner alarm jangled. *Watch the accent. You're not Conor Caldemeyer from the U.S.*

I could hear Bump's voice in my head. "Ye're Ryan Murphy from Dingle, Ireland." I touched my cheek where he'd slapped me when I protested. "It's who ya are. Do not forget it for a skinny minute. The Brits never forget—and they never forgive. Whatever really happened, they believe you killed a solider in Her Majesty's Army. They have informants and agents everywhere. Everywhere, I tell ya. The bartender who asks if ya want another, the kid who sells ya a bocadillo on the street, the fella traveler who strikes up a conversation. And when the next cute colleen drops her bloomers for ya, it won't be because ye're so damn charmin'. Let down your guard once and ya could be dead. If the Brits can't getcha somewhere with an extradition treaty, they'll content themselves with having someone put a bullet in yer head."

Bile rose in my throat before I could combat it and I retched over the stern. I heaved twice more before cupping a handful of salt water into my mouth, rinsing and spitting. I read the name of the boat upside down.

"*The Perchance*," I said to Lucky. "Seems about right for me to be on a boat named *The Mishap*."

Lucky nudged my leg. He was far more interested in breakfast than impressed by my rudimentary grasp of Spanish.

CHAPTER TWO

Lucky chomped away at whatever was in his bowl. It looked a lot like what I'd discharged over the stern and smelled like week-old fish, but Lucky chowed down like he was dining on a porterhouse.

I wonder if he remembers I saved his life, or if he would leave me for the next bowl of kibble.

I sat on the deck with my back against the portside wall—or whatever it was called—and tried to get myself together. Eventually someone was going to expect me to do something to earn my passage across the Atlantic, and when they told me to "Hoist the mainsail" or "Shiver me timbers" or something else I would not understand, I couldn't be fouling the deck with whatever was left in my churning stomach.

How did my life get so fucked up?

I decided to focus on the last twenty-four hours and work backward. Less than a full day ago, I was having a celebratory dinner with my girlfriend and a collection of newly minted Camino friends. Everything was just ducky until twangy-tongued Bump Olimeyer, garrulous host and former chicken feed manufacturer, switched to a brogue thicker than an Irish stew and disclosed he was, in fact, Oisin Byrne of the Green Liberation Front. His deception would not have thrown me so badly had he not also mentioned that Michiko, the raven-haired Asian beauty who had assumed the label of the latest "love of my life," was Major Ara Park of the South Korean National Intelligence Service, on loan to MI5 for the sole purpose of locating me and returning my well-toned ass (a 500-mile, thirty-five-day hike does wonders for the glutes) to England so Her Majesty could string me up like a prize capon.

Mom had been so happy when I decided to go to the old country with Alec. "The rest will do you good," she had said. She envisioned green hills, rolling pastures, and legions of sheep. She was not naïve enough to believe there would not also be rivers of Guinness and more than a jigger or twelve of good Irish whiskey, but in her wildest imaginings, she would never have foreseen the nightmare my life would become.

I was on the run. And if Bump/Oisin were to be believed, I would be on the run for as long as I drew breath.

Mom kept vigil at my hospital bedside from the moment Chief Longo informed her of the roadside assault until the day Dad wheeled me up the drive and helped me limp into the house. She'd hated my decision to become a cop, and I know damn well she prayed the rosary every day and asked the Blessed Virgin not to grant my life's ambition—to wear the Smokey Bear hat and mirrored sunglasses of a New York State Trooper. Her standing with the Heavenly Mother was obviously better than mine. She granted Mom's wish to get me out of law enforcement. My humble requests of starring in center field for the Yankees and marrying Raquel Welch were never so much as acknowledged.

Mom's face came into sharp focus in my head—the stunned look on her face when she learned (surely by now she knew) I had been charged with murdering a member of the British Army. And while I hoped with all my heart she would never believe her "little Conor" could do anything so heinous, somewhere deep inside, I heard her voice: "Well, he had so many bad blows to his head."

Mother's horrified expression gave way to another image of disappointed astonishment: Gwendolyn's. She had stared at the paper bearing the legend "Declaration of Major: SUNY – Oswego." I'd scrawled Criminal Justice. I could sense her disappointment even though she kissed me on the head. And I saw the evidence of her disapproval when I awakened the next morning in our off-campus apartment bed, and she was gone.

There had been other girls...then women...but no one captured my heart. I was not about to let someone Cuisinart my soul again. Well, not until I met Billi (ne. Wilhelmina)...and then Danielle (but any man would fall for a woman who saved his life, lived by herself in the woods, was gorgeous (and breathed))...and then Michiko.

God, Conor...no Ryan—fuck—Ryan...your name is Ryan. So—my God, Ryan, you are a hopeless romantic.

She'd broken my heart, Michiko. Hell, anyone who'd taken Psychology 101 would recognize she was a Far Eastern version of Gwendolyn, but I'd thrown caution—and warnings—to the wind and gone all in. Her companionship (well, that's the word I would have used with Mom even though Dad would have smirked while he sipped his Black Label) made the long Camino pilgrimage bearable.

"Maybe she loved me," I said.

Lucky looked at me with his deep, German Shepherdy eyes, deep pools of "What are you, an idiot?"

I simply did not want to believe the woman who had made love to me in a Spanish stream was the most accomplished liar I'd ever met. Damn, I thought she was for real—I wanted to believe she cared about me. No, I *needed* her to care about me—stranger in a strange land that I had become.

Lucky was still looking at me, his head to one side.

"I know what ye're thinkin', lad," I said, this time remembering I was supposed to be Irish. "Yer glad old Bumpo was a' watchin' me because I'm too daft to keep me mouth shut and me fly closed."

CHAPTER THREE

"Hey Hollywood, those nets aren't going to fold themselves. Get cracking mate." The voice came from an old codger on the bridge leaning on the helm. An Aussie? A Kiwi? I couldn't tell. I looked around. There were others—real sailors all—but none responded to his screech.

"Ya talkin' to me, old timer?" I asked.

"Yeah you, Hollywood," he said. "Time to pay your passage. And mind your pooch. You're gonna have a bitch of a time cleaning his piss out of my nets."

"Sorry 'bout Lucky," I said, "but you've no privy aboard."

"Hold him over the side," he said, "especially if he has to bog. Not having him going to the dunny all over the place."

"He weighs over four stone," I said.

"Then don't drop him," he said. "Sharks will finish him off before you can jump in."

Lucky looked at me with wide eyes as if he understood.

"I'll clean up his messes," I said. "And why t'hell ya callin' me Hollywood? Ain't a Yank, ya know."

"Don't know who the hell you are," he said, "And I don't wanna know. My instructions are to take you off the mainland and out of sight where nobody can find you. You're either some famous John Wayne type, or you're a criminal on the run. So, what are you, Hollywood, a killer or a cowboy?"

"Where are ya takin' me?"

"South." He looked down as if checking a bearing. Then he was back at me. "In the meantime, mind the frickin' nets."

"What do ya fancy catchin', captain?" I asked.

"Pilchards. What the Yanks call sardines. They come to the surface at night to feed on plankton."

He could tell I was disgusted. I was still probably a little green.

"Sonny boy, they are smelly and disgusting, but they afford me this luxurious life." He swept his hand over the deck like a monarch showing off his kingdom.

Something came flying at my head. I snatched it out of the air before it collided with my skull. Could barely hit my weight in high school baseball, but I made All-Conference with my defense. I could still pick it.

Red can...white lettering...five stars under the name: Mahou, a fine Spanish ale. I popped the tab and took a pull. Cool but not cold.

Beer for breakfast, I thought. *How the mighty have fallen.*

The captain smiled and nodded. "You'll fit in, mate. Whoever the hell you are."

We floated and waited for darkness. After they prepared everything for the evening's activities, the crew sat on the deck and swapped stories. Oil Can bragged about robbing banks in the Mediterranean Islands; Barbell claimed he'd gunned down a pimp in a bar fight in Bangkok. My favorite psycho, Billiards, had built a reputation as a mercenary. He'd carry a gun for anyone and any cause willing to pay. Even though I'd spent time with Irish revolutionaries and a guy back in New York named Whirlybird Atkins, Billiards was the craziest man I'd ever met.

He talked about slicing his own doctor's jugular with a scalpel. "Sumbitch took out my 'pendix and left a nasty scar. Looks bad with my Speedo." Billiards tipped the scale at about the same weight as a middle-aged rhinoceros, so the image of him in a banana hammock frightened me more than the tale of butchery.

Captain Kiwi stood at the helm. Only once did he speak. Shorty said something about having a one-night stand with a well-known supermodel when he was on shore leave in Barbados. No one spoke until he mentioned how impressed the woman was by his "endowment." The captain's quiet voice echoed across the sea (he'd cut the engine). "Shorty, you couldn't impress a horny hamster with your pygmy pecker."

Everyone howled. Shorty acted hurt, then switched to another, equally unbelievable but highly entertaining myth of his sexual exploits.

Different breed of cats, I thought.

Michiko and Bump were tough, brave, and dedicated to a cause. The guys swilling beer and swapping lies on the deck of *The Perchance* were dangerous—and wary. Although they never stopped talking—or drinking—they noticed every vessel in the area. They recognized them all, other fishing boats that moored at a respectful distance to avoid fouling someone else's nets.

"Any of you criminals recognize the ship off the starboard bow?" the captain asked. He had his binoculars up to his eyes.

"Ain't a Seiner, that's for damn sure," Oil Can said. "Ain't no fishing boat a'tall. Looks more like an old Point-class."

"What the hell would a cutter be doing out here?" the captain asked.

I peered over the side. "Any flag?" I asked.

The captain scanned the ship again. "That's odd," he said. "They just struck their colors, but I could have sworn they were flying a Union Jack."

"Fuck!"

"Don't worry, mate," he said. "They try anything foolish, the fellas and I got your back."

Darkness tiptoed its way from the east. The crew members nursed their last beers and sang the traditional Toast to the Pilchards.

> Here's health to the Pope, may he live to repent,
> And add just six months to the term of his lent,
> And tell all his vassals from Rome to the Poles,
> There's nothing like pilchards for saving their souls!

CHAPTER FOUR

Darkness arrived around 2130 and the men transformed from a motley collection of tall tale spinners into a well-oiled machine. They spread the nets while I stood out of the way and marveled at their precision.

The nets hit the water and we waited. Shorty cranked up the far side of the net but left the side closest to the boat untouched. Oil Can whispered instructions to me.

"Line up...side by side...one-two-pull...one-two-pull."

When we could move the nets no further, the men hit the winches. Billiards pulled the release and hundreds of pounds of slimy, smelly sardines fell into the ice-lined hold. We repeated the process all night.

"What in blazes do ya do wid all the fishies?" I asked.

"A crew of Portuguese women will meet us at the shore in the morning," Shorty said. "They gut the fish, cover 'em in salt, and hang 'em on the beach to dry."

He was in the middle of explaining how the women were often willing to engage in extracurricular activities—"if you can find one who don't mind the smell of abalone"—when a sharp voice from the ocean lowered the temperature of my blood by about twenty degrees.

"Ship ahoy!"

John Bull, I thought. With instinct born of training and terror, I reached under my shirt for the pistol in the small of my back until I remembered I hadn't carried one since before walking the Camino.

"Don't fret, mate," the captain said. "It's not the Brits." He stepped toward the port rail where another ship was tying on, then looked back. "And if you're carrying a piece on my ship, you better ditch it. If I see it, you'll be shark bait before you can sing *God Save the Queen.*"

Lucky had snoozed throughout the evening, oblivious to the activity, but the second unfamiliar footfall sounded on the deck, he was awake and on guard. His growls and barks joined a chorus of voices speaking Spanish, Portuguese, Gaelic, English, and at least two other languages I could not identify. I heard the voice again. "Ryan Murphy, grab your shite, you're coming with us."

I looked at the captain. "All good, mate. My job was to get you into the open sea and determine if you had any interested parties. My boys were ready to defend you to the death if it came to that."

I stepped onto the gunwale. Strong hands grabbed me by the arms and lifted me aboard the other ship. I'm still not sure if he jumped or if someone picked him up, but Lucky joined me almost instantly. This second ship was running without lights. I could feel Lucky's breath on my arm, but I could barely make out his form. I heard the voice again—to my left.

"Whaddaya know about the Brit ship over there?"

"Probably less than anyone out here," I said.

A moment's hesitation. "You're either a wise guy or a dumbass. Either way, we got work to do. Sit here and shut up. If that pooch so much as whimpers, he's going over the side."

The ship pushed off. Fifty feet away from *The Perchance,* someone switched on the running lights. My eyes adjusted to the dim light, and I gasped. There were about a dozen men huddled below the ship's railing armed to the teeth. I saw several AK-47s and a few M-16s. As far as I could tell, each man had at least one handgun and three of them clutched M26 fragmentation grenades.

It was not a social call we were making.

I heard the captain hailing the British boat. He was speaking Portuguese. The conversation sounded friendly enough, but given my ignorance of all languages save English, my captain could have been calling the other guy a scum-sucking, snail-licking pig molester. My live fire experience was limited, but I'd played enough sports to recognize men in "go" mode. The guys at the rail were ready for a fight. One of them even slipped a stiletto between his teeth. The image was so out of an Errol Flynn movie I might have laughed had the situation not scared me to the point of nearly wetting myself.

I stole a glimpse over the railing, making sure to hold Lucky down. I didn't need him to think it was play time. We were about twenty feet away. I saw the guy next to me pull the pin on a grenade. He didn't release the spoon, and I hoped to God we did not hit sudden turbulence. I did not relish the idea of heaving overboard into dark waters where I was sure some large things with larger teeth were hoping for some loose sardines—or fugitives from justice—might provide a late-night snack.

The captain's voice echoed across the water. *"Obrigado. Boa not."*[1]

I relaxed when the pin slid back into the grenade, and I heard safeties click.

A shadow loomed over me. "We'll let those lads live another day. They're just having fun drinking some beers and fishing. Half of them are pissed drunk and passed out. The only thing they're searching for is tuna and a hangover. You're safe now, mate. You and your dog can get up."

"Where we headed?" I asked.

Suddenly, no one seemed to speak English. I heard one word. "Algarve."

I had no idea what an Algarve was or if it were a country, an island, another boat, or someone's name. I would soon find out. We sailed through the night and stopped south of Lisbon for more fuel. The engine was still running when Lucky bolted from the boat and raced for the nearest lamppost like Secretariat running for home at the Belmont. When we were topped off, we chugged back into the deep water. The sea was quiet, the sunrise spectacular.

I remembered another rising sun. It was a spring morning in New York. I stared out of the apartment window at the light dancing across Lake Ontario with a warm beer in one hand and my major declaration sheet in the other. I finished the beer, dropped the can and the university form in the trash, and went home—for good.

---

1. "Thanks. Good night."

A noise like a squawking sea bird brought me back to the present. I looked around—no birds. Lucky pawed at my leg and made the noise again.

"Damn, boy," I said. "Now you do impressions?"

I found the galley—wasn't hard, this was not the *QE II*. All Lucky had to do was show his face, now pitiful with near starvation (or his best impression thereof, at least) and the pup was soon gorging himself on bread, soup, and some form of poultry that I hoped was not related to the absence of avian activity around the ship.

Around noon we could see land again. The crew secured us at the dock while I stayed below as instructed. Through a small porthole, I could see the captain and a few of his men jibber-jabbering.

An hour later I was still belowdecks and starting to sweat. A black van pulled into the parking lot. Two men who could have started on the O-line for the New York Jets walked over to the captain. An envelope was passed, hands were shaken, and I was ordered ashore.

"Go with them," the captain said.

One of the no-necks pointed to Lucky and spoke to me with a thick, indecipherable accent. "Leaf da dug."

"We're a package," I said, not sure about the origin of my new-found cajones. "He comes or I stay."

The man uttered a two-word response that anyone can understand in any language, but the discussion about Lucky was over and he trotted along beside me towards the van. My new handlers spoke only Portuguese in the vehicle. I heard "Lagos" and assumed it was our destination.

The sign over the front door of the building where we stopped read "Dormitory Lagos." I congratulated myself on my superior translation skills. We walked down a set of stairs. Thing #2 knocked three times, paused, then knocked three times again. I was about to comment on the masterful code, but I'd been around enough thugs in the last few months to recognize when guys were "strapped." Besides, not everyone reacts well to sarcasm.

The door opened. Thing #2 pointed. Lucky and I entered. The door shut. I turned around to face the person who'd let us in.

"My name is Leonar."

If she had told me she was Miss Portugal 1976 I would have believed her. Olive complexion, onyx eyes, long jet-black hair parted in the middle, and—despite baggy khakis and her older brother's flannel shirt—a figure most centerfolds would have killed for.

"Where am I?" I asked. I was hoping my witty repartee would make her swoon.

Her smile was dazzling and more than a little unnerving. "This apartment will be your home as long as you are here."

"Sorry, darlin'," I said, "where is here?"

"Algarve." She noticed the same blank expression most of my college professors had seen. "We are on the southern tip of Portugal. The area was first settled about three thousand years ago. Everyone's been here: the Phoenicians, the Romans, the Greeks, the Celts, and the Moors. Because of that, we have unique food that I am sure you will love, and a very diverse population. You'll like it here."

I'd already noticed her skin. Now I thought I could make out the hint of a Roman nose.

"Not sure why I'm here," I said.

"Mr. Murphy—"

"Call me Ryan, love."

"Well Ryan, I can't answer because I don't know your circumstances. My employer is well connected globally. When certain people have certain needs, they contact him. Historically, the Algarve's been the place where outlaws hide when they need to. Are you some sort of outlaw, Ryan Murphy?"

I did my best to sound genuine when I laughed. Not sure if she bought it. "Of course not, darlin'," I said. "I'm a victim o' mistaken identity. But no one had the grace t' let me plead me case." I paused because her face showed no expression. "Sorry, I do tend to go on. Diarrhea of the mouth, you know."

"Oh my goodness, you have diarrhea in your mouth? How foul!"

Now my laughter rang with a hint of veracity. "No, no." I held up my hands. "Just a way of sayin' I talk too much."

"Thank God," she said. She crossed herself. The look on her face told me that whatever inappropriate daydreams I was starting to have about her were not going to come to fruition. She gathered herself, shook a little like a dog after a bath, and stared at me with *those eyes*. She handed me a small cardboard box.

"Ryan, after I leave, you can open this. Inside are escudos—local currency. About fifty U.S. dollars. There is also a key to this apartment, emergency contact numbers, a Portuguese passport, and instructions for your new job."

"New job?" My confusion was growing more profound with each conversation. "I figured this was a way station—a stopover. How long am I here for?"

"I have no idea," Leonar said. "I'm just a go-between. There aren't many jobs here for people who aren't multilingual."

Hell, I can barely remember which flavor of English I'm supposed to be speaking.

"So, we had to decide. There was a bartending job in an Irish pub, a painter's assistant, and one with a septic company. But, we chose to put you in a local hospital—sort of an OR tech."

"What the feck," I said. My dismay was not faked. "All I know about a hospital is I never want to be in one again. Why not the bartender job? I know my way around pourin' a pint."

"I'm sorry, Ryan," she said. "It's too public. We're supposed to keep you safe and out of jail. The bar gets a lot of traffic—a lot of tourists. Did you know your face is all over Spanish television? They called you a dangerous fugitive."

"Leonar, 'tis a big misunderstandin'."

"Don't care," she said. "I am not a judge. I simply do as I am told. I will be here tomorrow to take you to the hospital. There are a few extra clothes in the closet. I guessed your size. Be ready at 0800."

Once the door closed, I looked around. There was food in the refrigerator, an assortment of shirts and trousers along with several pairs of boxers and some thick socks in the bedroom, and a handful of basic toiletries in the WC. There was no dog food.

Lucky and I went in search of canine sustenance. I stuck to the back streets and alleyways. Every van looked like the one I boarded at the dock. I felt like I was being watched. I expected Michiko to appear at any moment, throw a burlap bag over my head, and take me to some secret location where commandos in camo and balaclavas would wire my nether parts to a car battery.

I found a little bodega called Silva's and bought food for Lucky. The moment he saw the bag, he knew it was dinner time. The Acana brand was particularly popular in Spain; I'd seen it in a few stores. He bumped my leg all the way home.

I found a metal bowl and filled it. "It's got free range chicken," I said.

Lucky tore into it with such vigor I decided not to mention the carrots, red lentils, pumpkin, and (*glurg!*) kale. Lucky had a peculiar eating ritual. He took a mouthful, dropped it on the floor, slobbered it up from the tile, then repeated. He kept it up until the bowl was empty. The whole episode lasted about three minutes.

He looked up at me with expectant eyes.

"No more, boy," I said. "Don't want you to get sick."

Lucky narrowed his eyes, then curled up in the corner. He opened one eye, unleashed a thunderous belch, then went to sleep.

CHAPTER FIVE

Morning came quickly and Leonar was at my door at 0800 as promised. My first thirty days would be part-time as a trainee, 0900 to 1300. After that, I would do full shifts five to six days a week.

"Ryan, what will you do with your dog?"

"Nuthin'. He'll stay here. He might like the telly."

"You cannot leave him here. He'll mess the floor."

"Relax, lass," I said. "He was fine aboard the ship. He can hold his water for four hours."

§§

Lucky was going to have an easier time not peeing than I was not puking. The moment I entered the hospital, I flashed back. The alluring stench of antiseptic spray and bleach, mingled with human waste, made my stomach flip and sent me back in time to my own incarceration in St. Virginia Hospital. I had awakened from a three-week coma to the good news of a broken arm, a broken elbow, and six smashed bones in my left hand. My dreams of leaving the police department and sitting in for Billy Joel when he gave up the piano evaporated. How hard could it be to tickle the ivories once I learned how to read music?

But there was another odor, one threatening to bring on a PTSD episode. All the air freshener in the world could not mask the lingering smell of death. I saw O'Reilley's head explode and could feel his skull fragments hitting my face and shoulder. I heard the voice from the bridge. "This is Sergeant Major Pinkrall of Her Majesty's Army. You are under arrest. Drop your weapons and get on your knees or you will be shot. Do—it—now!"

I saw my life spiraling into a maelstrom of false identities, safe houses, code words, and days filled with dread. I was a guy from a small town in New York. How the hell had this happened?

Better choices would have helped. I could have refused to go on patrol with Robinson—a jerboa in a tiny police uniform would have been more effective than that lazy, retirement-seeking layabout. Someone competent would have covered my ass; I wouldn't have been beaten to within an inch of my life. I would never have seen the inside of the hospital. No one would have given me "extended leave" and I would have kept my scrawny ass in the Empire State instead of traipsing to Ireland with Alec, wouldn't have met Billi, could have—

"Ryan, Ryan!"

I returned to the present.

Leonar was shaking my arm. "You okay?"

I blinked a few times, and the hospital came into focus. "Right as rain, darlin'," I said. "What's wrong?"

"You were staring out the window in a daze. And there are tears in your eyes."

"Dust mites," I said.

She didn't believe me for a skinny minute, but she let it go. "Ryan, this is Alfonso," Leonar said. She pointed to a thirty-something man.

Tall and skinny with a head of hair Fabio would have coveted, he stuck out his hand. "Nice to meet you," he said.

I shook his hand.

"I'll be training you to work in the operating room," he said. "First two weeks are mostly classroom where you will learn to identify surgical tools. Then you will observe surgery for a while. By the fifth week, it will feel like you have been doing this your entire life."

I imagined bowel resections, floors covered in blood, doctors screaming, "Code Blue, Code Blue!"

Alfonso and I were quiet for a reverential moment as we worshipped the image of Leonar's tight backside disappearing through the sliding glass doors. Then, we went to work.

The first day was easy, but anxiety haunted me every minute. Lucky attacked me, leash in his mouth, every day when I returned home. We stumbled on a nice park where he met some furry friends. And I discovered the ancient truism was accurate—chicks dig dogs.

I met a very friendly, cute woman around my age. My extensive investigative training paid off when I noticed she wasn't wearing a ring. Unfortunately, my Portuguese was worse than her English, which was limited to "Al-lo," so our daily encounters never escalated past a nod and a pleasant smile.

CHAPTER SIX

When I started classroom training, I didn't know a curved (foraminotomy) pituitary from a rotating endoscopic Kerrison shaft. I recognized scissors (I'd been one hell of a paper doll cutter when I was five), but I had no idea there were different types—mayo and bandage—and I thought Metzenbaum was probably the name of my father's tax guy. I lost count of the types of forceps, but I remembered there was one named "Desjardins," which sounded like a fancy mustard. There were scalpels, different blades, and all manner of retractors—and a most disturbing implement called a proctoscope.

The pleasure cruise I'd enjoyed over the past months—being assaulted, blisters, heat rash in the most unpleasant places, pulled muscles, the constant threat of death by hanging—was over. I had work to do. In thirty-one days, some poor, anesthetized sucker was going to be at the mercy of my ignorance.

The next week was all about sterilization. I realized I'd never learned how to wash my hands properly. I operated the autoclave, a significant device scorching germs from all it touches with temperatures ranging up to 270°F.

One Wednesday, Alfonso tapped me on the arm. "We're going into the OR," he said.

"Great," I said. "T'will give me a chance t' get me feet wet."

"Oh, there will be no wet feet, my friend," Alfonso said, "unless you plan on stepping in the blood."

I looked at him like a Schnauzer fascinated by a dryer. "Huh?"

"You will be there to assist. It's an amputation."

My vocal cords suddenly atrophied.

Four minutes later, I was moving a somewhat less than enthusiastic patient from a gurney to an operating table. About the time the bone saw began to whir, I was glad I'd skipped lunch. When the carnage was over, I staggered for the door.

"Not so fast, my friend," he said. He swept his hand around the room with the flourish like Leonard Bernstein concluding a Beethoven symphony and said, "Clean it up and get it ready for the next procedure."

Four weeks in and I was a vet. I could do anything in the OR other than something requiring an MD degree. The night before my first day as a full-time operating room technician, I lay in bed and rehearsed every possible scenario. I concluded the OR was little more than a sophisticated assembly line. Wheel in the patient...knock the patient out...cut the patient open...close the patient up after every sponge has been counted. God help the attendant who said, "Weren't there thirty-eight sponges? We only have thirty-seven here," after the surgeon had removed his gloves.

§§

Day One arrived with all the fanfare of bird poop on a windshield. I had not expected a party, but I got nothing more than, "You're in Number 4 at 0730." Even when I was a cop I had never felt so responsible for a person's life. There was always the chance of shit hitting the fan when I was wearing the blue, but now I was hands on with over a half-dozen critically ill people every day. The first day I assisted with an appendectomy, a repair in an abdominal aneurism, and the removal of ovarian tumors. Alfonso admonished me to separate the procedure from the person. Strong attachment could lead to devastating emotional crashes, and I'd had enough of those in my life.

The first time I saw a doctor open a stomach with a scalpel I almost doubled over. Thirty days later, I didn't even blink. My focus was on helping to turn the procedure around in an expeditious fashion so we could be ready for the next one on time. The operations were invasive and—from the outside—gruesome. But they served a greater purpose, an end on which I focused whenever I felt the urge to empty the contents of my stomach inside my tight surgical mask.

Day Two began with an amputation of a leg below the knee. The gas-passer put the patient under, the surgical resident applied the tourniquet, and the carpenter, I mean surgeon, sawed his way to success. The doc was from the subcontinent and though his English was undoubtedly better than my Pakistani, I had a hard time translating his commands.

I handed him the wrong size scalpel because I thought he'd said, "Clam shell" and I guessed. He threw the instrument on the floor and cursed. When he asked for a Kelly clamp, I got it right. A minute or so later with his eyes locked on the patient, he extended his hand, palm up, and said, "Tame ting." I hesitated.

"Tame ting."

I froze.

His head jerked to the side. He pointed to a Kelly and said, "Tame damn ting."

My new nickname: Tame Ting.

Ninety days in, I was a pro. I felt comfortable with most of the procedures and had learned the idiosyncrasies of each physician. Lucky, who'd perfected his bladder control, met me at the door every day—rain or shine—and raced to the nearest tree as soon as I opened the door. He finished his business and waited for me to arrive with the leash.

Though I liked my colleagues, Lucky was my only companion. Almost every evening I could hear music and boisterous laughter from the Irish pub down the lane, but I had been warned to stay away from it. The Green Liberation Front seemed to be monitoring what I was doing. Based on what they knew of my history, they figured I'd screw something up, so I followed their advice.

I liked the Algarve. The shoreline rivaled any ocean view I had ever seen—real or in pictures. Most of the locals were genuine, friendly, and helpful. Lucky and I had a favorite beach and, after one raging coughing fit, my canine buddy learned not to drink the salt water. Steak was a luxury we could not afford (even if we could find it). We got our protein from the abundant fresh fish. A steady diet of seafood added luster to Lucky's coat. On the downside, his breath made him occasionally unapproachable and his gas took on the potency of a weapon of mass destruction. He seemed oblivious to his deadly emissions. While I gasped for breath on the couch with a pillow over my face and tears running from my eyes, he'd scratch his back by rolling around on the floor, then look at me as if to ask, "Hey, got any more of that bacalhau?"[1]

Lagos, Portugal

1. Salt-dried cod. Portugal's national dish.

CHAPTER SEVEN

Nights were tough. Falling asleep was easy, but I always awakened after a few hours. Sometimes I was running surgical procedures through my head. Commands ping-ponged in my mind: "scalpel, lap sponge, bovie, laparotomy pad, suture, mosquito, Crile, Kelly clamp, book walter, army-navy, ribbon, deaver, tourniquet, oscillating saw." I saw visions of bodies in various states of dismemberment; I heard cursing doctors.

But I occasionally jolted into consciousness in a hard sweat and gasping for air. The images weren't as clear, but the horror was real and the fear of being captured palpable.

I could usually soothe myself back to sleep by remembering the Camino. I recalled the beautiful scenery, the amazing people I met from around the world, the churches and cathedrals, the incredible architecture, the happy hours with fellow pilgrims. Locals offered me food and water. I smiled whenever I recalled a local man in the middle of the mountains who was selling fresh cherries at the side of the road or the country woman who held out her hand and gave me a fresh piece of piping hot (and delicious) pie.

A crone approached me one day. I was hesitant—she looked almost exactly like the witch from *Snow White*. In truth, I was

shamefully frightened by her stooped figure. She spoke Galician.[1]
I could not identify a single word, but I understood the gesture.
She wanted me to have whatever was on the towel-covered plate
she was extending with her gnarled fingers. I took the offering
with the enthusiasm of a youngster going outside to "get a switch"
for his mother. When I lifted the towel, I discovered the most
delicious crepes I'd ever had. I ate them while weeping with joy and
embarrassment.

The people along the route of the Camino are used to pilgrims
and helpful to those who plod along. In one village, I had blistered
my feet past the point of my ability to treat them. A rotund little man
named Tosco pulled me into a doctor's office and pushed me to the
front of the line. None of the people who were waiting protested.
They knew I would not be there tomorrow; they knew my need was
pressing. When I tried to pay, I was reprimanded in a most kind
fashion.

"The pilgrims, they are sacred," Tosco said. "It is our duty to the
Virgin and to Saint James to protect them."

He refused any payment and sent me on my way with a bag full
of raisins.

"You need your strength," he said. "You are frightfully thin."

On the rare occasions sleep proved elusive, I went back home
in my head. One moment I'd be thinking about how much I
hated speed trap duty—the inevitable equipment fubars, whining

---

1. A western, Ibero-Romance language. Galicia is located in
   northwestern Spain. About 2.4 million people in the world
   speak the language with fluency.

motorists, tough guys showing off for their girls by asking for my badge number—the next I'd be reliving my first kiss with Gwendolyn. I jumped from playing a high school baseball game to twisting my ankle on the French Pyrenees. The injury always segued into Danielle, the Angel of the Wild, who nursed and fed me before saying goodbye in a most spectacular and naked fashion.

I relished the sweet memories; I did everything I could to purge the unpleasant ones. But the night has a mind of its own and I went to sleep in dread more often than I cared to admit.

CHAPTER EIGHT

If I had listed my feelings about my new life, "fulfilled" would not have been at the top. I settled into a routine. It was predictable. It was probably as safe as I could hope for. It was relatively mindless. And it was boring as hell.

Whenever I asked about dinner time, Mom was fond of quoting, "Man cannot live by bread alone." Well, neither can he thrive on six days of work on his feet, one day of strolling through yet another park, and talking to virtually no one other than his dog. I knew where to meet people. And I knew meeting people invited danger.

I missed the company of a good woman. I tried to ask a nurse named Anna to go out for coffee. I would have lasted longer in the ring with Muhammed Ali.

"Hey, would you like to have—"

"No thank you."

The towel flies in from over the top rail...the bell clangs...the referee waves his arms like a hyperactive baseball umpire signaling "Safe!" The fight's over and two guys are carrying me out of the ring on a stretcher while Anna crinkles her nose in distaste.

I resented my every move being watched by the GLF.

Another Sunday rolled by. I clipped Lucky's leash to his collar, slipped on my backpack, and opened the door. We walked to the street and stopped.

"Which way, boy?" I asked. I was out of ideas.

Lucky turned left. We walked a few miles until we came to a small park—one we had missed somehow. We wandered along a trail. Lucky paused every so often to growl at an Iberian hare lest the ball of fuzz should decide to unleash an attack. I imagine my buddy was missing squirrels. When I noticed the absence of the little gray torturers of all things canine, I asked. Alfonso told me that Portugal had once had red squirrels, but they had died out in the sixteenth century.

"They wandered back in from Spain," he said, "but they live in the north. We are not cursed by their presence."

Maybe Lucky felt the same way, but I imagined he missed playing Wile E. Coyote to the little bushy tails' Road Runner at least on occasion. A blonde woman approached. She was walking a bear—at least it looked that way to me. Monster dog...about two feet tall, somewhere north of 110 pounds. It had a tri-colored coat of black, white, and rust, and a white chest.

Lucky did his "getting to know another dog" thing...sniffing, a little lick here and there, more sniffing. He batted at "Mongo's" head. Mongo batted back. They both growled, but in a "What's happenin', dude" sort of way—no hint of aggression. The beast dropped to the ground. Lucky lay down for a rest next to him.

I tried an ice breaker. "Eles se gostam,"[1] I said.

---

1. "They like each other."

She responded immediately in Klingon. I stared—blank.

"Sprechen sie Deutsch?" she asked.

"Nine," I said. *You are an idiot.* I corrected my pronunciation. "Nein."

"Are you British?" she asked. Her English was good, and alluringly accented.

"God protect me, no," I said. "Irish I am. The name's Ryan...Ryan Murphy. I was just sayin' the pups like each other, no?"

She nodded.

"And who do I have the pleasure of meetin'?"

My throat was getting tight. I was concerned my voice might crack like a pubescent teen's. She was blonde, leggy, and her smile would have stolen the hearts of movie fans everywhere if only they could see it. My stomach began dancing the merengue.

Down, big fella, she is soooo out of your league.

"My name is Heida," she said. "I'm from Switzerland. Your accent, you don't sound like others I have met from Ireland. You sound more Canadian or American."

I mumbled something about growing up in the States. In truth, I'd grown sloppy with—no, sick of—my façade. My brogue, as lousy as it was, came and went. Either the people at work didn't notice, didn't care, or were too polite to mention it.

"Impressive beast ya have there," I said. "Catabrian brown bear, is he?"

I laughed so she would not think I was a complete idiot.

She smiled again. My knees shook. Then she laughed and I thought I heard the angels singing.

You have been alone way too long.

"This is Gus," she said. "Bernese Mountain Dog and a trained killer."

I had been reaching out to pat him on the head. I yanked my hand back.

She laughed again. "He's gentle as a lamb," she said. "And he'll do anything for a treat."

I reached into my pocket for a Sancho Pancho whitefish dog biscuit. Gus's head snapped up from the ground. His eyes locked onto my fingers. I shifted the treat into my palm. The little bone shaped snack disappeared. I moved to wipe my hand on my jacket.

"He doesn't slobber," Heida said. "He's a dry mouth breed."

"Convenient," I said.

My capacity to sound stupid in the presence of a beautiful woman was the stuff of legend.

"Ah, there's a small pub, I mean café, down the way. Would you two care t' join us?"

El Charo had an open table. The waiter brought a brace of metal water bowls and placed them on the cement floor. Gus and Lucky drank like men who'd crawled across the Sahara.

"So, you're an American by birth," Heida said.

I was tired of pretending. I longed to be Conor Caldemeyer again—to speak in my own voice—to say things without trying to remember how I was supposed to pronounce them. I wanted to start over—and here was a chance.

Well, while honesty had its place, sometimes it's best not to be *totally* honest. I didn't think leading with, "I'm a fugitive from British justice under a death warrant for killing a soldier" was my best move.

"Yes, Ryan Murphy from New York. Moved to Ireland a while back and sort of adopted the patois to fit in. Don't do it very well, I'm afraid. I'm not gifted in linguistics. Been here less than a year, and you heard my only Portuguese back there on the trail."

She giggled. "Well, you're right about the accent. Good thing you're not running from the law."

My fists clenched under the table. I hoped she didn't see me gulp.

But she went on as if her comment had been simply an attempt at conversation. "Gus and I are new as well. I work for a Swiss shipping company. Maybe you and..."

"Sorry," I said. "His name is Lucky."

"Well, maybe you and Lucky could show us around town."

I dodged my natural inclination to say something clever—and stupid. "We are at your service," I said, and we made a date for the following weekend to take the dogs for a walk followed by lunch.

Not sure if it was love or lust at first sight. Maybe I was just so damnably lonely I would have glommed onto a friendly porcupine, but when I stepped into my apartment, I was floating. Sleep came slowly. My mind would not shut down. I saw her face, I heard her laugh, I smelled her shampoo. But when midnight came and I finally drifted off, I had the first dreamless night in months...until...

I awakened at 0512. I could hear the voices of the GLF.

"Ye're tinkin' wid yer tallywacker, Murphy."

"A trap it is."

"Ye're an eejit,[2] son. And you'll be dead straightway."

---

2. Idiot

I mopped the sweat off my brow, stepped out of bed, and turned on the shower. Lucky studied me. His look said, "If you're up, I should be eating."

"In a minute, buddy," I said. With one foot in the shower, I turned. "You think Heida's okay, don't you? I mean, there's no way she wants to hurt me, right?"

Just before I put my head under the water, I could have sworn Lucky spoke. "That's exactly what you said about Michiko, dumbass."

CHAPTER NINE

Everyone knew about my impending date, and everyone had a suggestion, one or two I might even use. I wondered if it was really a date or just a dog walk followed by lunch. My romantic life had been an unending train wreck. I promised myself to take things slowly, to let nature take its course.

Heida was standing outside my apartment when Lucky and I stepped outside. I never thought about inviting her inside. She'd asked to see the city, not for a tour of a nuclear waste dump. I had a route mapped out thanks in part to the OR crew. We began walking around the original city walls. My plan was to head towards the sea.

Thirty minutes into our stroll we stopped to admire the ocean. The azure palate of the water was broken in places by flashes of white wakes from sailboats. We marveled when an accomplished crew unleashed a spinnaker. The craft shot forward like a turbocharged Shelby Mustang, virtually flying across the water. The sun blazed, the wind blew, and everyone around us looked happy and serene.

Conversation flowed like warm syrup—no awkward pauses. More amazing, I managed not to say anything fatuous. I didn't try any inane pick-up line. I didn't slobber out ghoulish compliments. But more than once I could hear the Bellamy Brothers singing: "If I said you had a beautiful body, would you hold it against me." I had never met anyone from Switzerland, and I did a great job of feigning interest in the country's history and culture. My sole concern was a single blonde citizen of that bastion of neutrality.

A voice yanked me back from a daydream where Gwendolyn's face drew closer to mine, lips parted, and began to morph into— "Ryan...hello...Ryan, are you okay?"

"Yes, yes, Heida, I'm fine." I hoped I sounded genuine. "Just got lost in the moment for a second. Actually, I'm not fine—I'm great. This is a lot of fun. Let's get these dogs back on their feet and walk up to the castle. I bet there's a place for them to romp up there."

An hour later, we arrived at the Castelo Dos Governadores, also known as the Governor's Palace. Saying it was impressive was like calling Chicago "a nice little garage band." Heida had a degree in European History with a minor in American History. She said members of her family had emigrated to the States and she wanted to know something of the country's appeal.

The Governor's Palace

I heard myself saying, "You've got all the appeal anyone needs," but I managed to cough before I verbalized my inanity.

I am seriously out of shape, date-wise.

Her forebears had traveled to America just in time to tour some of the great battle sites of the Civil War—as participants!

"Not our nation's finest moment," I said.

She waved off my criticism. "America has had far fewer such episodes than most of the countries in Europe," she said. "Did you know these are the original walls?"

"Really?" I thought it was a better answer than "nope" or "huh."

"Built by the Romans about two thousand years ago. They were the primary protection from the Barbary pirates."

"Rrrrrrrr you serious?" I asked.

God smiled on me. She laughed. "You're silly," she said.

"I was going for adorable, but I'll take it," I said.

She ignored the opening and went back to the lecture. "Over the years, the castle has been occupied by the Romans, the Arabs, and finally the Christians in the sixteenth century."

I almost asked her if the red squirrels left then to find a better neighborhood, but I demurred.

"In 1755, a massive earthquake destroyed most of Lisbon and damaged Morocco significantly. Then came a tsunami. The waves measured over fifty feet. Casualties numbered between fifty and one hundred thousand souls."

I didn't really care about the tidal wave, but I could have listened to her all day. She had an odd habit of intermingling languages; she spoke six. She was fluent in German, Spanish, Italian, French, Portuguese, and English. "I've worked very hard to learn to speak to them without a German accent," she said. "How am I doing with English?"

"Very vell," I said.

She hit me on the arm. I almost swooned.

"You think it's too late for me to learn another language?" I asked. "I was too lazy to take French in high school. I'm afraid the opportunity has passed."

"Don't say it's too late, it's never too late," she said. "What language would you want to learn?"

"Spanish...or German," I said.

"If only you had a friend who'd been reared in a German speaking country," she said.

I raised and lowered my eyebrows and prayed I didn't look like someone who should own a windowless van.

"Tell you what," she said. "I will teach you to speak German, but only if you swear you'll never do that eyebrow thing again. It makes you look like a pervert."

Damn!

"Promise," I said. "Just so you know, I was going for irresistible."

"Didn't make it," she said once again bypassing the bait. "Another thing, you must do what I tell you and study hard. It won't be easy, but we'll have fun with it."

"How would you propose we have fun with learning a new language?"

"Well, would you be interested in learning about der Geschelechtsverkehr?"

"Sorry, the only German responses I know are 'ja' and 'nein.'"

"Well, choose the right one, because I was asking if you would like to learn about sex. Now do you see how we could have fun with this?"

"When can we start?"

There was a moment—I knew it, I could sense it—but I spoiled it, whether intentionally or not I was unsure.

"Where are the pups?" I asked.

I spotted Lucky watering a stone some Roman grunt had probably used as a pillow back in the day. Lucky and Gus were having a great time. They cavorted and snarled and thoroughly enjoyed terrorizing other dogs. They swooped in like fighter jets, ran circles around yapping terriers and quivering Malteses, then raced off loudly proclaiming their superiority of every other mongrel.

They careened over to remind us they had not eaten since the last time we'd distributed treats. I reached into my pocket. Heida rooted through her voluminous shoulder bag. Gus and Lucky chomped away, then sat on their haunches and waited for more. I patted my good boy on the head, unsure whether I should hug him or tell him to go away.

I chose the former. I was going to stand by my decision about relationships no matter how fucking lonely I was.

CHAPTER TEN

The walk back to Heida's apartment would only have been more awkward if I'd forgotten to wear pants. Silence dominated the first twenty minutes. When we stopped to look at something—I don't remember what—we started talking at the same time, which made us laugh. Things got better.

"Sorry for...ah...ruining the moment back there," I said. "I mean, unless there wasn't a moment—then, I apologize for thinking there was a moment when there wasn't—"

"Shut up," she said.

I was never good at following instructions, especially if I was in the middle of a lie.

"I'm still in recovery from a woman who used my heart for a speed bag and—"

She stopped and waited for me to...well...shut up. I ran through what I needed to tell her.

I need you to be honest with me. Are you working for the British government and looking for a way to bring me to justice for a crime I swear to God I did not commit?

I was close to saying it. I'd left a drugged Michiko in a fifteenth-century hotel room, swum across a river in the middle of the night, and endured a sea voyage on a stinky fish boat (I knew it was a "fishing vessel" but my mind was raging), and I was not going to endure more of the same. Gwendolyn, Billi, Danielle, Michiko—even I could see evidence of a serial bad relationship jumper-into-er.

Heida rescued me from my own insanity. "Ryan," she said, "I'm the one who needs to apologize. I'm really enjoying our time together. I should not have made the joke about sex. It was forward, misleading, and inappropriate."

Misleading? Damn!

"I hope you will forgive me."

"Hey," I said, "how could I stay mad at an expert in castles and tidal waves and such?"

The laughter eased the tension.

"Cards on the table," I said. "I like you very much and I would love to know you better. Like anyone else, I've made mistakes in my past and I don't want to mess this up. I want to take our time and do this right. Sound good?"

Her answer was a hug. Not a "meet and greet" and not a "pelvis rubber" —just a solid embrace with a really nice slow-motion release. I really wanted to kiss her, but I was becoming the master of self-control. Besides, by the time I decided to make my move, she had resumed walking.

We arrived outside her apartment and hugged again. If she had invited me inside, I would have been naked before I hit the door, but she decided it was the time men fear— "condition time."

"Ryan," she said. She held up three fingers.

"Go," I said.

"I want to know if you are married, if you are a wanted felon, and if I can trust you."

The moment of truth. I had been preparing for Judgment Day, the time I would have to be honest. Make or Breaks-ville. What did I have to lose?

I went two-thirds in. "Married, not a chance," I said. "And you can absolutely trust me."

"You never told me you were a politician, Ryan," she said. "I asked a trio of questions; you answered a pair. You skipped the part about being a felon."

"Sorry Heida," I said. "Short attention span—dazzled by your beauty."

It was cheesy and cheap, but it worked. She blushed.

"You know I am fully employed at the local hospital. Do you think they would be hiring wanted felons?"

Technically, I had not lied. The truth had become something poisonous—a substance I could not let into my mouth. Right then, I knew a life with Heida, a puppy, and a cottage on the shore with a white picket fence and a vegetable garden was never going to happen.

"Ryan, listen carefully," she said. "You made a commitment about learning German. We will meet every Tuesday and Thursday evening at the library, and I will give you lessons. I will also hold you accountable to study."

"Sounds great," I said. I needed more deflection. "Maybe after school, we can go out for ice cream, and I'll let you tell me more about der Geschelechtsverkehr."

She shoved me in a playful way. Then her face grew stern. "Now you will see the serious side of me, Ryan," she said. "This is not a date. You will be studying German and there will be no ice cream involved. We will meet for ninety minutes. When the lesson is over, we go our separate ways."

I nodded without enthusiasm. She headed for the door. I heard the key click in the lock. Then, her voice. "That leaves four more days in the week...for other things," she said.

CHAPTER ELEVEN

I had a lot to think about on my walk home. I was already looking forward to meeting her at the library in a couple days, even though the appeal of German instruction lessened with every step. I softened the pain by convincing myself that Heida had fallen for my clever, "Teach Me A Foreign Language, Baby" ruse.

Back at the apartment, Lucky kept glaring at me.

"It's okay, buddy," I said. "Harmless fun today."

More glaring.

"Nothing to worry about. You're my man. It's just you and me. She won't change anything."

The eyes narrowed.

"I'm not a monk, man. I can't stay cooped up here for the rest of my life."

He swiped at me with his paw.

"Want me to live in a monastery, chant, make beer. That what you want?"

He nudged his bowl at me with his nose. What he wanted was dinner. My imagination was beginning to get the better of me.

§§

Monday was just another day until the powers in charge put me in the OR for an appendectomy procedure with a new doctor. Well, he wasn't new. He didn't hold the scalpel by the wrong end or anything. He was just new to me.

Nothing about Dr. Sanchez was factory fresh. He was gruff, surly, arrogant, and smelled of mothballs. But the sumbitch knew how to operate.

We always played a little game in the OR. "Guess the music." Each surgeon preferred his (and they were all men) particular brand of audio poison. Since we were a teaching hospital, younger guys kept us guessing. I was hopeless when the tone-deaf young 'uns went for something from their own country—Diva, Pop Dall'Arte, Mão Morta—but I killed if they liked 'merican stuff: Mariah Carey, Backstreet Boys, and the like. Once, when the surgeon was in his fifties, I took a shot and guessed Dylan. Won a case of La Letra beer.

The older surgeons were harder to unravel. I pegged Dr. Sanchez for a classical guy. Just when I was preparing for "Lacrimosa" from Mozart's *Requiem*, AC/DC's "Thunderstruck" blared through the speakers. The good doctor walked in, gowned and scrubbed, and proceeded to remove the inflamed organ with the deft touch of a safecracker. Twenty minutes from the opening stroke to the last suture.

My kind of sawbones.

When he left, I sidled up to the circulating nurse. "What's his story?" I asked. "Seems like an interesting guy."

She looked around and motioned for me to step outside.

"What do you want to know about Dr. Sanchez?"

"Just seems remarkable," I said. "About seventy-five years old—listens to metal. I'm not a veteran in there but I bet not many folks have ever seen anything like his skill. He was like Don Larsen in the '56 Series—sheer perfection."

"I don't know anything about American football," Nurse Velasquez said, proving she didn't know anything about American baseball either. "Dr. Sanchez is a special surgeon, but he finds it difficult to find people who will work with him. He demands perfection and can be brutal to those who do not meet his standards." She leaned in and whispered. "I have never been one to start rumors, but I have heard that Dr. Sanchez was the personal physician to Generalissimo Francisco Franco."

"Is he still dead?" I asked.

Nurse Velasquez had obviously never seen *Saturday Night Live*. She looked at me like I was mentally deficient.

"Franco led the Nationalist forces and overthrew the Second Spanish Republic during the Spanish Civil War. After Franco's death, Sanchez allegedly fled the country and came here. He witnessed a lot of death during and after the war in the concentration camps. He made it his life's goal to help as many people as he could. He is what you gringos call 'a born again Christian.'" (My accent had obviously not fooled her either.) "He volunteers all his time here. Will not accept any payment." She got right up in my face. "Do not mention any of this around him."

"I won't," I said. "Thanks."

§§

Tuesday came and I met Heida for my first German lesson at the library. I had been worried about it, but Heida made it easy. At the end of the session, she said, "Once you master conversational German, I'll teach you about der Geschelechtsverkehr."

"How long will that take?" I said. I hoped I didn't sound too eager—or desperate.

"Based on tonight, and assuming you do the at home studies, two to three months."

I promised to be the best student in the history of the Rhineland.

The weeks passed. More time with Lucky, Gus, and Heida. More lives saved. A few folks who didn't make it. When I wasn't thinking about Heida, I was obsessed about Dr. Sanchez and his odd history. I felt a strange kinship with him. Here he was in the final years of his life trying to make up for past misdeeds. He was carrying a great burden, and it showed in his personality, or lack thereof. I wondered if I would turn out the same way.

Somewhere north of eighty...retirement home stinking of urine...sitting in my own filth awaiting a diaper change...begging for the merciful hand of God to end my life. Or would I be eating grubworms in Her Majesty's Prison Wakefield? Interesting: I couldn't decide which scenario frightened me more.

Chapter Twelve

I awakened Sunday morning with anticipation just short of dread. I had a date with Heida. The plan was to walk the pups, enjoy some ice cream near the sea, return our four-legged companions to their respective homes (which sounded a lot better than "ditch the dogs"), and then have a private dinner. The anticipation seemed natural. The apprehension arose from my recurring ability to screw things up—or miss golden opportunities like the chance I had to kiss her previously.

On the long walk to meet Heida, I couldn't stop thinking about Dr. Sanchez. Why had our paths crossed? Was the meeting some signal from the Universe, a divine tap on the shoulder, or was I simply the only OR tech willing to tolerate him?

I tried to get into the good doctor's head. I could not imagine a situation like the Spanish Civil War. Admittedly, I was ignorant of the details other than that there was a civil war...and it had been in Spain. And my father wondered why I had not made detective.

What I recalled of Franco wasn't good. He was a Fascist with ties to Hitler. Not something anyone wanted on a resume. Wait...it was coming back to me.

Among her other multitudinous talents, Gwendolyn knew more about art than anyone else in my circle. Of course, I ran with a guy whose parents named him Stumpy, so we weren't exactly the Algonquin Round Table. Anyway, the woman who still held a majority share of my heart was fascinated by Picasso's work, particularly *Guernica*.

Franco's army was attempting to take control of the north to put an end to the war and Franco wanted a little help from his buddy Adolf. The German Luftwaffe attacked the city of Guernica on Market Day when thousands of people were visiting to buy fresh food from the local farmers. They called it "terror bombing" because civilians were targeted in hopes of driving the population to capitulate.

I wondered what part Dr. Sanchez played in the attack. Did he know about it in advance? Was he privy to Franco's strategies, or simply taking care of the Generalissimo's balky prostate? Given the physician's quest for absolution, I concluded he knew all about the scheme to bomb the innocents and did nothing to abort it. As penance, he was on a quest to save as many as he could while banging his head to the finely tuned voice of Bon Scott. The staff saw Sanchez as a miserable man and went to great pains to avoid him.

I figured he was a man in search of his lost soul...like me.

§§

Lucky usually heeled pretty well for a dog I'd found wandering through Spain. But the closer we got to Heida's apartment, the more he strained on the leash. By the time we got to her steps he sounded like someone being strangled with a clothesline. He didn't care at all when the Swiss Miss appeared. He absolutely lost his mind when Gus followed her into the street.

The dogs jumped all over each other—twins reunited after a three-decade absence.

Weirdos.

Heida held her arms open in invitation. Being a gentleman, I accepted and hugged her with Sunday school decorum. *Two Mississippi...three Mississippi.* I relaxed my grip. She strengthened hers. When she determined it was time, she let go. On the way out of the embrace, I broke my own code and kissed her on the cheek.

She smiled.

We watched Tweedle-Dum and Tweedle-Dee for a moment, smiles spreading across our faces.

"Such joy," Heida said.

"Such idiots," I said.

"That too," she said.

"So," I said, "are you ready for our big adventure? I've been working hard on the German...strictly business and all that. This, senhorita, is a one hundred percent, certified, Grade-A date."

"Excellent," she said. "I'm ready for a wonderful day and I am especially looking forward to some vinho tinto."

"Not much of a red wine connoisseur," I said, "but I imagine we can find someone qualified to give us some good suggestions."

Her smile was natural and radiant. "And while we are at it, we can mix a little business with our pleasure."

"How's that?" I asked. We started walking.

"Your final exams," she said.

I stopped like an uncooperative mule. "This is supposed to be purely social," I said.

"I am thinking we will shoot down a brace of pigeons with a single shot."

"Do you mean kill two birds with one stone?"

"That's what I said."

I let it go. "What's your idea?" I asked.

"First, we spend the day speaking only German."

I made a face. I was very mature.

"Second, at dinner tonight, you translate the menu into German."

Desperate for a loophole, I said, "What if the menu's in Portuguese?"

"Then you get a pass," she said.

"I'm sure you are going to explain to me why I would want to foul up a lovely afternoon by struggling to communicate."

I swear to God, I'd never seen anyone's eyes twinkle before that exact moment.

"Well, the quicker you pass your test the sooner we start learning about der Geschelechtsverkehr"

"Wann fangen wir an?"[1]

---

1. "When do we start?"

"Wir fangen jetzt an!"[2]

We talked about everything, jobs, dogs, food, the Algarve, and our lives back home, all in German. Heida asked about my time in Ireland, Northern Ireland, France, and Spain. She had the roadmap; now she probed.

With her eyes staring into the distance, she said, "So, Ryan, I thought a lot this week about our last conversation. You've covered a lot of ground since you arrived in Ireland. Can we talk more about that?"

"Sure," I said hoping I sounded, you know, sure. "Ask me anything." My face burned. I was glad she was deliberately looking anywhere but at me. I knew we were walking into the abyss of decision time.

"You told me about being injured on the job when you were a cop," she said. "All better?"

"Healthy as a horse," I said. "Well, not a Sweepstakes winner, but you get the point."

She was not amused. "You went on vacation to Ireland but decided not to return home with your friend. What kept you there?"

"Well," I said. "It sounds more interesting than it really is, but it involves a woman."

"Sounds about right," she said. I was sure she'd noticed the absence of my phony brogue, but was less interested in my linguistic inability than in my story.

"Billi invited me to stay and meet her family," I said.

"Agreeable boss you had in the States," she said.

---

2. "We start now."

"I was still on medical leave," I said. "I got beaten pretty badly." I paused. "Alec had to go home. Billi took me to Northern Ireland, and I got a job running a pub. It was fun—met a lot of interesting people. But the place shut down. It's a tough business. Everybody in Ireland thinks all they have to do is have Guinness on tap and the money will roll in."

"Like selling chocolate or watches in Switzerland," she said.

"Exactly," I said. "Anyway, I'd figured out that Billi and I would be better friends than...ah...partners—"

"It's okay, Ryan," she said. "I figured a good-looking man like you has enjoyed a continual stream of...ah...partners."

I figured I needed to move the story along. "So, I packed my meager belongings and decided to walk the Camino de Santiago."

"How did you hear about it?"

I should have said something about all good Catholic boys growing up longing to slog through the mountains towards the burial site of James the brother of Jesus, but I screwed up and told the truth.

"Heard about it from a woman named Shannon."

"Ah...Billi...Shannon...I am sensing a pattern. A girl in every port, sailor?" she asked. There was no malice in her voice. Instead, she sounded playful...and interested.

"I've met a lot of people in my travels."

"Amazing...all women," she said.

"No, no, nonononononono," I said. "Guys, lots of guys, lots of hairy, smelly, unattractive guys."

"I assume the women were the same way," she said.

"Not at all," I said, not sure why I felt the need to defend Billi and the others I had not mentioned. "No, Billi was very pretty. Reminded me of someone from a long time ago."

Heida had the decency not to ask. "You seeing anyone now?"

"I don't know," I said. "Am I?"

She stopped and took both my hands in hers. "Play your cards right and maybe you'll have an answer later."

Chapter Thirteen

I would not have been surprised to see Gus and Lucky jump a steamer and sail to Tahiti. They chased each other, splattered every sign and statue they passed, and generally acted like buffoons—they were two kids at the county fair. On the way home, we all had ice cream.

The walk back was weird, almost as if we were talked out.

"You still want dinner?" Heida said.

"Absolutely," I said.

"Still willing to take the final test?"

"Wer nicht wagt der nicht gewinnt,"[1] I said.

She clutched my hand. We did not talk; we did not look at each other. We tried so hard to be cool, it soon became obvious we were trying too hard.

I stole a few glances, which was not easy because every time I looked at her, I had to fight the urge to stare. She took "beautiful" to a Hall of Fame level.

I could have pulled back when she hugged me at her door. I could have turned my head when she kissed me. I could have ignored the

---

1. "Nothing ventured, nothing gained.

sexiest moan I'd ever heard. But I didn't, and all the way back to my apartment, I was sure I was floating on air.

I began talking to myself.

"Do I feel comfortable moving forward?"

"What kind of a question is that? Of course."

"Any chance this is Michiko redux? Another British agent sent to capture you?"

"Doubt it, but who gives a crap?"

"You thinking with the big head or the other one?"

"What do you think?"

§§

Lucky was glad to arrive home. He was exhausted and he knew it was dinnertime. I fed him, showered up, studied my German, and rested for an hour just in case I needed extra stamina at the end of the evening.

I arrived at Heida's door at 1925. I almost didn't recognize her. She was, as the saying goes, "foxed up." Her hair was down; she'd ditched her usual jeans and jacket for a tight sheath dress. The hemline was eight inches or so above her knees. She was braless.

Without apology, I stared.

"Do you approve, or should I change?"

"Uh...ah...glurg...hell no."

"You seem uncomfortable."

In ways you do not want to imagine.

"Heida, you look amazing," I said. "I've just never seen you with your clothes on."

Mother of God, you are a dumbass.

She laughed—full-throated and genuine. She took my hand and pulled. "Come here, smooth talker."

The kiss started at the front door and moved to the couch. Just about the time I was sure we were headed to the bedroom, Heida broke off and looked at her watch.

"Time for dinner," she said.

"But—"

She looked at me with mock sternness. "Someone has not yet passed his final exam."

She was gracious enough to excuse herself to freshen her makeup. Her departure gave me time to "adjust" myself and to lower my pulse rate. When she returned, I moved in for another kiss. She stiff armed me. Walter Payton would have been impressed.

The restaurant was a few blocks away. We held hands on the way. Maybe I thought about holding Gwendolyn's hand as we strolled across campus, but if I did, it wasn't for long. I was determined to live in the present—at least for one night.

Martim, the owner of Piri-Piri, was the brother of the OR team member who'd shot me down when I tried to ask her out. Anna had bragged about the restaurant for months and pleaded with us all to go there for any special occasion. When I told her—and everyone else—about my upcoming date with Heida, Anna called her brother and set everything up. Martim set us up with a great table overlooking the Bensafrim River. Heida had told me she was fond of rosé. A chilled bottle of Mateus was waiting at the table. We sat, the waiter poured, we perused the menu. I was beginning to sweat the upcoming interrogation when a man appeared.

"Mister Ryan," he said. "I am Martim. English not so good. But hope you enjoy with your lovely lady friend who is elegant."

"Obrigado Martim," I said. "And your English is far better than my Portuguese."

We had just toasted our first dinner together when Pedro appeared. He presented us with complimentary fried fish and explained the seafood specials for the night. They had all our favorites: cod, grilled shrimp, lobster, monkfish, and pargo. Pedro's English was non-existent. I did the best I could with my limited Portuguese.

The fried fish looked familiar.

"Pedro, o que é isto?" I asked.

"O nome do peixe e pilchard," he said, apparently relieved he would not have to attend to yet another American who believed anyone could understand English when it is spoken slowly and loudly enough.

Pilchards. I knew it.

"Sardines," I said. I sounded like a six year old who'd tied his shoes for the first time.

Heida looked at me with something akin to pity. "You had to ask?" she said.

I took a few onto my plate. She passed.

We sipped our rosé. Something touched my leg. I didn't want to look for fear of finding a rat or something really disgusting. The sensation crept up towards my thigh. I looked at Heida. She was smiling in a less-than-virginal way.

"That you?" I asked.

"If you have to ask, I'm not doing it right," she said. She delivered a parting poke to my knee and reached across the table for my hand. We sat in the candlelight holding hands like a couple of moonstruck teens.

We were...easy. That's the best word for it. Conversation was effortless as long as we stayed away from the kryptonite of my past. I knew I'd better enjoy whatever we had, because when I eventually told her the truth—and the moment of disclosure would surely come—the next time she kicked me, it wouldn't be a playful nudge...and the target would not be my knee.

"You have a family back home?" she asked.

"Wonderful, yes. I miss them every day. Try to call them from work whenever I can."

Was my nose beginning to grow?

"That's so sweet." She hesitated. "Would you like to come to my apartment?"

"That would be great," I said. I was halfway out of my seat.

She waved her napkin. "Whoa," she said. "Not what you're thinking. I have a phone in my apartment. We'll call my folks. They know all about you and are eager to meet. Then you can call your folks from there—tonight."

Before I could answer, Pedro arrived with two spectacular salads. I realized he'd never asked us what we were going to eat.

"Pedro, podemos pedir agora?"[2]

---

2. "Pedro, can we order now?"

What little Portuguese I knew related to food and drink. I ate in the hospital cantina each day. It was learn the language or starve.

"Sem menu, os pedidos de Martim para voce!"[3]

I smiled.

"Ryan, what did he say?"

"I'm pretty sure our host has ordered for us," I said.

Inmates in a French prison movie don't scarf up food like we did. We were polishing off the salads when Martim appeared with a tray. A pair of cloches awaited the unveiling. Martim sounded like a prize fighter after a bout.

"Mr. Ryan and Miss Heida, Martim cook for you—my own self. Fishes caughted tonight—two kilometers away. The vegetables are from Martim's garden. Enjoy."

Martim's Dinner Creation

---

3. "No menus. Martim orders for you."

He bowed from the waist, deeply enough to impress Henry VIII, then stood and snapped his fingers. Pedro materialized from the ether.

"More wine for the lovers," Martim said.

Heida blushed a vibrant shade of scarlet. But she was smiling. And a solitary tear scrolled along her perfect cheekbone.

Pedro filled our glasses.

Heida raised hers. "Here's to us, and the hope we will get lucky later tonight."

I held up my hand. "Check, please!"

Pedro came over. Heida laughed and shooed him away. He nodded, but as he turned, he gave me a knowing smile.

Dinner was amazing, but I could have eaten, as the saying goes, "the ass out of an elephant" and I would not have noticed. I was ready to go, but Heida had made her "get lucky" comment after a couple of glasses of wine. I wanted to make sure she was okay with where we were headed. I was not going to foul this up.

"Can I ask you a personal question?"

"Ask me anything."

"It's about the...ah...'get lucky' comment. Can we talk about that?"

"Did I offend you?" she asked. "The way we kissed—I assumed you are not gay."

"No, nothing like that," I said. "I just want to make sure you feel okay with everything. I mean, there's been a lot of wine and I don't want to take advantage—"

"Mister," she said, "I have every intention of taking advantage of you. You are a wonderful man, Ryan Murphy, but you are lousy at reading signals. I was wondering if I needed to stand in the doorway in my all-together and wave road flares. I hope you rested up this afternoon, because tonight, you're not going to get any sleep."

"Heida, I love you!"

Oh shit. Did I say that? Damn, I said it. Can I walk it back?

She was a mind reader. "Do not even consider taking that back," she said. "I love you too. Now, we are going to take our time and eat our dinner. Because we're going to need all the nutrition we can get when I get you home."

Dinner took four and a half days. My lord, the Portuguese believe in leisurely dining. By the time Pedro served chocolate cream parfaits and limoncello, both of which were lovely, I was ready to start screaming: "Doesn't anyone care that I am trying to get laid!"

We paid for dinner, bid farewell to Martim and Pedro, and promised to return another time. We were barely out of the door when she kissed me—with sinister intent.

The traffic was normal, which meant crazy. Cars honked. Drivers shouted. Scooters weaved in and out like motorized snakes. Pedestrians crossed streets at their own peril. Tour boats cruised the river. Fishing vessels chugged for home.

We would have made better time if we hadn't stopped to perfect the art of making out on the sidewalk. We were like a couple of crazed teens. Mid kiss number forty-something, my mind shot back to the night of my high school graduation.

We'd waited, Gwendolyn and I, waited because she insisted. She was not going to be "the girl you banged in high school." She wanted to be sure we had a future. And it never occurred to her that I would ever be daft enough to blow said future to smithereens.

It was a little too on the nose, but our first time was in the back of my dad's car. We were kissing—and some other stuff—when Gwendolyn hit the pause button. She reached into her pocketbook and removed a condom.

"You know how to put it on?" she asked.

I lied. "Sure."

She knew I was lying when I unwrapped it and attempted to put it on backwards—or upside down—or whichever way prevented it from unrolling in its prescribed fashion. While I was being outsmarted by an inanimate piece of latex, Gwendolyn was getting naked. By the time I had "sheathed the sword," she was too impatient for me to undress.

Just over forty-five seconds later, we were done. I was not exactly Ron Jeremy.

"Sorry," I said.

"It'll get better," Gwendolyn said.

And boy was she right.

Heida licked my neck and snapped me back to the present. For some reason, I did not feel the least bit guilty.

CHAPTER FOURTEEN

By my reckoning we were about three blocks away from nudity when we heard a screech, the squeal of rubber, and the dull, sickening thud of vehicles colliding. It was the intersection we had just crossed. I stared for four seconds before I turned into Pavlov's policeman. The wreck was worse than anything I had ever seen. I grabbed Heida's arm.

"Get to a phone box and call for help, I'll see what I can do."

I ran into the scene. There were two cars, one billowing smoke, and a mangled motorcycle. I didn't see a rider. The driver in the smoking Saab was slumped over the wheel. The inside of his vehicle looked like a Jackson Pollock painting. I reached through the open window.

"Senhor," I said. "Senhor." I tapped his cheek, very lightly. No response.

I moved to the mutilated car in front. The driver was comatose.

Heida ran up. "They're on the way," she said. She stopped, eyes toad-like. "Oh God, Ryan. Are they dead?"

"I don't know," I said. "I'm gonna try to help. See if you can find whoever was riding that."

I nodded to the twisted metal that moments before had been a Casal motorcycle. Then I pointed past the front of the first car. "He's going to be up there somewhere. I'm betting he went airborne."

People crowded both sides of the street. Looky-loos—worthless as tits on a boar. I checked the Saab driver again. Pulse was weak and thready. Then I heard a word from the crowd. Even if I had not understood, I would have figured it out from the tone.

"Incendio, Incendio!"

Flames licked from under the hood. Cops never moved crash victims from cars for fear of inciting paralysis—never—unless there was the possibility of drowning-or burning to death.

I wrenched the door open and slid my hands under the driver's shoulders. I'd never attempted to lift anything as heavy as a comatose human body. I pulled. It felt like he pulled back.

I looked over the accordioned roof at the crowd of lemmings. "Ajude! Ajude!"

Two big guys trotted over. They were never going to die of any stress-related illness. I made signs to be gentle. They reached in and pulled on the man with the finely tuned touch of a pair of alligator wrestlers. The guy in the seat did not budge. I looked into the car. His foot was wedged under the brake pedal. The driver was going to turn into Johnny Storm's Human Torch if I couldn't get him out. Without an acetylene torch, I was shit out of luck. Unless...

"Faca?"

They looked at each other and shrugged.

"Faca, dammit!"

One of them reached into the small of his back and extracted a Kamura Tanto knife. I'd seen pictures during my training. Six-inch

Damascus steel blade with a sawtooth back. I didn't bother to ask why he had it.

I reached in and sliced away the man's pant leg. I felt around the ankle. Compound fracture. I stepped out of the car.

"Alcool," I said. I held out my hand.

The other guy reached into his hip pocket and pulled out a bottle.

"Obrigado," I said.

I splashed the booze over the blade, then poured the rest of it over the wound. It wasn't close to OR standards, but the liquor would kill some of the topical germs. Couldn't hurt.

I looked back. Both guys were leaning in.

"Cinto!"

No hesitation. A belt slapped into my hand. I tightened it around the man's calf, said the quickest Hail Mary of my life...and stopped. I'd seen this done more than a dozen times. Amputations are not delicate, but I suddenly realized I'd never carved a turkey at Thanksgiving dinner, much less a human being's lower leg.

I glanced around. The fire was spreading.

I cut.

The bone was splintered pretty badly. Getting through it with the saw blade wasn't hard, but the heat got to me and I think I passed out. By the time someone splashed water on my face, someone else (I assumed the big guy who wasn't clutching at his waistband to keep his trousers up) had pulled me and the now one-footed victim from the burning wreckage.

I took a long swig from a water bottle a bystander shoved in my face, watched an ambulance drive away with my first "patient," then went to help the others. We got the two folks from the lead car and carried them a safe distance away.

When I heard more sirens, I realized I had not seen Heida since she departed in search of the flying motorcyclist. I stepped to the curb and called her name. I heard a whimper of response.

She was curled in a ball and sobbing. She'd found the rider. He was impaled on a fence post. The stake was protruding from his back just under his left shoulder.

"Heida. Heida!"

She looked up.

"Go get a medic!"

She did not move. I knew she was in shock—I'd seen it before. But I didn't have time to attend to her.

I cut away the cyclist's jacket. About the time I got his shirt off, three EMS attendants showed up. The post was three inches wide and made of wood. The medics cut the post away from the fence with a reciprocating saw and packed the area around the post with gauze. We carried him to the ambulance.

By the time we loaded him up, there were other ambulances, two fire trucks, a raft of news crews, and about a dozen cops. I checked on the other victims, who were being carted away to the hospital, then turned to go back to Heida. Someone grabbed my shoulder.

The man's windbreaker declared "Policia."

"Nome?"

"Ryan Murphy."

"De onde voce é?"[1]

---

1. "Where are you from?"

"A—" I stopped. *Damn.* "A...Ireland."

"What happen?"

I told him what I knew...in my brogue...like I had been told.

"What cause it?"

I said I did not know.

"You cut foot?"

I nodded. He walked away. Before I took three steps, I heard a voice.

"Murphy!"

I'd seen smaller refrigerators. The plainclothes cop was 6'4", easy, and solid. A gold badge was clipped to his belt. Though accented, his English was very good.

"Mr. Murphy, witnesses tell me you cut the man's foot off to save him from the fire. Is that true?"

I stood a little taller and prepared to act humble.

"I did indeed, sir. Only way t' get 'im out. Etherwise, he mighta gotten toasted."

"You better hope he makes it."

"I do indeed," I said.

His next words wiped my self-satisfied smile from my face.

"If he dies, Mr. Murphy, you could be held responsible."

CHAPTER FIFTEEN

Inspector Oliveira was neither impressed by my heroism nor swayed by my reasoning.

"What makes you the expert on amputating a man's foot, senhor?"

I explained my position at the hospital. "I've assisted on several amputations." I realized I was begging. "The man woulda burned to death, he would."

Oliveira took my name, address, and employment information and said he would "be in touch." When I turned to look for Heida, I was blinded by lights from a camera crew. A reporter started firing questions at me in Portuguese. I got some of it, but decided to use the go-to, "I'm guilty as hell" response favored by members of the Mafia and crooked accountants, "Sem comentários."[1]

I walked away and scanned the crowd. Heida was sitting on a park bench about fifty yards away. Palms under her legs, she rocked back and forth. She had the thousand-yard stare. As soon as I touched her, she started weeping, all the while looking at something and nothing at the same time.

---

1. "No comment."

"You okay?" I asked.

She saw me for the first time and barnacled onto my neck. We held each other and she cried.

Another moment in my life where everything went south in an instant...

...a traffic stop leading to a hospital stay...

...an exploding bridge and a dead British soldier...

...that fucking declaration of my college major...

Whoever said "Life is funny" was either stupid or ignorant. Life has no humor. Life is cruel.

I didn't look up until the finger tapped my shoulder a third time. I wiped my eyes and looked at a uniformed officer. Instinctively, I held out my wrists. He shook his head then jerked his thumb over his shoulder. A woman with raccoon eyes stood about ten feet away. "Talk to you," he said and stood to one side.

"Meu nome é Beatrix Lopez," she said. "Meu filo..."[2] her voice broke. "No carro..."[3]

Great heaving sobs came from somewhere deep inside and she grabbed me like a woman clinging to a floating mast to keep from going under. "Obrigado," she said. "Muito obrigato."

She released me and stumbled towards the ambulance onto which medics were loading her son. The cop, whose English was worse than my Portuguese, made signals.

"He's offering us a ride," Heida said.

---

2. "My son..."

3. "In the car..."

"Got it."

More waving arms. Heida pointed to me, then to herself. She interlocked the fingers.

"You're coming home with me," she said. "I don't want to be alone."

"Me either," I said.

A few minutes later, we stepped out of the cop's cruiser.

A while ago, after dinner, I'd envisioned our entrance...the door flying open...panting bodies slamming into the wall...fingers fumbling with uncooperative buttons and stuck zippers...tongues dueling...clothes strewn across the floor...and lamp-shaking, furniture-breaking sex on the couch, the floor, the counters, and up against the wall (which experience had told me was not nearly as easy as Hollywood made it look).

Instead, we collapsed on the couch and resumed the crying jag. Then we fell asleep, curled up on the couch in each other's arms. Lust was no longer on the menu.

I awakened to horrible breath—Gus.

"Geez, buddy," I said, "you need a breath mint."

Heida was already awake and making breakfast. There is no more distinct smell than bacon frying. My clothes were stiff with dried blood.

Heida had showered. She had on a silk kimono. Her hair was still wet. She looked like a goddess. I wrapped my arms around her. "Morning," I said.

She proffered a piece of bacon over her shoulder. "Your breath is worse than Gus's," she said. She pivoted. That smile...wow! "And you smell like a compost pile." She looked over my shoulder. "If you hurry, you can shower and make it to work on time."

I hustled down the street with a handful of bacon and a warm bagel in each pocket. When I unlocked my door, Lucky raced outside like his tail was on fire. I left the door open for his return and walked into my bathroom.

The image staring at me from my mirror could have starred as the victim in a slasher movie. Besides the rust-colored stains on my shirt and pants, there was dried blood all over my arms and face. My hair spiked up—red tinged.

My clothes went into a trash bag, and I stepped into the shower where I watched the crimson reminder of the previous evening's nightmare swirl down the drain.

CHAPTER SIXTEEN

I looked like every other hospital worker on my way through the double glass doors—a significant improvement from the derelict I had presented thirty minutes earlier. I knew the day would be counting sponges and sterilizing equipment, but last night's upheaval had given me a new understanding of the patients. I only saw them when they were on the table. I never thought about the trauma they endured before someone put a mask over their faces and told them to count backwards from one hundred.

We weren't slapping bumpers on Fords, we were making decisions that would affect people long into the future. And I wasn't sure this was a place I needed to stay.

We started the morning with a trio of appendectomies followed by a cholecystectomy. I'd gotten over the "yuckies" long ago, so I ate lunch with the gusto of a high school wrestler the day after the season ended. God—or Fate or something else—smiled on me because no one asked about my night o' romance. I could handle the carnage of the OR but I knew I would never get through lunch if I had to regale my compatriots with the story of the speared motorcyclist. And I certainly did not need anyone giving me an amputation-based nickname like "Quicksaw Murphy." I listened to accounts of other first dates, snoring husbands, and a baptism. For reasons I will never understand, a tech named Gloria decided we wanted the most intimate details of her marriage.

"Eduardo cuts his damn toenails and leaves the clippings on the table. It's been going on for years. I've been warning him about it and all he ever does it laugh. Well. I showed him. I found his nails on the table again on Saturday. He was watching the football match, so I asked if he wanted lunch. He was most pleased when I gave him his favorite—a tuna fish sandwich. He loved it. He asked if I'd added sesame seeds or something. 'No,' I said. 'Something is crunchy,' he said. 'Quite delicious.'"

Every person at the table put down their sandwich.

"Did you tell him?" I asked.

"Not until later. After the game, we were drinking wine. He made overtures—you know—sexy time. He rubbed my shoulders and kissed my neck. I made a great show of moaning and such. He took off his shirt, grabbed my hand—he has never been the gentle sort—and pulled me into the bedroom."

A chorus of "ooooo" and "ahhhh" erupted followed by a cascade of questions.

"What did you do?" "Did you tell him?"

"'Hector, darling' I said, 'you know I love you and I always want to make love with you, but why do you ignore the things I ask of you?' He was confused. He stood in the middle of the bedroom with his pants halfway off. 'What do you mean?' he asked. 'I love you, Gloria. Right now I want to show you how much. You know I will do anything you ask.' He gave me *that* look. 'Anything at all.'"

The men all chortled. The women looked disgusted.

"I undid a few buttons on my blouse," Gloria said. "His eyes were getting big."

"Among other things," one of the women said. There were howls of laughter.

"You promised not to tell, Maria," Gloria said. Everyone laughed again.

"'Hector, my love,' I said, 'you always leave your toenail shrapnel lying around. You know it upsets me. I've been asking you to throw them away—you still leave them on the coffee table.' Well, he took me in his arms. 'I am sorry,' he said. 'I will do better, but right now, we have more important things to consider. I will clean them up just as soon as we are finished.'"

"'No worries,' I said. 'I took care of them.' He was not paying attention, so I said, 'Did you like the sandwich for lunch?' He looked a little confused. 'Yes, I did, but this is not the time—' I interrupted. 'Crunchy with the chips in it like you prefer.' 'Very crunchy,' he said. 'New chips?'"

Giggles rippled through the room.

"'Oh, I added a special ingredient this time.' 'I know,' he said. 'You added love—now why don't you show me a little of your special ingredient?'"

By now, Gloria had to shout over the chorus of hoots and catcalls. Everyone was smiling.

"'I added your toenail clippings, you dolt!' I said. His eyes bulged. I could see him struggling to swallow. He ran to the bath and threw up. By the time he came out, I was naked on the bed. 'Come get some, big boy,' I said. He walked right out of the room and did not speak to me the rest of the day!"

CHAPTER SEVENTEEN

We headed back to surgery with smiles on our faces, but by the time we entered the OR, we were all business. I was in OR 6, not my favorite—mostly spinal work. Because of my inexperience with more complicated procedures, the nurses had to split time between doing their intricate jobs and babysitting me. Sometimes they got a little cranky.

Today's menu was spondylosis.

"What's that?" I asked.

"Spinal fusion," she said. I swear she rolled her eyes.

We moved the patient onto the operating table and positioned him face down. The gas-passer did his thing and I cranked up the entrance music for Dr. Estevez: "Jumpin' Jack Flash." He took a scalpel and waited. I switched music to his "incision" song: "Paint It Black." Any time there was a pause between songs, he stopped until the music cranked back up.

The guy was eccentric, but from what I could tell, he knew his way around a spinal cord. He went through three Stones albums before the procedure was completed, but when the last suture was in place, he looked around and said, "Ben feito."[1]

I was swabbing the floor of the OR when the PA crackled. "Ryan Murphy para Administração. Ryan Murphy para Administração."

It's over.

I cleaned up and headed to the Administration Office. I didn't bother changing out of my scrubs. Maybe appearing before a judge in surgical garb would buy me some sympathy.

He has atoned for his sins, your honor. We ask for leniency.

I rounded the final corner and braced myself for the sight of armed Brits—maybe a SWAT team. I started wondering about local extradition laws. On the way through the door, I reminded myself to "be Irish."

"Ryan Murphy t' see the boss," I said.

The secretary smiled and picked up the phone. I heard "Ryan Murphy." The rest was a stream of warp speed Portuguese. She never took her eyes off of me.

"This way," she said after she cradled the phone.

I decided to take a shot. "What's going on? Am I in trouble?"

Her English was perfect, with only the slightest hint of an accent. "You don't know?"

"I assume I am being fired," I said.

She laughed in a "you dumb bastard" sort of way. "Hardly," she said.

---

1. "Well done."

The conference room was full of people, most of whom were smoking. I'd been in New Jersey bars with cleaner air. The secretary said, "Ryan Murphy," and the place erupted in applause.

A slender man in his fifties approached. When he grabbed my hand, I recognized the touch of someone who wouldn't know which end of a shovel to hold—soft hands, puttyish grip.

"Santiago Pereira," he said. "Hospital President."

I looked around and did not recognize anyone. "Nice to meet you," I said. *Might as well rip off the Band Aid.* "May I ask what this is about?"

"Ah, direct, to the point—a man of action," he said. "Precisely why you are here."

Someone moved towards me from the corner of the room. This one I recognized: the reporter from the accident.

Pereira was still talking. "We understand you saved some lives last night and we want to show you the honor you deserve. We are very proud when our staff members help people in need outside of our walls. The story of your courage last night overwhelms every one of us, and we want to commend you for taking charge."

He threw his arm around me. A flash went off. While I was still blinking, Beatrix Lopez came through the door, followed by an orderly pushing a hospital bed. I recognized the face on the pillow.

I blinked again—hard, and not because of any flashes. I did not want to break down in front of all these people. Without warning, I felt like I had a piano on my back. My legs wobbled, but I righted myself. The stress and trauma of the previous night hit me squarely between the eyes.

Beatrix introduced her son Rodrigo. He smiled faintly. He was on pain meds and spoke no English, but I could read his eyes. They screamed, "Thank you—you saved my life!"

I let the moment—and my ego—sweep me away. All of a sudden, I was the center of *positive* attention. Beatrix was rattling away. I made out "herói"[2] and that was pretty much all I needed. Two days ago, I might have smiled, ducked my head, and fled back to the OR. Now I was holding court and explaining every aspect of my newly discovered field medic talent. I turned into a pseudo-Irish version of television's Charles Emerson Winchester, a bloviating self-promoter who could not shut up about my exploits. Yes, I camouflaged it all in a veneer of humility—lots of "aw shucks" type crap—but I was damn proud of myself.

A translator fired a question at me from the reporter. "You took this man's foot. He will never walk again. Did you do the right thing? Is this a good example? Other people may see your story and try to do the same thing."

I froze, instantaneously aware I had flown too close to the sun. This wasn't talking about sexual escapades or bitching about egomaniacal surgeons with my co-workers. My face was going to be all over the news. Sure, maybe I was in some backwater part of Portugal, but still.

Pereira came to the rescue. He eased between me and the camera and, in a way known by executives the world around, began to take credit for what I had done. According to el Presidente, I'd been trained by the finest nurses and techs in the area, all of whom he

---

2. Hero

had hired. The standards of excellence he had established since his arrival...blah...blah...blah.

The reporter left and we celebrated my work with hors d'oeuvres and champagne. When I reached for the door, Pereira touched my shoulder.

"You are done for the day, my friend," he said.

"I only had a sip of champagne," I said. "I'm fine."

His capped teeth, at least one size too big for his mouth, glistened. "Oh no," he said. "You are to go home and relax. You have earned a week off—paid—for your gallantry and quick thinking. You have brought great honor to our hospital. It is the least we can do."

I headed for Heida's.

I wish I hadn't.

CHAPTER EIGHTEEN

She answered the door after I sat on the bell for a solid thirty seconds. She was not the vision she had been when I awakened. Her cheeks evidenced tears; her eyes were swollen and vacant.

"Hi," she said.

"Hi yourself," I said. "May I come in?"

"Wish you wouldn't," she said.

I froze with one foot inside. My head swiveled. She was looking through me.

"What's wrong?" I asked. "What did I do?"

She probably didn't wait forty-five minutes before she answered, but it felt that way.

"What didn't you do?"

Once again, my high school debate training paid dividends. "Huh?"

Another interminable wait.

"Go on," I said. I had retreated back out the door by now.

Heida took a deep breath. "Last night was wonderful at first. The dinner...the conversation...the kiss—"

Moron that I am, I tried to be funny. "Only one good kiss." I wilted in her glare. "Sorry," I said.

"Anyway," she said—she sounded like a teacher who'd just sent the problem kid in her class to the principal's office— "it was all great and then…"

I waited to be sure she wasn't going to speak. "I know," I said. "Pretty awful."

"Didn't seem that way to you," she said. "I was curled up in a fucking ball—"

I knew I shouldn't interrupt again but I felt compelled to lighten the mood. "Don't beat yourself up about that. You did great. You found the motorcycle popsicle guy—"

"Goddammit, Ryan! You think that's funny?" Now she was looking at me and the effect was not pleasant. She might very well have been inspecting something unpleasant she'd scraped from the bottom of her shoe. "The man was impaled, and you make a joke? What the hell is wrong with you?"

Shit!

I blanched, opened my mouth, then bit my lip.

"You bounded around the scene like Superman. All you needed was a red cape."

I made sure to eliminate any trace of sarcasm from my voice. "Well, I was a cop, you know."

"You told me you were basically a traffic cop. You never said you were one of those guys who kicks in doors and shit. What you did last night wasn't normal. There was gore everywhere and you never flinched. There's something you're not telling me."

"I…I…I…"

"Don't try!" She was not aware that she was screaming, but I was. I tried to move her inside. She wrenched her arm away. Her voice sounded like the loudspeaker at Fenway Park. "Nimm deine verdammen hände von mir."[1]

I was not an expert in German, but anyone could have understood.

"Heida, I won't touch you again," I said. "But please calm down. People will think you're being attacked."

She blinked five or six times in rapid succession—someone coming out of a trance. "Sorry," she said in a way that indicated she was not. "I saw something in you last night—something odd—something frightening. Maybe I was just in shock. Maybe I am humiliated by my inaction. I don't know. But I know one thing. I cannot see you anymore."

The door shut and I was alone in the street.

---

1. "Take your fucking hands off me!"

CHAPTER NINETEEN

The bar was empty. And pretty soon, the bottle of wine was as well.

My first sip was accompanied by thoughts of *It'll be fine. She's just upset.* By the time I reached the bottom of the second bottle, I couldn't think at all.

I wandered my way home and collapsed on the couch. Lucky was curled up on the floor. The last thing I could remember was something one of my buddies on the force had said: "Falling in love is pretty good. But remember, it's not the fall that kills you; it's the sudden stop at the bottom."

I had the dream again. It always came with a few variations, but the theme was consistent. I was on a beach with half a coconut in my hand. A straw and a cute little umbrella leaned from the shell. I sipped, said "ahh," and looked at my naked body. Gwendolyn smiled at me from the neighboring chaise.

She smiled in her knowing way, the signal she was ready to make love—an act destined to render everything else inconsequential. She moved closer. A cooperative breeze blew her hair away from her torso. I was mesmerized by the beauty of her nakedness. I put out my hand to caress her. Her skin was...

...hairy.

I shot upright. A strong hand covered my mouth. Someone was holding me. After struggling for a few seconds, I surrendered, lay back, and prepared for the bullet in my brain.

They found me.

A voice came out of the darkness. "We're not here to hurt ya, lad. I'm gonna take m'hand away, but if ya scream, Blarnard'll lay ya out with his sap. Ya understand?"

I nodded.

The light came on. Two men, both stocky, stood next to the couch. I'd seen the type before—I didn't want any part of these guys.

"Whaddya want?" I asked.

They looked at one another. "Gotta hand it to him, Blarnard," the first man said. "He's still tryin' to pass as Irish."

"Might fool a Yank," Blarnard said, "but he won't get past a true son of Erin."

"Fuck it," I said. "What's up?"

"M'name's...well...call me Sean," the first man said.

"'Cause that's his name an' he's too much of a ludder to come up with sumptin' on the fly," the other one said.

"Shut yer pie hole," Sean said. He looked at me. "Ya made a hash o' yer situation here, lad. Yer face is all over the news. Ye're a fecking' celeb, ya are."

"Who the hell saw the interview?" I asked. "We're in the middle of nowhere."

"True," Sean said, "in the middle of nowhere that a Tommy general decided to use as his family holiday spot. Our intel says the

Brits are on the way t' the hospital right now. That puts them about thirty minutes away from here, tops."

"Ya got three minutes to pack," Blarnard said.

I took my time getting up.

Sean slapped me across the face. "Shake yer arse, Murphy," he said.

I had not completely forgotten my training. I had a "go bag" ready. I spent my allotted 180 seconds rounding up Lucky's stuff. My new friends were well briefed. They didn't even try to talk me into leaving my dog—my only friend.

"Where we going?" I asked.

Their answer was to shove me into the back of yet another van, in which we drove to yet another destination in the middle of yet another night of fear and confusion.

CHAPTER TWENTY

No one spoke. The few attempts I made at conversation were met with icy stares and muttered curses. When we drove past the city limits sign, I ran numbers through my head. I'd been in Lagos for over a year. Now I was hoping they would hide me in the country, a place where Lucky would thrive, and Heida could visit on weekends.

Heida...she of the smiling face and luxurious kisses.

Heida...blonde and beautiful.

Heida...who apparently never wanted to see me again.

My dreams of passionate afternoons dissipated like morning fog vaporized by the rising sun—and we kept driving. About ninety minutes later we entered a town called Faro. Despite the early hour, the place looked busy. Shops were already open. I could smell salt in the air.

"This the last stop?" I asked.

"Handin' ya off, lad," one of them said. "Ya get t' be the pain in someone else's arse."

Thus ended the verbal exchange.

We stopped in front of a pub named Clancy's.

Clancy's

Irish, seems about right.

"Follow me an' don't say a feckin' word."

I had visions of tending bar again. I was a good bartender. I could sling suds with the best. I was affable and a good listener—

A palm struck my face. "I told ya not t' speak. Are ya daft? Ye're back there muttering like the motor to yer mouth is stuck."

I was third through the backdoor and guided to a walk-in cooler where I sat at a table wedged in the middle of the stacks of Guinness cases. Lucky lay on the cool floor, let out a contented sigh, and went to sleep. I patted him on the head. "Good boy," I said.

When I looked up, Lucky and I were alone.

I could hear music through the door, which made me question the cooler's insulation. "Jug of Punch" was blaring away. Pretty early in the morning for a drinking song on the jukebox, but I figured the barman was probably bored.

One pleasant evening in the month of June, as I was sitting with my glass and spoon, a small bird sat on an ivy bunch and the song he sang was "Jug of Punch."

Toor-rah-loora la, toor-rah-loora-lie,
toor-rah-loora-la, toor-rah-loora-lie.

I closed my eyes and mouthed the words. I knew them all from countless nights behind the bar at Simpson's in Belfast. I was rounding the corner into the second verse when the door opened and a large, bearded man wearing an apron and an Irish wool tweed cap entered the cooler. The lighting was poor, but something about him rang a bell. I couldn't quite place him. He stood, hands on hips, and shook his head.

Then... "Hello, Ryan."

I knew the voice.

"Bump," I said. I smiled and stood to shake his hand.

"Sit the feck down! What is wrong with you? You promised me you would stay off the grid, instead you put your sorry arse on television."

I had only heard his brogue for about half a day. The rest of the time during our acquaintance on the Camino, Oisin Byrne had affected the twang of an Arkansas chicken farmer while posing as Bump Olimeyer.

The face was covered with a mass of tangled hair, but I would never forget the booming pronouncements of the soldier from the Green Liberation Front. He had saved my ass in Santiago, Spain. His last words had been, "Ye're on the run from now until there ain't no monarch in England. Good luck to ya, Murphy. May God hold ya in the palm of his hand." A sweet blessing, but the implication was that he never wanted to see me again.

"Oisin, calm down, it wasn't my fault."

"Nothing's ever yer fault, is it Ryan! Can't ya follow a simple order? All ya had t' do wuz keep yer feckin' face out of the limelight. Instead, ya plaster yer ugly mug all over Portuguese television and dare any Brit within three hunnert miles t' come and get ya. You're feckin insane, I tell ya!"

"Can I at least explain?" I realized I was begging. "If you knew the situation, I think you'd understand."

"Screw yer understandin'," he said, "And while ye're at it, may the lamb of God stir his hoof through the roof of heaven and kick you in the arse down to hell."

"Wrong place at the wrong time. It wasn't intentional, trust me."

"Trust you, really?" Oisin's characteristic smile was absent. I wondered if the grin had been Bump's artifice—yet another layer of deception in a ruse I had bought completely.

Like Michiko, I thought. *She loved me...she wanted to be with me...always. I thought...*

The memories vanished in the face of Oisin's persistent verbal barrage. "Yer story don't matter," he said. "Ye're here 'cause ye're an awful eejit. Ya know, ya wouldn't be the first one to disappear from this cooler. A lot of people have walked in here and been carried out in pieces."

An ice pick of fear ran up my spine. "You going to kill me?" I asked.

The pause was long...longer than it needed to be...for effect.

"No," he said. "Not now anyways. I'll find ya a cot. If I know where you are, maybe I can keep you out of trouble. At least in here, ya won't be ag bualadh craicinn[1] with some wench ya picked up strollin' about."

I was about to launch into a defense of Michiko's honor when I noticed the steely set of Oisin's jaw. I wasn't too far from "sleeping with the fishes," like Luca Brasi in *The Godfather.*

"Tomorrow, ye'll be getting' on a boat."

"Are we going back to the Algarve?"

"Ya never left," he said. He chewed on his lip for a while. "I don't know where ye're headed yet. I'm waitin' on a call from Belfast. I can guarantee ya one thing though, mate. Ye're gonna hafta learn a new language. That fake brogue wouldn't fool an Irish setter. Lovely animals, but dumber than a box of hammers, they are." I would have protested but Oisin's eyes were pinpoints of fury. "Yer little appearance on the telly means we're outta English speakin' options unless they put ya down under."

I gulped. "They're going to kill me for being interviewed?"

"Jesus, Mary, and Joseph ye're dense, boy," he said. "If they were gonna do ya in, ya'd already be pushing up daisies. Down Under...Australia."

I had a brief vision of kangaroos, koala bears, and platypuses...or was it platypii? Oisin was still talking.

---

1. Slang for sexual intercourse: Literal translation – "whacking skin together."

"Ya need t' know, if they'd told me to off ya, it'd be done—a double tap behind the right ear...always my preferred side. Come on, then."

I was still shivering when he led me to the stairs, and it wasn't from the cold. These people were different...ruthless...true believers. They didn't care about me. It was all about the cause.

A rickety army surplus cot stood guard in the corner of an upstairs office.

"It'll take a minute t' git yer travel documents in order, so ya've got three days here," Oisin said. He pointed to a door. "There's the loo. Don't even tink about leavin' tis room," Oisin said. He held two fingers to his temple and mimed shooting himself in the head. "I'll send some food when I feel like it."

CHAPTER TWENTY-ONE

The days crawled by. The nights were slower. Whoever was in the bar had a big time. I heard shouts and songs and clinking glasses well into the wee hours. I might have joined them, but I kept seeing Oisin's very unsubtle warning in my imagination.

Oisin waited until I was a little scraggly to take my passport photo. He said the stubble would help disguise me a little. My hair was longish and, thanks to the Mediterranean sun, a little lighter. Still, Oisin bleached my hair. I looked a little like Hardy Krüger in *A Bridge Too Far.* I was spared the ignominy of wearing the itchy fake mustache they'd forced on me when I left Belfast.

"Ya best not feck up this time," Oisin said. "We've done all we can wid hair and the like. If ya have to move again, it'll mean face-altering surgery." He paused. "And a bullet is much cheaper."

The departure day arrived. When I awoke, I smelled something foul. I looked at Lucky. "You stink, buddy," I said.

He cocked his head; his ears stood at attention.

I sniffed again. "Sorry," I said. "It's me."

I hadn't bothered to shower. Depression makes personal hygiene an afterthought. Yep, I was way past "worried" or "blue." I was in the depths of personal despair. Once again, I'd walked into a room marked "A Happy Life" only to trip on my own ego and screw it up. Heida didn't know where I was—and probably never would. If she even cared.

"I was so damn close," I said.

Lucky looked at me. Skepticism painted his face.

"I'm not talking about sex," I said, although I'd had more than a few dreams about Heida and the delights I might have found in her unclothed company. "I mean...shit, never mind."

Lucky lay on the floor and crossed his paws over his nose.

"I get it," I said. "I get it."

The water was cold. The soap was grainy and smelled slightly of gasoline, but when I was finished, I felt a little less ursine.

I was still drying my hair when a bowling ball of a man opened the door. He jerked his head towards the stairs.

"Should I bring my stuff?"

He nodded.

Lucky trotted along behind me. Oisin and two others were seated at the bar. The remnants of what looked like breakfast for two dozen people littered the counter. I raised a hand in greeting. Oisin threw me a biscuit and pointed to the back door.

The van rolled out. We rode in silence for a while until Oisin decided to speak.

"Ya know, Murphy," he said. "I can't figger out why the GLF keeps protectin' ya. Not fer the life of me. When ye're not thinkin' with yer lad" —he inclined his head in the direction of my crotch— "ye're not thinkin' a'tall."

There was nothing I could do but shrug. He had a point.

"When they sent me here, they wanted me t' fit in a bit, so they bought me a boat. A fine little craft it is—a little fishin' rig. Truth be told, I've dropped more bodies in the sea than I've taken fishies out it."

"Sounds like a threat," I said.

"Trust me Ryan, if I had my way, the sharks would have been feastin' on yer bollocks last night. They feed at night, and coming across a naked body tied to some concrete blocks at the bottom of the ocean is like winning the lottery for them boys."

I almost mentioned an elaborate plot to kill James Bond but thought better of it. This was not the time for my classic sarcasm. "If you're not going to kill me, what are you going to do?"

"I didn't say I would never kill ya," he said. "Let's just say ya got a temporary stay of execution. What happens next is up to Belfast, but I promise: if ya feck up again, the order will come, and sure as shite, I'll make it happen. Savvy?"

"Loud and feckin clear," I said. "Now, where are we going?"

"Don't get yer knickers in a bunch," he said. "I'll tell ya when we're away."

The *Night Cap* was a thirty-two footer rigged for sport fishing. The name was perfect, at least for Oisin when he'd been disguised as Bump—always springing for another round, never leaving until last call. Bump was fun.

Oisin was an asshole...a dangerous one.

While we loaded the gear, I chatted with Oisin, mostly to calm my nerves. He decided to act more human—at least for a while.

"Much luck?" I asked.

"Know fishin', do ya?" he asked.

"Enough to spot a marlin lure when I see one," I said. "Catch anything special?"

"Nuttin' much over four hundred pounds," he said. "But, like I mentioned, we ain't really here for the sport."

Declan, Patrick, and I finished hauling stuff on board. Oisin fired up the motor. It purred like a well-fed tiger. We cast off and moved out to sea.

Declan took the helm and Oisin motioned me to the bow. Lucky, curled in a corner at the stern, never thought about moving. After he tired of busting my balls, Oisin settled in on our destination.

"Ya know, there were plans to get ya back Stateside in another two years," he said. He saw me perk up. "Don't get excited. Ain't gonna happen now. Now that ye're the hero du jour, everyone'll be lookin' for ya."

"Okay," I said. I could feel my shoulders sag. It seemed to me that I'd been on the run for decades. "Where to now?"

"Casablanca," he said.

"As in Morocco?" I asked. "Like in fucking Africa?"

He touched his nose with his index finger.

"I won't make it thirty minutes," I said. I tried to keep the panic out of my voice—without success. "Somebody will cut my throat. I've seen movies about that place, and the ending never goes well for people who look like me."

"At least ye won't die hungry," Oisin said. "The couscous is to die fer."

"I like Chinese food," I said, "but that doesn't mean I want to live in Motuo County."

Oisin's eyebrows raised. "How do you know about a remote province in China?" he asked.

"I may be a dumbass," I said, "but I am not ignorant."

Declan opened the throttle a little. Oisin had to raise his voice to be heard. He didn't mind. He liked yelling at me. "I don't make the rules, Murphy. Ye're the one who fecked up. My orders are t' get yer arse out of harm's way—again, I might add. There's a massive manhunt for ya rampin' up on the Iberian Peninsula now. Ye're photo's everywhere, even at that hospital where ya somehow managed not to kill anyone."

Now was not the time to proclaim my excellence as a healthcare professional.

"No one thinks ye're a hero anymore, lad. With any luck, we'll get ya to Morocco and everyone will stop thinking about ya after a while."

"So, I need to learn Arabic?"

And I thought Portuguese was tough.

"Nope," Oisin said. "We keep ya there till the radar stops searchin' for ya, then we'll put ya on a plane. Right now, ye're too hot to travel much of anywhere.""Where to when I finally move?"

"Yer travel agents at the GLF are gonna give ya a choice: Greece, Turkey, or Germany." He waited. "Well?"

"I choose now?"

I could tell Oisin was trying to rein in his temper. "Christ on a cracker, boy, it ain't like asking for a pint at the bar. These things take time...planning...coordination...forged documents. Now choose before I make the decision for ya—and it might not be so pleasant."

I took a long, deliberate moment to stare over his shoulder into the water...the very deep water.

"Greece is going to be hotter than hell," I said. "Like living in Mississippi only without good barbeque. I saw *Midnight Express* a while back. No way I'm risking a Turkish prison."

"It's settled then," Oisin said. "Germany."

"I didn't pick," I said. "I was ruminating."

"Like you thought you had a choice," Oisin said. "Ya'd stand out like a street walker in a convent in those other places with yer pasty-ass complexion and yer masterful grasp of languages."

That stung a little.

"Well, I would have picked Germany anyway," I said. "I can get a job slinging suds in a beer hall."

My head snapped back. Oisin was loading up to hit me again. I threw my hands up to protect my face.

"This isn't a feckin' joke," he said.

I rubbed my cheek. "I know," I said. "I try to be funny when I'm nervous.""Well, ya'd best learn to do better," he said, "'cause ye're gonna be livin' on the edge of the razor for the next few years."

CHAPTER TWENTY-TWO

Oisin radioed my new destination to someone as we sailed through the Gulf of Cadiz. We docked briefly to take on fuel in Barbate, Spain. Lucky bounded onto the dock in search of the nearest tree before we tied off.

"Well trained pooch." It was the first time Patrick had spoken. He sounded a little like an asthmatic parakeet. I knew better than to tease him. Somewhere along the line, I'd learned two things about him. He'd been exposed to sulfur gas, which explained the voice. And he was a trained assassin, which explained why I shut the hell up about the first point.

"He's a good boy," I said.

"Had him long?"

"Over a year," I said. "We sort of found each other a while back."

"Nothing like a good dog," Patrick said. "Good companions. And if push comes to shove, they ain't bad if ya roast 'em right. Tastes a little like mutton."

I'd been watching Lucky run around the dock. I turned to see if Patrick was kidding.

He wasn't.

Refueled, we shoved off. A few hours later, we arrived in Tangiers, the northern-most tip of Morocco. We moored and slept on the *Night Cap.*

I awakened to screeching gulls and the glare of the sun rising over the Mediterranean. Declan and Patrick hitched a ride to the dock on a private dingy. Forty minutes later, they came aboard with eggs flavored with dark Moroccan olives, and a salty, crunchy pastry called Harsha along with Jben.[1] I loved the food of Portugal and Spain, but this brought cuisine to a whole new level.

"Don't fall in love with the haji food, Murphy," Oisin said. "You won't be here very long." He stuffed a piece of cheese in his mouth and licked his fingers. "Hope you like käsespätzle."

"And gas," Declan said. "Sauerkraut gives me the wind something awful."

I tried not to think of the vile smells that might emanate from the mountain of a man. Oisin saw my nose wrinkle and laughed. "It's as bad as ya think, lad," he said. "Wondrous toxic it is."

Apparently, food made Oisin chatty—or he was just pleased by the thought of being rid of me.

"Before ya go, ya have t' try the spiced lamb. They serve it up with black olives and roasted potatoes. Trust me, it's better than sex."

Declan's chirp skipped across off the water. "Pretty hollow advice from a fifty-year-old virgin!" He looked at me. "The food's good. The rides on the women are better—a lot better."

---

1. Soft cheese, usually made from goat's milk, Jben is often flavored with herbs or honey. It's the closest thing to ricotta in Morocco.

Oisin wiped his mouth on his sleeve and stood. Breakfast was over. "Alright, ya bunch o' perverts," he said, "back to the task at hand. We gotta get Murphy so far away that I'll never have to save his arse again."

My inner smartass emerged from hiding. "I know you're going to miss me, sweetie," I said.

I had misinterpreted the mood.

"Call me that again and I'll slit yer throat." He looked at his crew. "We have six hours to make Casablanca. HQ put a rush on the docs. Passport, driver's license, health card. Everytin' will be ready an' waitin' on this gowl[2] at Mohammed V International. If we make it, the night's yer own t' do wit as ya please."

Patrick and Declan exchanged knowing glances and set to their tasks with renewed energy. I watched the receding shoreline and went back to memories of my carefree life before any of this. Growing up on Lake George in the Adirondack Mountains of New York was special. Lake George, the queen of American lakes, meant loading up a boat with one-part guys and about twelve parts beer. Nothing beat circumnavigating the thirty-two mile shoreline in search of female companionship while reducing the beer-to-bro ratio as rapidly as possible. It was never dangerous...until it was, but I chose to reflect on the good times.

We always cruised south and stopped along the way. We docked at bait shops and bars. We chatted up locals and hit mercilessly on anything with a bustline. God, we were incorrigible. And not particularly bright. All the way down was warm and sunny, but the

---

2. Annoying person. Pronounced gow-el.

return trip—northward into the dark clad in wet swim trunks—was invariably miserable. But, aside from my moments with Gwendolyn, they were the best times of my life.

Without thinking, I looked around the *Night Cap* for a case of beer. When I didn't spot any, the reality of the moment smacked me in the head like a swinging boom on a sailboat. I was on the move again, destined for a country I didn't know anything about other than the WWII lectures I'd ignored and movies like *Stalag 17* with Bill Holden and *The Dirty Dozen*. If pushed, I might have admitted to believing most Germans looked like Karl-Otto Alberty from *Kelly's Heroes*, white blonde and spooky.

Damn, I am ignorant.

We motored across the water for another four hours, a lot of time for reflection and plenty of opportunities for Oisin to rag me about one thing or another.

He was a weird duck. One minute, he was threatening all manner of violence; the next, he reverted to his alter ego—Bump Olimeyer—and sounded like he was ready to jump in a Chevy for a cross-country road trip.

Finally, I summoned up my courage. "Oisin, you going with me?"

"Hell no," he said. "Once I get ya t' Muhammed, we're done. It's slán leat.³ Ya won't see me again. Cause if I come back, ye'll never see me comin'."

"Okay," I said, "so it's time to clear the air."

"Fire away mate, but be careful what you ask for."

---

3. "Health to you."

"Okay great, easy question," I said. "Is Oisin Byrne your real name?"

"Are you taking the piss? Bloody hell no; you take me for a fool?"

"I'm not surprised. How'd you get tangled up in all this?"

Oisin stared out over the water. He was gone for a moment, transported somewhere deep in his mind. When he came back, his face was a little softer. "Raised in Derry by a Catholic family, I wuz," he said. "Me mum tried, but I was a bad kid. Got pinched one too many times. The resident magistrate gave me a choice: prison or the military."

"Pretty easy call," I said.

"I thought so," he said. "Truth to tell, I wanted to be a hooligan, but me ma said the Blessed Virgin would strike me blind. So, I joined the Royal Marines, and they made a soldier out of me. I was sent to fight in the Bush War in Southern Rhodesia."

"You were good, I bet," I said.

A hint of a smile. "Damn good," he said. "Too good. Killin' came easy. Worked my way up to lieutenant."

"Surprised you didn't make colonel."

"Might have, but I had...well...let's just say I occasionally had differences of opinion with some of the field commanders."

"Imagine that," I said. I instantly regretted the comment, but Oisin smiled.

"After Rhodesia, was assigned to the Middle East, anti-terrorism. Really enjoyed the work."

"Seriously?"

"Where have ya been, Murphy? I got to kill people whenever I damn well chose."

He was still smiling but there was something reptilian behind the eyes—a hungry croc stalking an unsuspecting tourist.

"Still," I said, "sounds like you were being trained to track down people like me instead of helping us escape. Something happened, didn't it?"

"Not as stupid as you look," he said.

Oisin's face, a picture of contentment not long before, transformed into a malevolent mask. Fury bubbled beneath the surface of a thin, pasted-on smile.

He'd gotten out after six years. The discharge was honorable, but no one had fought his decision to leave. He intended to work in the Derry shipyard like his grandfather and father. When he turned the corner to his old neighborhood, what he saw were hulking ruins, something out of a war movie.

Some local kids had been harassing the British troops. The army evicted the entire row of houses and forced several hundred tenants into the squalor of public housing. While the residents were still on the street collecting their belongings, a trio of Chieftain tanks rolled down the street, stopped, and used the simple but happy former homes for target practice. When all that remained were smoking ruins, the war machines turned and clanked away like they were in a parade.

"One of the arseholes in the lead tank had a portable tape machine and some powerful speakers," Oisin said. "He cranked up the volume and played 'God Save the Feckin' Queen.'"

I didn't say anything. I couldn't speak.

His younger brothers were sent to prison without benefit of trial. When Oisin filed an official complaint, complete with a profane verbal assault, he was shipped off to HMP Magilligan for six months on the charge of suspected terrorism.

"The guards knew I was ex-military," Oisin said. He was staring through me. My hair could have been on fire and he would not have noticed. "They beat me twice a week for sport. They wanted to see if they could get me to fight back. They're only alive today because I wouldn't."

They suspected his two younger brothers of being a part of the gang that was harassing the British.

The day of his release he went to a pub where a friendly stranger stood him a pint. The new acquaintance was a recruiter for the GLF, which was currently sending its soldiers to North Africa to be trained by the Palestinian Liberation Organization. Financial support for the GLF came from the Republic of Ireland, friends in the U.S., and the Balkans, but there was increasing pressure for the organization to separate itself from the PLO.

Once the brass learned of Oisin's extensive training, he was put in charge of teaching guerilla warfare. He instructed his students in hand-to-hand combat, munitions, bomb making, and battlefield first aid. When the organization pushed away from the PLO, the money faucet opened wide.

"One night, someone sent some commandos to our site. They were Billy Badass Boys, or so they thought. We'd just finished our trainin' regime, so ever-one was up t' speed. When it was over—and it was over quick—there were four dead Brits and one more who was wounded and didn't live to see the sunrise. My boys didn't have so much as a hangnail. Turned out the attackers were mercenaries hired by the PLO. It was the last time they fecked with us."

We sat for a while and watched the dolphins bob up and down next to the hull. Oisin slapped me on the knee. "Ya know kid, I kinda like ya. I pick on ya a lot, but I think ya got some big bollocks. Ya been through a lot. In a way, I wish I wuz goin' t' Deutschland wid ya. Instead, I'm going back to my bar to sell pints of Guinness and live a quiet life."

He saw something flash through my brain.

"Oh no, lad. If ya ever wander into m'bar, I'll put a bullet in your skull. Got that?"

"Loud and clear Oisin...or Bump...or whatever the fuck your name is today."

The landscape changed from the barren dessert to a more urban area. Patrick announced we would soon be arriving in Casablanca Morocco. When we anchored, we shook hands, and I attached Lucky's leash. He had the look of a dog who really needed some foliage. We stepped into the dinghy.

Oisin handed me a few bills. "Fer the taxi," he said.

I nodded but turned back when he said, "One more ting."

"What?"

"Ya can't be travelin' wid da pooch. By now, ever-one knows about Lucky. Ya try to take him on a plane and ever copper will know who y'are. Best ya leave him wid me. I promise ya, I'll watch after him like he was me own."

I knew if I argued, I could keep Lucky. I also knew keeping him was a mistake. I handed his leash to Patrick. Lucky growled but went with him. I stared at my shoes to avoid the look of betrayal.

"Thanks for the ticket," I said.

I turned my back on the boat and wandered towards the crowd on the quay. Halfway along its length, something inside broke.

And I wept.

§§

The dock was a shit show. Every vender in Africa wanted to sell me something—trinkets, jewelry, shirts. No one was selling booze outright because it was only legal in licensed bars, but I was sure I could ask around and get something. There were a few shady looking guys who were only a fur coat and a feathered hat removed from being a New York pimp. I avoided eye contact.

Mo, the taxi driver, knew exactly one word in English— "airport" —but the language barrier did not stop him from yakking the entire time. He unleashed a constant stream of Arabic at full volume, sometimes at me and sometimes out of the window, directed towards some real or imagined offender.

The street reminded me of all the bathrobe dramas I'd seen at home when I was a kid—you know, children dressed like Mary and Joseph and shepherds on Christmas Eve and Dad sitting in the audience because he wanted to make sure no one spilled anything on his best lounging attire.

This was not small-town America. People mashed together. The place was a swirl of color and movement. We passed so many camels and food vendors, I stopped noticing them. A guy skewered meat in a lot next to an abandoned car with no tires. With the cab's window down to assuage the stifling heat, I could hear voices raised both in anger and excitement. One moment, I would catch the smell of something vile—the next, an aroma that set my mouth drooling.

An hour later, we pulled into Mohammed V International Airport. I jumped out of the taxi, paid the fare and the tip in Spanish currency. This time I had no trouble understanding the intent of the driver's shouts. He drove off and waved at me—middle finger extended.

Mohammed V Airport

I could hear Oisin's voice. "Go to Draga's. Find a gal wearin' a pink blouse and a big green hat." I scanned the place. No pink blouse. No green hat. I walked back into the breezeway.

A diminutive woman in a pale pink top (it was a sweater—what did Oisin know about fashion) and a baby's-first-year green hat the size of the jump circle on a college basketball court grabbed my elbow.

"Nice hat," I said.

"Follow me," she said, unmoved by my sarcasm.

We went to a back table in Draga's. She opened her satchel and handed me a one-way plane ticket, a German passport, a train ticket, and a sheaf of papers.

"Read. Memorize. Burn," she said.

I glanced at the photo and the new name.

"What do I need to know?" I asked.

"All in there," she said.

I scanned a few of the sheets and looked up to ask a question. I saw her hat flopping past the front desk. Once again, I was on my own. I returned to my reading.

Fly into Frankfurt...spend the night in a hostel on Grune Street near the zoo...board a train for Heidelberg...find 245 Langer Anger Street. My rent was paid for a month. After that I had to fend for myself. There were some employment suggestions.

I went over my new life until I had everything cold. I was Klaus Schneider, an independent businessman from Newark. My grandparents had seen the writing on the wall and left Germany in 1936. My father, Helmut, had met my mother, a Georgia girl name Sophie Madison, and they'd married in 1965. I'd come along a few years later followed by two younger brothers, Karl and Stefan. I attended community college in New Jersey before completing my degree at Rutgers where I played baseball.

Upon graduation, I'd returned to my native land where I met my late wife, Helga. She died in a fire after we'd been married for six months. Her death drove me to despair, which explained why I was "independent." I spent my time traveling, financed by the money I'd inherited from my grandparents, who had founded a successful employment agency in New Jersey after the war. There was more—a lot more—but I worked my way from one page to the next and back until I had it cold.

Throughout the course of my lessons, I'd ordered a few Casablanca lagers. I paid the server. He scowled at me, but let it go because I overtipped him. Across from the restaurant was a currency exchange machine. It gouged me on the fee, but I needed to have some dirhams in my pocket. At a newsstand, I bought an English copy of *Sports Illustrated* and a pack of cigarettes. (I needed the free matches.)

After lurking outside the men's room for an uncomfortable amount of time to ensure it was empty, I went in, moved all the trash from one can to another, dropped my "resume" into the vacated can, and burned it. I waited around to ensure no one came in to play hero and put out the fire, then washed my hands and went in search of my departure gate.

I had about thirty minutes before boarding. I spent the time trying not to think about Heida, a wasted effort because she was all I could think about.

By now she knew I was some crazed serial killer from Ireland who had left a string of bodies (and broken hearts—I added that part) across Western Europe. I felt bad about leaving without a word. I could see her face. I could smell her hair. I could hear her laugh.

An attendant called my flight and I stepped into the line. By the time I found my seat, I had erased every memory of Heida from my mind—right along with those of Michiko and Gwendolyn.

Yeah...right.

CHAPTER TWENTY-THREE

I'd been settled in my seat less than three minutes when the flight attendant showed up and took my drink order. I'd never been asked *before* takeoff, so Turkish Airlines jumped to the top of my preferred airlines list. I ordered a Spanish white wine.

"We only serve Turkish wines," she said. She could tell I was surprised, probably because I made a face after I remembered the burning tar stench of Turkish cigarettes. She came back. "This is Sadalan. You will like it very much or it is free."

Better be careful offering free wine to an Irishman, I thought. Then I remembered I really wasn't Irish—and I was supposed to be German now.

The direct flight was scheduled to take four hours. A fit young man with a brush cut sat in the window seat. When the attendant came to top off our glasses once we reached cruising altitude, the conversation started. His name was Zach Grant, U.S. Army. He was returning to his base in Germany following a thirty-day leave. I knew he was from Brooklyn before he told me. (He said he'd had a "bawl" on his trip.) His mother was Jewish, so most of his time off had been in Israel—at her request.

A big fan of CSN,[1] he'd taken the time to replicate Nash's train trip described in "Marrakesh Express." The second he said the title I was back in school, Gwendolyn in a tee shirt and panties fixing dinner while the song spun on her portable stereo. When dinner finished, she'd flipped the 45, set the player to "repeat," and we made love while the trio sang, "Helplessly hoping, her harlequin hovers nearby." Never did figure out what the words meant. All I knew was it drove Gwendolyn into a sexual fever, so I didn't give a damn.

I returned to the present and listened to Zach droning on about the trip from Tangier to Casablanca to Marrakesh.

"First-class was four dollars," he said, "but it wasn't like in the States. I learned first-hand about—how did Nash put it—oh yeah, 'ducks, and pigs, and chickens call; animal carpet wall to wall.'"

I finished the line. "American frauleins five-foot tall in blue."

"Hell yeah," he said. "Gotta respect a man who knows his bands."

"You like it?" I asked.

"Figured out why Nash was so bored he wrote a song. Damn blue-haired women complaining about bad service in restaurants and some Brit talking about his polo league. I swear to God he had a monocle like he was the Monopoly guy."

"Rich Onkel Pennybags," I said.

"Who?"

"Dat's de fella in the game. Rich *Uncle* Pennybags."

Zach cocked his head. "You sure know a lot about America—rock and games and shit. And that's the worst fake German accent I've

---

1. David Crosby, Stephen Stills, and Graham Nash

ever heard. Sounds like you're trying to do Sergeant Schultz from *Hogan's Heroes.*"

Damn! Think fast...think fast...think fast.

"I grew up in America. German immigrant parents. German citizenship. Went to college at one of the SUNY campuses for a semester exchange program," I said. "Growing up with German parents, I sometimes channel their accents without thinking about it." I hoped he would leave it alone.

He didn't. "Whatcha been doin' since?" he asked.

I was about to come up with some lame answer when the plane bucked a little. The attendant came on the intercom, told us to check the security of our seatbelts, and announced we were descending.

"Where you staying in Frankfurt?" Zach asked. "I'll give you a call. We'll have a beer. I know all the great beer halls."

"Don't have a place," I said. "Been wandering a while. I think the Amerikaner would say I was trying to find myself."

"Lucky you," he said.

Exacerbated by the simultaneous arrival of three international flights, the line at customs stretched down the hall. No problem. It gave me a chance to run through my new background in my head. I couldn't have another awkward encounter. I had to know who the hell I was and how I was supposed to talk.

I hadn't been nearly as good at the Irish thing as I'd thought. About seventy-five percent of the people, I'd encountered knew within three minutes that I was about as Irish as linguini. Fake German had to be easier. And Zach was right. I loved *Hogan's Heroes.*

Now I was Klaus fricking Schneider from Cranberry, New Jersey. I would have preferred something easier, but I guess Karl Marx was out of the question.

"Bitte ihren reisepass!"[2] I got that much and handed over my passport.

"Herr Klaus Schnieder, sag mir, was ihr zweck für die einreise nach Deutschland?"

I was ready. "Ich bin hier im Urlaub und plane, überall nach Verwandten zu suchen. Englisch, bitte.[3] I have never lived here."

"Where do you intend to do this, Mr. Klaus Schneider?"

"I'm spending the night in Frankfurt and travelling to Heidelberg tomorrow by train. I have many cousins I'm trying to locate, hoping for a family reunion."

I heard the pleasant sound of the passport being stamped, collected my documents, and moved into the crowd.

"Nächster!"[4]

I didn't like traveling. Forged documents are seldom perfect. The best one can hope for is a fatigued and/or bored civil servant who is thinking more about what's for dinner than worrying about undesirables entering the country. My instructions directed me to a hostel on Gruene Straße.

---

2. "Your passport, please."

3. I'm here on vacation and plan to look for relatives. English, please."

4. "Next!"

A short stop at a bank to update my Portuguese and Moroccan currency to Deutsche Marks, followed by a quick taxi ride brought me to a filthy, crowded hostel. It made some of the dumps where I'd stayed on the Camino de Santiago look like the Ritz Carlton. The front desk attendant (a stoner listening to Hendrix's "Voodoo Child") said, "Dude, you wanna pay for the communal meal?"

I analyzed his accent. *Somewhere in Jersey by way of Zig Zag rolling papers*, I thought.

I hesitated.

"No place else to eat that close," he said. "Not great, but you won't get the runs."

Based on his three-star Michelin rating, I paid for the meal and went to my room. It was furnished in early dorm room. I searched for bedbugs. When I didn't find any of the little critters, I relaxed.

I took a short nap in the lower bunk. When I awakened, I headed for the shower. I had gotten my shirt off when a woman exited a shower stall sans towel. I tried not to stare. I apologized. She smiled before commencing with her drying technique, which involved what I considered an inordinate amount of unnecessary stretching and moans. I turned to avoid further embarrassment and sat on a bench to untie my shoes. I looked up into the hairiest ass I'd ever seen (not that I was an expert). When I was unable to muffle my shriek, the owner of the posterior turned, his "equipment" about eye level.

"Mein fruend, you look as if to have a...how you say...ein schlaganfall."

The woman behind me said, "A stroke. Amerikanisch. Probleme mit nacktheit."

Hairy Ass laughed. "Seriously? If you have a problem with people being naked, you are in the wrong country."

I grinned like a man on a church pew trying to ignore a boil on his butt. "Just want to make sure I'm in the right place," I said.

"Vell," he said, "get used to it...ah...buddy. No one here cares. Nothing we have not seen before unless you are...ah...a pornostar."

I didn't think it was time to play show and tell. "Don't want anyone to be offended," I said.

"I'm Peter from Denmark. Nice to meet you." It was the first—and I hope last—time I shook hands with a naked man. "Please go ahead. Undress. Take your shower. Vill you be joining us for dinner?"

"I'm Klaus," I said. I stepped into the shower. The water would have made the Arctic Ocean shiver. "Y...y...yes. Dinner."

"See you there," he said. "I will introduce you."

When I got out, everyone was gone. I dried off remembering my last frigid bathing experience—a Belfast dungeon. When I'd come out, the keeper had taken a look and said, "Maybe I'm wrong, but guessing you 'aven't had a lot o' invites from de adult entertainment industry, 'ave ya?"

I dressed and found my way to the dining hall. It was happy hour. Peter was yakking it up in the corner. I made my way over. He poured a beer, handed it over, and introduced me. About twenty minutes later, we were seated at a long table.

Five minutes into the meal, the conversation zeroed in on "the new guy in the shower." The girls talked about nudity and sex like they were ordering a Big Mac.

"Listen everyone," I said, "once and for all, I am all for naked people. I just wasn't ready to meet Emilia in all her...ah...natural glory."

She smiled in a way I was inclined to interpret as invitational. "It's okay Klaus," she said. "Tomorrow morning, the water will be warm. We'll share a shower at 0700. No excuses about shrinkage."

The room erupted in laughter at the same time the servers entered the dining room with large platters of assorted sausages, sauerkraut, veal, and rolls. They returned with more pitchers of beer. We looked like we hadn't eaten in a month. My first meal in Germany did not disappoint. The best hotdog I'd ever had in the U.S.—a loaded offering at Fenway—was nothing compared to this. I looked across the table.

Emilia had speared a brat. She waved it back and forth in front of her full lips.

"Klaus, this is what I'm expecting from you in the morning. I believe it's called 'morning wood.'"

"Just don't bring the fork," I said.

After dinner, we sat in a large room. The beer hadn't stopped flowing. Emilia surprised me by sitting on my lap. She whispered, "Promise me you will not disappoint tomorrow."

I decided not to push it. "The way you were announcing the water temperature, I figured you had invited everybody."

She stuck her tongue into my ear.

When I stood, she managed to keep her feet.

"Sorry," I said. "Nature calls."

Her eyes were slits of either lust or inebriation. "Want some help?"

I left without answering and retreated to my bed. Most of the night, I catnapped. While the possibilities offered by Emilia's invitation held considerable appeal, the thought of trying to perform in front of the dozen or so weirdos who would no doubt appear did not.

CHAPTER TWENTY-FOUR

At 0500, I got out of bed, grabbed my stuff, and snuck out of the hostel. I knew my train would be on time.

Fifteen minutes before departure, the loudspeaker directed me to Track Eight. We rolled out of the station at 1100 hours on the dot.

The car was full of college kids. Sally, a petite redhead from Burlington, Vermont, sat next to me. I introduced myself as Klaus. I'd visited her area in my youth. It was only an hour away from my hometown.

"I spent a lot of time in Ticonderoga," I said. "My parents used to rent a cabin every summer. Ever heard of it?"

"Oh my God yes!" she said. She bubbled with Tri-Delt enthusiasm. "My sister dates a guy from Ticonderoga. He attends St. Michaels College. His family has a beautiful place on Lake George. We have spent soooo many weekends there. It is soooo picturesque. The bar scene is totally rad. We always go to a place...ah...Blood Something. You know, I'm usually pretty wasted by the time we get there, so—"

"The Bloody Bucket?"

"Oh my God, that's it. How do you know?"

"We drove by there all the time," I said. "I went there once with my father for lunch. We got cellophane-wrapped sandwiches. I think they were left over from the Korean War."

Her face went blank. "You mean Vietnam," she said. "I heard about that. Terrible."

I left her minimal understanding of U.S. history alone. "Anyway, I guess all they focused on was beer. Dad told me the bartender's name was Mad Dog."

"Like I would remember," she said. "We were partying hearty."

"What's your sister's boyfriend's name?" I asked.

"Mark Lawson. Great guy. They are talking about getting married. I don't think they care, but they are tired of trying to act like they aren't doing it, you know." She winked.

I didn't react. I was a little freaked out.

I knew Mark Lawson. We'd been buddies in high school. Played a little ball together. He told me about someone he was dating, said it looked promising.

My heart rate increased. *Home.* I'd tried not to think about Mom and Dad for a long time. Had gotten pretty good at compartmentalizing my memory. But Ms. Sorority had sledgehammered the carefully constructed wall blockading my memory. Suddenly I saw my mother's face the first time she visited me after I'd been beaten—the look of terror that someone had brutalized her baby. I could feel my father's hands adjusting my batting grip and hear his voice from the bleachers, "They got you played to pull, son. Fire one over first base and you'll run all day."

When's the last time I talked to them?

Gwendolyn's intense eyes came into focus, and I had to blink back tears. I tried to lock back in on the droning monologue to my left.

"Anyway, he is so awesome. It's pretty radical for my sis to be dating someone older. I mean, he's like ancient...he's almost *thirty*."

I cleared my throat. "Don't think I know the guy."

"Hang on," she said. She started digging through a backpack large enough to support a platoon of paratroopers. She came out with a photo album.

Who takes one of those on a backpacking trip through Europe?

She flipped a few pages, then pointed. "Here...see...he's the one holding the telephone pole."

I didn't bother to tell her it was called a "caber," a feat of strength at the annual Scottish games at Fort Ticonderoga. I hoped my expression didn't disclose my lie. I would have known Mark anywhere. His voluminous muttonchops were his pride and joy and a target of many a jibe.

College smartass #1: "Hey. Lawson, you giving your pet racoon a ride on your face?"

College smartass #2. "That's no racoon; it's a chinchilla. Get it...*chin*-chilla?"

Same joke every time, though not always as PG.

She turned the page. My stomach twisted. Mark was participating in the tug-of-war. His biceps bulged. His face was tense. His mouth was open. He was screaming, "Pull you pussies!"

How did I know? I was two behind him yelling the same thing. I looked at Sally to see if she recognized me. After a few seconds, I realized she would not have recognized a naked Burt Reynolds...well, maybe if he were naked.

She was consumed by her own dialogue. I hadn't been listening to anything but the memories in my head. She moved to another page—eight guys and one girl.

"My sis is hot, huh?" she said. "But so is Mark. And look at the cuties he's with. My sister introduced me to them but wouldn't let me go out. She said they were a bunch of crazies."

Her sister had good judgment. I was on the back row, third from the left.

What the hell, I thought.

"I think she was right," I said. "I mean, look at them. Psychos, one and all." I hesitated for effect. "Seriously, look at that one." I pointed to my younger self. "He's got Ted Bundy eyes."

Sally studied my slightly blurry photographed face. "Yeah," she said after a moment. "I know what you mean."

What a dingbat, I thought.

We heard an announcement for Heidelberg. Sally put the album back in her pack.

"You getting off here?" I asked.

"No," she said. "I'm with some other girls. We're going ahead."

"How come you're not with them?" I asked.

"There are five of us," she said. "We play 'One Out' every day. Four sit together. The other one had to sit with a stranger. The other's watch out in case he's a weirdo or something."

"Sounds like fun," I said. "Bet you meet some interesting people."

"You have no idea," she said.

The train stopped. I gathered my stuff and bobbed my head.

"Nice to meet you, Sally," I said.

"Nice to see you, Klaus, or should I call you 'Ted'?" she said. "I'll tell Mark I ran into you."

I didn't stop running until I was a half-mile from the station.

CHAPTER TWENTY-FIVE

Hyperventilation was not far away by the time I arrived at 245 Langer Anger Street, an odd name but the least of my concern. For the first time since I'd left America, I'd been spotted. Despite the phony name I'd given, if Sally ever got home and started going through old pictures with her soon-to-be brother-in-law...

Shit!

"What are the chances?" I asked. "Four thousand miles from home and someone recognizes me from a picture *they've got with them?*"

I'd dodged so many bullets, real and figurative, that I believed my own bullshit. Surely, no one would know who I was. Sloppy Irish brogue? Didn't matter. Fall in love with a way out of my league woman in the middle of the Pyrenees? Sure—happens all the time. Save someone from a burning car, broadcast my mug over hell and half of Spain without attracting any notice? Why not.

"Caldemeyer...Murphy...Klaus Schneider...whoever the hell you are—get it together! You are a fugitive on the run from the English military. Her Majesty is never going to forgive...never going to forget...and even when she dies, her government will have my face plastered on cork boards of every law enforcement room across the

Empire. Hell, you got spotted by a college chick who probably hasn't been sober since she landed on the Continent."

Thirty minutes later, I had composed myself sufficiently to walk into the rental office and introduce myself.

The man behind the desk could have passed for Alfred Einstein, assuming the Noble Prize winning physicist had a chubby younger brother. "We've been expecting you Mr. Schneider," he said. "Papers."

I handed him my passport. He examined it with the zeal of a toddler searching through *Where's Waldo?* He returned it along with a large thick envelope. He escorted me to my room and outlined the rules in copious detail. He repeated the part about "no loud parties" several times and made it clear he also meant occasions where I might be in the room with "a companion."

The minute I stepped in, I missed Lucky. He would have loved the extra space, but I considered how difficult air travel would have been on him and convinced myself—sort of—that he'd be happier with Oisin. After vowing to retrieve the pup one day, on a date I intentionally left vague, I explored the place a little.

The apartment had a small kitchen (complete with an empty refrigerator), a water closet and shower, and a single bed—it might have been a hammock. For the first time since leaving Ireland, I would have a private telephone, though I had no idea who I might call or who might want to get in touch with me. There was a brown leather wallet on the bed. It held a German driver's license and a thick stack of Deutschmarks. I looked at the window and beheld a landscape that made Newark look like a botanical garden. This was the industrial sector.

The old no frills tour, I thought.

On the ground floor, I'd noticed a barbershop, a couple of bars, a small café, and a grocery. I trooped downstairs to shop for a few essentials. When I returned, I opened the envelope and inspected the contents.

The first thing out was a credit card in the name of Hans Mueller. I complained to the wall. "They got me a credit card in *the wrong name!*" There was a Swiss passport in the same name and a note: "In the unlikely event that your current identity is compromised, destroy everything and use these."

The passport smacked against the headboard on the other side of the room. At least I still had a decent arm. I began to pace...and fume. I was furious, without any idea towards whom I should direct my outrage. I was in my fourth...no, sixth...foreign country. I'd lost track of how many identities I'd attempted. I'd met and been discarded, or betrayed, by four stunning women (five if I counted Gwendolyn) and was close to breaking. The image in the bathroom mirror bore no resemblance to the carefree kid who'd joined the police department seven years ago.

"Fuck!" I slapped at the cheap fiberglass sink. "Fuck...fuck...fuck!"

I was no therapist, but I knew the best way to release the pressure threatening to initiate an embolism: beer. Surely, I could find a place full of bigger losers than I was.

I stopped in the first bar downstairs. Tears For Fears was singing "Shout" from a vintage jukebox. There were a half-dozen well lubricated gents slumped on barstools. I took the first vacant seat I could find and ordered a beer.

"Vat kint?" The bartender was approximately the size of Rhode Island.

"Hefeweizen," I said.

"Ve only got Erdinger," he said.

I was going to go all asshole American because I was at the end of my rope but the guy next to me chuckled. "He uses dat joke on every new person."

I took a few pulls. Good stuff. I drained it pretty fast.

"Another, bitte," I said. For reasons I did not bother to understand, I pointed to the guy next to me. "Und eins für meinen freund."[1]

"Danke," the man said. "Thomas."

Shit, what is my name?

"Klaus," I said remembering just before it became obvious I had no idea what my name was.

He shook my hand. When he let go, I glanced to make sure all my digits were still intact.

I flexed my fingers. "Work with your hands?"

His English was good, his accent thick and Teutonic.

"Did I hurt you, fraulein?" he asked. He smiled. He was missing his right canine. "I am a stone mason. Sometimes I forget not everyone is so strong." He said about nine words in German. When he saw my eyes glaze over, he switched back to English. He was working at the local university, building a wall.

"Your boss mind drinking on the job?" I asked.

---

1. "And one for my friend."

"This is not drinking," he said. He drained his stein and signaled for another. "This is beer—water to a German. We have beer breaks in the morning, at noon, and in the afternoon. Everyone is responsible. Not like you Americans."

I started to protest, then remembered what my college buddies looked like every Monday morning in class, bloodshot eyes, vacant stares, holding their head in their hands.

When I returned to my apartment, I reviewed the other things from the envelope. There was a list of potential employers. None of the jobs involved significant contact with the public—no bartending this time. The instructions for phone use were underlined: <u>Phone for local calls only unless contact with Spanish personnel urgently required</u>. "Spanish personnel" —Oisin.

I put my head back and took a sip of beer. I didn't wake up until morning.

CHAPTER TWENTY-SIX

I woke up in a relatively good mood, thankful I left the bar when I did. I shifted into find-a-job mode. I only had thirty days of prepaid rent and I was pretty sure a career as a highly paid gigolo would not end well, so I went out in search of a taxi.

Twenty minutes later, I came across a cab dropping off an unhappy American man with an unhappier wife.

"This is supposed to be a five-star," she said. "I don't think so."

"This was *supposed* to be a golf trip in Scotland," he said.

The driver was about half a giggle away from no tip. "Hey," I said, "you guys mind if I take this?"

The man looked at me, then at his wife. "We ain't using it," he said. He handed the driver a lot of money and followed his wife into the hotel.

The driver looked at me. "Let's go before he figures out he tipped me triple the fare."

I climbed in. "Doesn't understand the exchange rate, huh?"

"Typical Amerikanisches arschloch," he said. He winced. "Sorry," he said.

"No problem," I said. "You call 'em the way you see 'em. Lots of my fellow citizens are assholes." I'd abandoned any hope of learning a new language or passing myself off as anything other than American.

"Jurgen," he said.

"Klaus," I said.

In the rearview, I saw him roll his eyes. "If you say so...Klaus. Where to?"

"Looking for a job. Got a list. I'll pay you for the tour."

He held out his hand over his shoulder. I gave him the sheet. When he looked at the first name, I saw his shoulders buckle with a stifled laugh. He let me off at Holzkohle-Unternehmen. This time, he made no effort to hide his amusement.

"What's so damn funny, Jurgen?" I asked.

He pointed to the building. It could have been Sing Sing Penitentiary. Columns of thick black smoke plumed from twin chimneys.

"You just don't look like a coal worker to me. Most of the guys in there just got out of prison."

"So, not a good idea?"

"How do you Americans say it: it should be the final vacation."

"I think you mean 'last resort,' but I catch your meaning. Tell you what, go down the list and pick where you think I have the best chance of not getting shivved."

At Heidelberger Stahlunternehmen, a stainless-steel manufacturing plant, an efficient secretary showed me to the office of Helmut Rheinfurt.

After twenty minutes, he said, "You are not qualified for any of the floor level positions, but we might have a place for you in our international sales division. You will need to sharpen your German skills...ah...significantly, but you seem like a bright young man. At least at the beginning I think we would limit you to English speaking locales. I will call you in a few days with details about your next interview."

I strutted out of the building and climbed into the cab. "Nailed it, Jurgen," I said.

"Great, let's go have a beer to celebrate!"

What he meant was, "Let's go and you can buy me more beers than a bull elephant could drink." Damn that guy could put away the suds. But I was feeling better than I had in a while, so I paid the bill without complaint with money I had not earned.

Not unless you count risking my life and living on the run. Details.

We drank and swapped stories. I screwed up and mentioned soccer. Jurgen launched into a good natured lecture about fußball.[1]

Four beers later—three times as many for Jurgen—he offered to drive me home, "On the residence."

I didn't bother to correct him, but I'd long ago quit riding with guys who were hammered. We were only a ten-minute walk from my place, so I headed to the apartment after we exchanged numbers in case I needed further use of his services. Why he wanted mine was a mystery—until a little later.

I had been on the couch long enough to stretch my legs on the coffee table when the phone rang. Jurgen.

---

1. "Soccer" for Americans. "Football" for the rest of the world.

"Mein frau heard all about today," he said. "I had to tell her because she thought I was out with some flufigg.[2] She told me to invite you for dinner. I don't think she really cares to meet you, but she wants to check out my story."

How could I turn down such a warm invitation to act as a referee for the Battling Bickersons? After all, I hadn't eaten much other than bar food in the last few days. A home cooked meal sounded good. How bad could it be? After eating Irish food, I wasn't afraid of anything.

I gave him my address and about ten seconds after ringing off, I began to get suspicious.

What are the chances I meet a random taxi driver who agrees to chauffeur me around, goes to have beer, then invites me to dinner? I could hear Oisin's snarky caveat: "They have informants and agents everywhere. Everywhere I tell ya. The bartender who asks if ya want another...the kid who sells ya a bocadillo on the street...the fella traveler who strikes up a conversation...and when the next cute colleen who drops her bloomers for ya, it won't be because ye're so damn charmin'."

I let it go. If I let paranoia rule my life, I'd go crazy. Of course, I might live longer...

The week dragged along. I didn't bother applying for more jobs. I knew the interview was locked. When Saturday came, Jurgen pulled up exactly as planned.

Damn, these guys are punctual, I thought.

---

2. Floozy.

We headed south out of the city and crossed the Rhine River. Jurgen never quit talking. He and his wife Renate lived in the small town of Dierbach, an hour's drive from Heidelberg. He couldn't make a living driving a taxi in a small town. He commuted every weekday.

Jurgen gave me a history lesson. We were leaving the state of Baden-Wurttemberg and travelling to Rheinland-Pfalz. German states were divided into landkreise, counties. He lived in the Sudliche Weinstrabe district of Rhineland-Palatinate Kreise. The landscape changed dramatically on the other side of the river. The cityscape disappeared. I felt a wave of nostalgia. I remembered growing up in the blissful surroundings of the verdant Adirondack mountains and I was overwhelmed with the spectacular job I'd done in screwing up my life. At that moment, all I wanted to do was go home, a possibility that grew more remote every single day.

"You like what you see, yes?"

"Jurgen, it reminds me of home. Great memories."

"Now you see why I don't live in Heidelberg. I only go there for the money, to make a living for my family, no other reason."

"Come on, Jurgen," I said, "something good came of it. If you didn't work in the city, I wouldn't have bought you so much beer and I would not be visiting in your home."

"This is true. I hope it is a good idea. My wife is not fond of Americans."

I figured Jurgen for fifty-ish. He'd have been younger than ten during the war. I assumed his wife was the same age. She might not have the greatest memories about Americans,

"Wasn't this dinner her idea?" I asked.

"Sort of," he said. "I lied a little about her worrying about another woman. She knows me too well to think I would cheat. I may have encouraged her a little."

I decided to address the five-hundred-pound gorilla. "The war?"

"What about the war?" he asked.

"Something bad happen to her?"

"No, no, no," he said. "If you really want to know, I will tell you."

"Nothing ventured," I said.

"Huh?'

"Just go ahead. Tell me."

He took a deep breath. "Growing up there were many American military bases in the Rheinland. Soldiers came to town. They were not always on their best behavior. They drank, got in fights, picked on the locals. They thought throwing the word 'Nazi" around was funny."

I pictured the typical young GI—a guy fresh out of high school, or new to the Army because some judge said, "Son, it's the service or jail." Brash, full of hormones, assholes.

I'd been that kid. Might have ended up in a military unit in Germany except for Gwendolyn.

"Your wife think I'm just another drunk American?"

"I told her you were very nice, very generous. I told her you speak a little German and are trying to fit in, unlike most of the soldiers we met. She decided to give you a chance to redeem your nation's reputation."

Nothing like a little pressure. "I'll do my best," I said.

"Just be yourself and you will be fine."

The village reminded me of Lake Placid, where I'd attended the 1980 Winter Olympics with my father. Jurgen was very proud of his town.

"This is the Dierbach area," Jurgen said. "It's named for the river we just crossed. Over here is Fischer's, best candy store in all of Germany. They have the most wonderful dominostein anywhere." He saw my blank look. "Chocolate covered jelly and gingerbread."

He pronounced the word "chen-cher-bret."

"Sounds delicious," I said. I was the master of witty banter.

"Next door is one of the two gaststätten." (I knew 'restaurants.') "Then we have the Metzger and our famous backerei. We buy our bread fresh every day. You are, no doubt, aware of Germany's wonderful cakes."

"I really like bee sting," I said.

Jurgen was impressed. "Not many Americans know that one."

I was about to launch into my extensive study of all things fattening, then decided I was talking too much.

It was a beautiful scene. Couples walked along the road arm in arm. Everyone appeared to know everyone else. There were smiles and shouts and waves. Motorists signaled cars into the traffic without a single "one finger salute." A bucolic...sweet place.

Jurgen pointed. "The brauerei where we get our beer."

"Very nice," I said. "You go there to buy it?"

"No, we have home delivery."

"What?"

"We put in our order, and it arrives. Daily...weekly...whatever we need. I get deliveries on Mondays and Fridays. My neighbor across the street gets his every day. Nothing as good as fresh German beer. The breweries are governed by der Reinheitsgebot."

"Huh?" Again...talk show guest quality conversation.

"The German beer purity regulations. They have changed some throughout the centuries, but they have been in effect since the days of The Holy Roman Empire in 1516."

"Amazing," I said. I meant it. "People in America get excited if something is a hundred years old."

"Jugendliche."

"Youngsters, indeed," I said. "What are the purity laws?"

"They outline the four ingredients for beer."

He coaxed his aging Mercedes through a series of turns while he explained about water, barley, malt, and hops. The homes were more spaced, the tracts bigger. We slowed and drove down a gravel drive. Jurgen switched off the car and we got out. Pride spread across his face.

"My home," he said.

CHAPTER TWENTY-SEVEN

The cottage was small and well kept. A stream ran along the eastern side about a hundred meters away. In the background, I could see the Odenwald Mountains.

"Stunning" was all I could manage.

"Like an Otto Ackerman painting," he said.

I nodded as if I had some idea of the name he mentioned. He could have said "Otto von Bismarck" and I'd have just nodded and smiled.

"Germans are hospitable people, Klaus," he said. "My wife would have invited you regardless of her memories. Here in Germany, we put the unpleasant things behind us and focus on eine hellere Zukunft."

"As soon as you offer me a beer, we will toast to *a brighter future*," I said.

Jurgen was pleased with my understanding.

Thoughts of home assaulted me again. I felt something akin to an entire waffle stuck in my throat. I stared at the hills.

"Klaus? Klaus, are you okay? Let's go inside so I can introduce you to Renate."

"Sorry Jurgen. Just remembering."

"Klaus, I have been to New Jersey. Nothing like it," he said.

"Ah..." I fought to remember my most recent fictionalized life. "...it's a town. Lots of...how do you say..." I didn't know shit about where I was supposed to be from. Sloppiness waved its finger at me.

"Bauernhöfe," he said. "Farms. So, what do they grow on your farm in New Jersey?"

Fuck! I took a shot. "Cranberries." I hoped the doubt in my head had not made my statement sound like a high school student searching for the name of Juliet's boyfriend.

Roberto?

"Ah," Jurgen said. "But of course. You Americans with your original names. They float on the water, right? I would be fascinated."

"It's...ah...like nothing I've ever seen anywhere else," I said. Probably the most honest thing I'd said in over a year. "My parents used to take me to upstate New York when I was younger. You know Lake Placid."

His eyes lit. "Of course, all Germans know where Lake Placid is. We Germans did very well in the 1980 Winter Olympics. We won twenty-eight medals."

"I know...great," I said. I decided it would have been rude to point out how he'd combined East and West Germany, as if they were not mortal enemies at the time.

"Mike Eruzione, Jimmy Craig, and the crazy coach, Herb Brooks." He threw his fists into the air. "U.S.A. ... U.S.A.—amazing!"

I was about to launch into my infinite pool of worthless information to replay the semi-final hockey game with the Russians.

Dad had gotten tickets "on a hunch" —more likely because we couldn't get in to see Linda Fratianne get jobbed out of the gold medal in Women's Figure Skating. But then the door opened. A woman motioned for us to come inside.

For a moment, I wondered if she was the reincarnation of Freyja, the Germanic goddess of love, beauty, sex, war, gold, and magic. Tall and shapely, Renate's long hair shimmered in the afternoon sun. Her jawline was squarish but when combined with her high cheekbones, she radiated—there was no other word—magnificence. I tried not to stare on the way inside.

I failed.

Jurgen noticed. "She has the same effect on every man who sees her," he said.

I looked him up and down. "Does she have a mental problem, or were you assigned to her as punishment for crimes in one of her former lives?"

He laughed, full and genuine. "Every man has that reaction as well."

He embraced his wife. They kissed with affection bordering on passion. Just before things got uncomfortable, they broke off.

"Forgive us," she said. "We are still on our flitterwochen."[1]

We were now at uncomfortable. "I'm so sorry," I said. "How long have you been married?

"Thirty-two years next month," she said. "Every day with my liebesmaschine is like the first time I saw him."

Love machine? I was not about to ask.

---

1. Honeymoon.

Three cuckoo clocks screamed at each other three times. The interior was busy—a lot of pictures, decorations, and random pillows—but hospitable.

The goddess extended her hand. "I am Renate," she said.

"Klaus," I said. "Charmed."

I wondered if I was expected to click my heels and kiss her hand. I decided against it.

"Welcome to our home," she said. "Jurgen said you were very insistent on visiting and learning more about us Germans." I shot him a sideways glance. He had taken a serious interest in a doodad on the entry table. "I am sure he told you of my lack of affection for Americans. You appear more mature. I'm sure you will demonstrate best behavior when visiting my home, yes?"

"Ah...sure," I said. Other than my grandmother, with her clear plastic furniture covers and written list of house rules, no one had ever lectured me about decorum at the *beginning* of a visit.

I explained my phony background and how I wanted to know more about my roots.

"You said 'roots,'" Renate said. "Did you watch the show by the same name on the fernsehen? Quite upsetting. Do you own slaves?"

This is off to a roaring start.

"No...no, I don't. No one in the U.S. has owned slaves in over a hundred years. My family was never involved." *What the hell, go for it.* I freelanced. "In fact my great, great grandfather on my mother's side was an artillery commander at the Battle of Gettysburg where the Union turned the tide of the Civil War."

I hoped to God she was not an American history buff.

In for a penny. "My father's relatives were very active in the Abolitionist movement. Dad claims one of his people served as Frederick Douglass's bodyguard for a while."

Go big or go home!

"Fascinating, though I must be honest. I do not know this Mr. Douglass."

Thank you, sweet and merciful Baby Jesus.

"Well," Renate said. "This is a good start. Make yourself at home. We have a lot to talk about between now and the time you go home tomorrow."

I looked at Jurgen again. He shrugged.

Renate showed me to my room on the second floor. The view of the forest was mesmerizing.

We had a delicious repast of rinderragout. The beef was tender, the vegetables fresh, and the stock hearty. "I hope you like the bread," she said. "I made it myself."

I remembered my manners, something easily abandoned during the life of a fugitive, and swallowed before I answered. "Everything is delicious."

I helped with the dishes, over Renate's objections. Jurgen never left his seat by the fire.

At Jurgen's request, I fished two beers from the fridge. I looked at Renate. "Want one?"

"She's having her tea," Jurgen said.

Renate sipped on a cup of tea and outlined the rules of engagement. "No sports. Nothing about war."

Jurgen did not object. Renate ruled with an iron fist in a titanium glove. There would be no question about where she stood on any issue.

"Renate, we had a nice drive today from Heidelberg," I said. "The scenery improved greatly as we were approaching Dierbach. This area reminds me so much of back home."

"I won't ask you where you're from because I don't know much about the states. I have heard of New York and California, and I have some cousins who moved to Wisconsin, but that is the extent of my knowledge in that area."

"Can I ask you about fishing?" I asked. "Or is that sports?"

The Dierbach River looked like a serious place for trout.

"The river is full of trout, but we are not allowed to fish without a special use permit," Renate said. "It gets expensive; Klaus is not very skilled. It's not worth the trouble. So, we go to Millers for what we need."

"What is the employment situation around here?" I asked. "Do the locals work here or truck into the city like you, Jurgen?"

"There's not much employment here," he said. "A lot do what I do. Others work at the American bases."

"How far are the bases?"

Renate piped up. "There is an Army base near Busenberg, and an Air Force base in Dahn. Both are very close, that is why we see so many soldiers. They seem quiet when they arrive, but drink too much and act foolish."

"What do the Germans do at the bases?"

"Mainly construction. The Americans are always fortifying their bases or building something new. Your country must have a lot of money because it doesn't care about costs. They hire locals to do mechanical work inside the bases and administrative type jobs, depending on how good their English is."

"Perfect, I'll get a job at the base and rent a room from you." My comment generated some nervous laughter.

Renate shot back, "If you wanted to work at the base, you must live much closer. Our home is too far away. No, no, it wouldn't work here."

"I'm joking, I'm sure I have a job with the steel company in Heidelberg. I'm just waiting for the official call to bring me on board."

Renate excused herself to do something to get ready for the party they were holding in my honor. "I hope you like sauerbraten, Klaus."

"It's a favorite," I said.

Jurgen and I finished our beer, and we stepped outside for a walk. As I suspected, Jurgen was a very popular person. We were gone well over an hour, but probably walked less than two miles. Every person working on their home invited us inside for coffee, a beer, or an apfelschorle (apple cider spritzer), which is a very popular German drink.

It was clear everyone loved Jurgen and Renate. I halfway listened. Most of the time, I thought about Heida and how grateful I was that she had taken the time to teach me German. All the discussions with the neighbors were in German, but I had a solid enough fundamental understanding to follow. Speaking gave me problems—although everyone appreciated my infantile attempts at speaking in the vernacular.

A cuckoo clock sang away at 1700 hours, and Jurgen stood up as if programmed. "Time to go," he said. "We must help prepare."

On the way home, I said, "You really don't have to do this. It's not like I'm anyone famous or important."

"The neighbors are coming over to meet you. It's no fuss...a little tradition. Germans use any occasion for a party. Renate has been cooking her sauerbraten all week in anticipation of tonight, and baking fresh bread. Each family will bring food and I had a special home delivery of beer yesterday."

When we walked in the door, Renate asked us to prepare for the guests. Klaus and I were about the same size, so he took me to his closet for something a little dressier than my jeans and flannel shirt.

I stood in the foyer and met the Mullers, the Kohlers, the Webers, the Peters, and the Krugs. Several couples brought their children. There was food everywhere. And there were several bottles of excellent homemade schnapps. I sampled from each just to be polite.

My German was a little better than I suspected. Franz Kohler looked me right in the eye and asked Jurgen if I was just another drunk American soldier.

Ass Hat! I answered in German. "I am not in the military, but I am looking forward to getting drunk with Jurgen."

Ass Hat looked like he swallowed ear wax.

My secret unveiled, questions peppered me from every angle.

"Where is your family from?"

"When did your family leave Germany and why?"

"Why are you in Germany now?"

"Are you married?"

"Where did you learn to speak German?"

I guess studying the notes of my pretend life paid off, because I answered all their questions easily. I stuttered through why my relatives left Germany in 1936. The official line was that they'd seen the writing on the wall, but Jurgen had warned me about bringing up the war, so I manufactured a tale about my grandfather always wanting to live in Wyoming or something equally ridiculous. The second I mentioned the American West, everyone wanted to talk about cowboys, Indians, Roy Rogers, and stuff I could bullshit my way through without disclosing that I had about as much German blood as Emperor Hirohito. Most everyone was pretty well lit. By the next morning I was sure they would remember nothing more than my sparking personality.

Renate announced it was time for dinner, so we made our way to the kitchen. I immediately recognized Renate's sauerbraten, platters of bratwurst, knockwurst, and traditional hot dogs, but needed Renate to explain everything else. There was pork schnitzel, large pretzels (brezelns), several variations of braised cabbages, potato salads, potato dumplings, potato pancakes, meat dumplings called maultaschen, white asparagus (spargel) and mountains of bread.

We ate, drank, and shared stories. The discussion circled back to me and my intentions.

"I want to find a job here and stay. I love it here. No one left in the U.S. for me."

Of all the lies I'd told that one hurt the most.

"I took him for an interview. He feels he will be getting a job at Heidelberger Stahlunternehmen. If that doesn't work, he's considering getting a job at one of the American bases."

Florian Krug said he lived between Dahn and Busenberg. "They are hiring at the Air Force base in Dahn. They hire right out of the local bar. If you're an American with some German language ability, they will sign you up on the spot."

"What do you mean they hire out of the local bar? Don't you have to complete some kind of application?"

"Of course, but Germans know how to bypass the process. When someone wants work, they go to the bar and ask the off-duty soldiers who they should see. They get an introduction to someone who is socializing there, and the door is opened."

"What do you think, Jurgen," I asked, "should I skip the job at the steel company and move out here?"

"Klaus, stick with the bigger company. German steel is the best, you know. But the base is a good backup plan."

I looked across the table. "Pieter, would it be hard for me to find a room to rent in Dahn?"

"Dahn is a busy little town with many people coming and going; there are always rooms open for rent."

Jurgen stood. "Now we go to the back and make holzkohle."[2]

Everyone rose. The women cleared the table. When I picked up my plate—Mom would have been so proud—Jurgen gave a slight headshake. I put it down and followed the men into the backyard.

Jurgen and Pieter built a small fire. The other men, all of whom had obviously gone through the process before, loaded a thirty-gallon aluminum garbage can with small chunks of oak and applewood. They drilled vent holes in the lid.

---

2. Charcoal

Jurgen spread the fire; he and another guy lowered the can into the center of the pit with the precision of someone disarming a nuke. Then everyone stacked firewood until the can was out of sight.

Eight of us stood around the fire sipping beer.

"Wouldn't it be easier to buy a bag at the market?" I asked.

What little respect I had garnered fluttered away like a fart in the wind.

Kohler shouted at me. "How can you say such a thing? Maybe you Americans have enough money to throw it away on something any dummkopf could make, but Germans are too savvy. We respect our wages."

Muller put a hand on his "well oiled" belligerent friend. "Klaus," he said, "please excuse Uwe." He extended his thumb, miming a bottle, and tipped it into his opened mouth. "You seem like a smart man, but we don't understand why you would question this."

Otto was next. "Men, he's obviously joking with us. I recognized earlier that he has a good sense of humor; he's trying to be funny."

Uneasy, disbelieving chuckles rippled through the group.

"Sorry guys," I said. "Just never saw anyone make holzkohle. We buy it at the local market, or we cook with gas on our grills."

I had apparently denied the divinity of Baby Jesus. They stared at me with the same expression Gwendolyn gave me when we watched *Carrie* for the first—and only—time.

"You cook with gas...outdoors?"

I started backpedaling—a defensive back trying to cover someone way too fast for him. "Ah...I prefer charcoal for the flavor, but some people have natural gas lines run to their outdoor barbeques. Very convenient." I threw a Hail Mary. "But it tastes like schuhleder in scheiße getauchtscheiss."[3]

Victory! Everybody laughed. I was no longer the idiot American.

"When my brother moved to Wisconsin twenty years ago," Otto said, "I visited. He cooked with store-bought charcoal. I was so embarrassed, I stayed up all night making holzkohle for him as my parting gift. He was so grateful, he cried."

My God, these guys discuss charcoal the way guys back home talk about the Yankees and Raquel Welch's body.

I was lost in my mental fog for a while until I realized they'd pivoted from their fascination with backyard cooking fuel. Kohler was talking about his first visit to America—as a prisoner of war.

"That's when I met Muller here—on a prisoner transport train out of New York City. It was June of '43. Everyone on board had just received medical clearance to continue to a POW camp in Chickasha, Oklahoma."

I braced for a rendition *of* "Deutschland, Deutschland über alles," but no one started singing. The mood was pensive but not bitter. Kohler was focused on the far wall as if staring through some window into the past.

"That's when we all understood how the government...how der Führer and his goons...had lied to us. We'd been told that America was falling apart, a nation in moral and economic decay. We were sure the citizens were at one another's throats, but the longer we traveled—in relative comfort I might add—the more we saw men and women, families, living and working together—people

---

3. "Shoe leather dipped in shit."

absolutely dedicated to preserving the wonderful life they had. They were without sugar, meat, flour, tires, silk stockings, and all sorts of other things, but they went about their days without complaint. In fact, most of the people we encountered were almost jovial."

Muller took up the tale. "Mostly, we could not get over the scope of the nation. We were on a train for four days and still in the same country. The landscape changed by the hour, but it was all America. When we arrived at the camp, we expected privation and punishment. We were treated with respect and given jobs. We were paid almost two dollars a day. I'd been a medic in North Africa, so I was assigned to Borden General Hospital. Kohler worked on a farm. The local farmers shared their produce with us. In fact, when the war was over, we wanted to stay, but we were sent back."

Quiet ambled across what had only minutes before been a garrulous assemblage. Each person absorbed a story I was sure they'd all heard before, but one whose impact never changed. The thought of enemies treating former foes with dignity was as moving as it was convicting.

The party broke up shortly after and, if everyone were like me, the attendees all went to bed that evening wondering if such civility would ever show its face again.

CHAPTER TWENTY-EIGHT

The next morning, the sound of pots and pans making love in the kitchen alerted me to get my ass out of bed. I dressed in the only clothes I had and went to the kitchen. Renate and Jurgen were preparing food. For reasons I still do not understand, the Mullers were there...or still there. They were wearing their party duds.

I sipped on some orange juice, which I assumed had been squeezed from secret German trees out back in a hidden German garden.

Otto grinned at me. Oral hygiene was not one of his stronger points. "Klaus, we had you going last night about the holzkohle," he said.

"Sorry I sounded so stupid."

Otto and Jurgen laughed.

"As you say in America, the joke is on you," Jurgen said.

"Huh?" Again, with brilliance.

"Germans also cook with gas and use store bought charcoal; we were just messing with you."

"Really?"

"Germans are well-known for our humor," Otto said. I almost coughed. "We could barely keep our composure when you reacted with such discomfort."

Real downhome humor. Humiliate the guest. Good one, boys.

"I am equally sorry," Otto said. "But I thought it was funny too."

Renate scowled. "Klaus, you should have stayed with us, you could have avoided these childish men."

"It's no problem. I'm just happy I didn't upset anyone while making a fool of myself."

Renate served a wonderful breakfast. The farmer's omelet of eggs, ham, peppers, onions, and potatoes was accompanied by blueberry and apple pancakes, pastries, and sausage.

Renate refused my offer to help with cleaning, so I went outside with Jurgen and Otto. The fire had mostly disappeared, but Jurgen warned me it was still hot. He put on fire gloves, hoisted the can, and dumped the contents on a concrete pad. It was the most perfect charcoal I had ever seen.

"Go get some clothes from my closet," he said. "We will go to mass before I take you home."

I would have preferred to head back. Mass every Sunday until I left for college and eight years of Catholic school had sated any desire I might have had to explore the mysteries of theology and faith. I never went to church anymore, but I knew my way around a Hail Mary and the Our Father, so I was sure I would not replicate the great holzkohle fiasco of the previous evening.

The walk to church reminded me of an old Andy Griffith episode where everyone arrived at church simultaneously. Everyone from the night before was there. The other guys busted me about the charcoal. I grinned and bore it.

All in good fun—you simpletons!

The songs were the same as back home, only in German. I followed most of what the priest said, stood and knelt at the right times, and got to the end without embarrassment.

After mass we all went back to their home. Renate and her posse of women from the night before cranked up lunch. I figured I'd have a sandwich, maybe a doggy bag if I was lucky, and jump in the Mercedes. Somewhere around my fourth beer, I wandered over to Jurgen.

"Time to go?""Oh no, my friend," he said. "Relax. Sunday is a very special day."

"Church...I know. I was raised as a Catholic."

"Oh, much more," he said. "It is a special rest day. We get together with friends for breakfast, then we dress up, go to church. We've just had lunch. Soon we will go for a walk, then head to the gasthause for dinner. Don't worry about getting back to your apartment. You know the company will not be calling to hire you on Sunday."

"So, will we be returning tonight?"

"No, I will take you back in the morning. Are you having fun?"

"Yes, I just don't want to impose."

"You are my guest," Jurgen said. "More importantly, you are my *friend*."

Thirteen of us hit the road for our walk. Once again, we stopped every block or so to talk to yet another set of neighbors or to charge up onto a porch to greet a blanket swathed oma[1] enjoying the sunny afternoon from the safety of her rocker.

Eventually we left the pavement and went on what appeared to be an old logging road. The sights brought back my days on the Camino. It was peaceful, very green, and the temperature just right. We walked about three miles before returning to the road.

We stopped at a bar for a bathroom/beer break. The beer came in enormous steins so picturesquely decorated they could have been used in any Hollywood biergarten scene. This time, I decided to listen more and talk less. No reason to give these guys any ammunition.

I was transported in my mind to the Adirondacks—family and friends. Uncle Frank and Aunt Martha were mad at each other as usual but would make up by the end of the evening and gross all the kids out by playing kissy face. Uncle Tank, always with the slightly dirty jokes, and Aunt Laurie, acting as if she didn't approve but with a twinkle in her eye, never failed to slip me a few bucks so I could buy candy or soda. Mom and Dad were there, along with my siblings who were my constant playmates. My older sister and her husband sometimes came, but their appearances diminished over time because she was always pregnant. Dad preferred to believe the conception was immaculate. My siblings and I were grossed out.

And there was my cousin Burt, the coolest guy I ever knew. He wore his hair long, listened to Iron Maiden and Black Sabbath (later, Slayer and Mötley Crüe), and talked about "reefer" and "blow" and other stuff I didn't understand until I got older and realized he was

---

1. Grandmother.

a stoner, dropout moron who was destined either for prison or an untimely visit to the morgue. Still, those were the halcyon days of my youth.

Nothing better.

"Klaus, what do you think of the German people and our way of life?"

When Renate spoke to me, she was a little too close. I was aware of her sensuality. I backed up a little while trying not to be obvious about my discomfort. "Renate, it reminds me of my life back home. You are all wonderful people and I appreciate your close friendships. This has been a special treat and I hope I can visit again."

Everybody heard me. There were instantaneous invitations and promises of reunions. I'd heard similar promises before from people I'd never seen again, so I nodded and smiled.

Out of nowhere, Uwe Kohler made a proclamation.

"You'll be back! Heidelberg is not going to work out for you. You don't know anyone there. And it's a city. City life is schrecklich."[2] (There were murmurs of approval.) "You are more of a landjunge.[3] I think the base is a better fit."

I tried not to show my irritation at his presumptive charge into my personal affairs. "I really liked the man who interviewed me at the steel factory," I said. "He seemed confident about hiring me."

"Was he wearing a suit and tie?"

"Yes, of course"

---

2. "Terrible."

3. "Country boy."

"Trust me, he's lying to you," Uwe said. "He's telling you what you want to hear to get you out of his office. We Germans are known for our social graces."

Let's review. Social graces...knee slapping humor...yep, that's the world's view of Germans.

His wife joined the parade of unsolicited advice. "Klaus, he knows what he is talking about. He worked in the corporate world all over Germany including Heidelberg. He used to wear a suit and tie until he got sick of the trickery and deceit going on with the executives. He never regretted his decision to quit and come here."

I looked at Jurgen, hopeful he would tell everyone to back off. Nope.

"You said your rent is paid to the end of the month. You don't have much time to find a job. I suggest you go see the man at the steel factory tomorrow. If they do not hire you on the spot, take Uwe's suggestion and apply at one of the American bases."

The group cheered and my future was decided by voice vote. Apparently, I was an ex-officio member of the "Future of Klaus Schneider Committee." I had no vote. We finished our beers and moved toward the gasthause with the precision of a drunken marching band. I was overdressed for the walk and happy hour, but way underdressed for the dinner. The men were dressed in their finest leather pants worn with a dress shirt and a hat called a gamsbart. The women were in a bright outfit called a dirndl, which consisted of a long skirt, a blouse, and an apron.

The fellas enjoying their Sunday

The secret German national telepathic communication network alerted the waitstaff of our need for beer. Once again, steins the size of two-liter Pepsi bottles clunked onto the table. Our crew members were regulars.

After a few sips, Jurgen touched my arm. "Come with me," he said.

I met Becker, Wagner, Kaiser, Walter, Berger, and a dozen more. All the men were cherry faced and well into their n^{th} beer, although unlike the guys at Frank's Tavern back home, these guys showed no sign of inebriation. I decided if the Olympics ever put in Beer Drinking as an event, everyone else would be chugging for third place behind the Germans and the Irish.

I had to answer a lot of questions once they knew I was American, particularly about my work. When we got back to the table, I leaned into Jurgen. This was not going to be one of our public conversations where I received group advice. "Is there something I should know about?" I asked. "You told those guys I was going to be working at the American base."

"My friend," he said, "you and I both know you are not going to be with the steel company. If they were serious, they would have contacted you by now."

Not sure how. I've been gone all weekend and I left my Dick Tracy watch in the apartment.

"I'll check first thing tomorrow," I said.

"Good idea," he said. "Now we eat!"

The dinner was family style and excellent. We had at least four different kinds of sausage, schnitzel, two types of cabbage, pork knuckle, huge pretzels, some kind of beef roll, and my favorite, sauerbraten. Judging by the copious amount of cabbage we consumed, I was determined to be upwind on the way back to Jurgen's.

Jurgen, Renate, and I sat by the fire and sipped Riesling. Renate said she was pleased to have found at least one satisfactory American.

"You are welcome here any time," she said.

"You have been most gracious," I said.

Early the next morning, Jurgen fired up his taxi and we returned to Heidelberg. On the way, we strategized and decided I should wait until Tuesday, just in case the steel people called me on Monday.

"You do not want to seem desperate," Jurgen said. He dropped me off at my apartment. "I will call tomorrow, and we will determine when you should go to the factory."

After all the camaraderie of the weekend, the apartment felt empty and lifeless. I reviewed my spectacular succession of failed relationships and idiotic decisions. Depression decided to sit with me for a spell. I considered my position. If I came clean about everything, I might be able to convince the Brits of my innocence. The bridge exploded...the young soldier died...I was present but not responsible for either event. And I hadn't been the one who drugged their sultry, Korean agent. All I'd done was...well, things I still would not tell my mother. Surely, by now, cooler heads would have prevailed.

I got off the couch, picked up the phone, and dialed zero. The voice at the other end was German and not the least bit hospitable or jovial.

"Polizei, geben sie ihr geschäft an!"[4]

I hung up and hoped they did not have a tracing system. I was living in a dump, but it was a luxury suite at the Pierre compared to a prison cell in Northern Ireland. Of course, I might not have to worry about fighting the rats for a crust of bread after I stood trial. I was pretty sure a guilty verdict would end with me at the business end of either a rope or an SA80.

I went back to the couch and reviewed the weekend of lots of drinking, eating, and socializing. My mind jumped. One minute I saw myself hawking steel to Canadian industrialists; the next I was working at an American military base doing whatever an American military base needed me to do.

I went into the kitchen and rummaged through the drawers. I found a carving knife with a six-inch blade. Wüsthof. German steel. Even in a pit like this, German pride shone through.

---

4. "Police, state your business!"

I scrapped my thumb across the blade. Damn thing would have split a hair longways. I'd seen a few lacerated carotids in my time on the force back home. Quick bleed out.

I stroked the blade along my throat. The steel was cold, hard, and menacing.

Yep, this'll do it, Conor, old boy.

Then I remembered some of the botched life ending attempts I'd seen in the hospital. Messy and debilitating. Given my track record, I'd end up in a wheelchair with a feeding tube.

I hurled the knife across the room, expecting it to stick in the wall. It hit handle first and clattered to the floor.

Par for the fuckin' course. I curled in a ball on the couch and cried myself to sleep.

The morning was dark, gray, and wet, but my sleep had proven palliative and the despairing savagery of the previous evening was gone. When I stepped off the couch, I saw the knife against the wall and shivered. I decided to call the steel company.

I waited until 1000 hours. When the receptionist answered, she put me right through to Mr. Rheinfurt—or so I thought. After a minute of being on hold, the attendant came back, told me Mr. Rheinfurt was unavailable, but would call me shortly.

I stayed in the apartment all day. Only called back twice. I was proud of my self-restraint. Jurgen called at 1700.

"Sorry," he said. "Busy day with the rain. What time tomorrow?"

"Buddy, I've called three times. Can't get the toolbox to talk to me. He's dodging my calls."

"We tried to warn you," Jurgen said. "Right now, I bet some clown is rushing home to tell his wife about his promotion. They will have a great celebration."

"I hope she gets pregnant...with triplets," I said.

Jurgen laughed.

"I really wanted that job," I said. "I would have killed it."

"No doubt," he said. "You are what I believe your countrymen call 'a people person.'"

Yep, that's me. Ol' people pleasing, women screwing, soldier killing Conor Ryan Klaus Whatshisname!

"You think the offer for a job at the bases is still open?" I asked.

"Certainly," he said. "There is a bank holiday on Thursday. I will pick you up on Wednesday afternoon and take you to my home. Thursday morning, we will investigate."

"I think I'm done here in Heidelberg," I said. "If you don't mind, I'm going to bring all my stuff—it's not much. In addition to looking for work, I'll find a room in Dahn on Thursday. I'm feeling goot about this."

I spent the rest of the day doing laundry and drinking beer. I finished off what little was left in the fridge and packed up. On Wednesday, I took long walks, drank beer, and told the guy in the front office I would not be renewing my lease. He did his best to disguise his relief.

Jurgen and I had a great time on the drive to his home. Renate greeted me with the enthusiasm of a lifelong friend. She had made a nice stew in honor of my return.

"I am so happy you are back," she said. "Just promise me you will not turn into one of those drunken fools who cannot keep their hands to themselves."

"I promise," I said. "But with any luck, I might find a cute fraulein to date. Got a sister?"

She blushed. "I'm afraid you are on your own," she said.

The next morning, we stopped outside of Busenberg and picked up Krug. Dahn was near the French border. Krug explained the bases.

"The Air Force base will pay more," he said. "It needs more people who speak English and German."

"You think my German is good enough?" I asked.

"You are not translating for the UN," he said. "So as long as you don't try to negotiate a disarmament treaty, you should be fine." He roared at his own joke.

Ah...those witty Germans.

We passed the bases on the way to a Tudor style home. Krug walked to the door and knocked. A woman answered, and when she saw him she threw her hands in the air and gave him a big hug. There was a brief conversation. My deep acquaintance with the Gospel of Luke told me what was going on.

"No room in the inn."

We drove to a home on Gartenstrabe. This time, after another embrace—the guy knew everyone in Germany—I saw a nod and a smile. The woman showed me to a lovely room on the second floor. It would have done, except the WC was downstairs. We tried another place on Trifels.

The second-floor room had its own half-bath. The shower was down the hall. I signed some papers, put down a deposit, and received a key.

After I unloaded my stuff, which took all of three minutes, we went for the traditional "move-in beer." While we drank, the guys shared their advice. Get to know the locals. Participate in the local Volkswanderung. Join a hunting club, meet the local Forestmeister, and participate in a hunt. Be careful about dating. German guys weren't wild about local girls dating the soldiers. They would assume I was a GI.

"What's the Volkswanderung?"

"The 'people's hike.' There are many walking trails around the mountains and on Saturdays, everyone shows up for a hike. It's very organized with beer, medals, and German bands. Most of the people in town come."

"That sounds great. What is a Forestmeister?"

"He oversees all licensing and permits. If you want to hunt or fish, you must get to know the Forestmeister."

I didn't have any questions about the women. I figured I could foul that up without any help.

We walked back to my new home. Jurgen and Krug waved and drove off, the Mercedes blowing out enough smoke to set Smokey Bear into a frenzy. I sat on the edge of my bed. The realization sat on my chest like an overweight rhino.

I was totally alone...again.

CHAPTER TWENTY-NINE

A new room, a new town, a new identity (even though it was a week or so old), and a new job...probably. I was tired of posing as someone I was not. In a word, my life was lunacy. Like they say, "You can't make this shit up."

I took a walk downtown to scope out what Dahn had to offer. I wanted to find the bar near the entrance to the base that supposedly had an in-house American Human Resource department. It was 1600, too early to get crazy, but a good time to get to know my new town. Like Dierbach, it was clean, picturesque, and homey, but much livelier.

I found a restaurant called Wildschwein. The sign in front featured a giant boar as fierce as any Arkansas Razorback I'd ever seen. The menu offered whatever you wanted as long as it originated inside a pig. I ordered a beer, and a Schweinefleisch, a pork sandwich. It came with potato salad and it was delicious. The woman serving my food looked about my age, so I told her I was new in town.

"I just moved here today from Heidelberg and don't know much about the area. Could you suggest a place where I could meet people?"

"Germans or Americans?" she asked. "A fraulein, perhaps?"

"This is my new home, so I want to meet both."

"If you like beer, you go to Schmidt's and meet the local men. If you are looking for frauleins, there are some late-night clubs you could visit. If you want to meet Americans, you'll find them in most any bar in town."

"How about if I wanted to find a job working at the Air Force base?"

"Flightline Bar," she said. "It's close to the main entrance to the base. They are always hiring people. My boyfriend works security at the base."

Boyfriend.

Since I'd already started enough international incidents, I put my best opening lines in cold storage for another day, thanked her, paid the bill, and continued my walk. I stopped by another place called The Independent. I needed a little more liquid courage before I went to Flightline. Inside, The Independent was creepy, very dark with red and black lights in the ceilings. It was the kind of place a cheating spouse would go on a date. I could tell there were people in the booths but couldn't make out any faces—and I was a trained law enforcement official. Well, I had been somewhere two, three, or four lives ago. I was losing count.

The bartender looked like an extra in a James Bond movie. He gazed right through me with "I am going to conquer the world" eyes. This guy had never lost a staring contest.

Ninety minutes later and certain I had contracted any available airborne social diseases, I headed for Flightline. When I got there, I was ready for Porky's—I'd seen the movie just before leaving home for Ireland. I assumed there would be a mud wrestling pit in one corner, burly, tatted-up pool players squabbling over quarters in another, and fistfights about to break out at every other table. All I wanted to do was enter the place, speak to someone about a job, and get out before I became a statistic on a police blotter. Before I opened the door, I could hear "Pour Some Sugar on Me" by Def Leppard. Ron Savage's bass line pounded my chest. I was about to break out in memories, but when I opened the door, I was too confused to remember any of them. The place seated close to three hundred, but the only people inside were a bulging biceps bartender and me.

I took two steps. The barkeep worked the tap, filled a three-gallon stein, and slid it towards the place he anticipated I would occupy. I caught it before it crashed to the high-gloss oak floor. I took a sip. Heaven in a glass.

The bartender switched off the music and approached. "Name's John," he said.

I broke into my best Billy Joel impression. "John at the bar, he's a friend of mine—"

"Fuck off," he said. "And don't bother finishin'. I don't give nobody drinks fer free."

He couldn't have been more British if we'd been touring the Tower Bridge.

"Liverpool or Manchester?"

"The fuck are you asking, mate?"

"The accent, sounds British."

"Well, ya got two strikes against ya now, Yank. I'm from Port Isaac, a small town in Cornwall. I'm sure no American has ever set foot in my town, so don't make the mistake of saying you know where Port Isaac is."

"Sorry man," I said. "Just trying to be friendly."

"Not yer fault, mate," he said. "I quit makin' Yank friends a long time ago. The doughboys come; the doughboys go. Not worth the effort to meet 'em."

"I'm not a soldier," I said. Some primordial anger bubbled just under the surface, but I decided not to push it.

He took my mug—without asking—and topped it off. "If not a soldier, you must be with the Agency," he said.

"John, if you took the trouble to get to know who I really am, you'd be bored to tears."

"What brings ya here then?" he asked. "Ya chasing skirts? Ya looking for a poof? Don't care. None of my business who ya shag."

I sipped some beer to buy time and fashion a response. "I was living in Heidelberg," I said. "Couldn't get a decent job. Some folks told me I might get a job at the Air Force base in Dahn. When I got here, someone else told me to come here to investigate what was available."

"Ya got the right place—ya got the wrong night. Thursdays are slow. The Non-Com Club on base has a band every Thursday. The slags will all be there."

"Not opposed to meeting a young lady, but right now I need work."

"What kind? Ya good at anything other than parking yer ass on a barstool?"

This guy had apparently not attended every session of his Dale Carnegie course.

"Hell, I'll do anything within reason," I said. "Just need a paycheck. But, as I said, I wouldn't say no to a date."

"Be careful with the locals," John said. "The Germans haven't been happy with Yank soldiers since 1959."

I crawled through my mental files. "Ah...right," I said. "Elvis. He...ah...sampled a lot of the local fare, did he?"

"Anything with a skirt until he met Priscilla in '59," John said. "Regardless, Germans are pretty sure that soldiers are only interested in one thing—and it ain't marriage, a family, a picket fence, and a Weimaraner."

"Well, I'm not in a hurry to start a family either," I said. "But it would be nice to meet someone."

"Ya want to meet girls, ya should work here," John said.

"What do you need?"

"A bouncer, a bartender," he said. He sized me up. "Let's go with bartender. Ya look like a stout wind would blow ya over."

I hadn't put back any of the weight I lost on the Camino. "I can hold my own," I said. I was a little offended, even if he was right. "But, if you're offering a choice, I know how to tend bar."

John threw a hand towel at me. "What's the difference between a Boulevardier and a Negroni?" he asked.

"Equal portions of sweet vermouth and Campari. Bourbon in the first; gin in the second."

"Okay," he said. "I can hook ya up for a fee."

"A fee?" I had visions of protection money and pinstripe suited guys named "Vinny the Nose."

"Favor," he said. "Ya work when I say. If I need a wingman for a date, ya go out with the other bird even if she's an uggo."

"I'll pass," I said. "I want to work on the base."

"Suit yourself, mate," he said. "Ya want to meet some girls. This is the place to do it, but if ya want to polish some general's Mercedes..."

When I finished the beer, which John kept filling like a breadstick basket at Olive Garden, I took the short walk back to my room. I had about a month's worth of cash. If I kept striking out, I'd be pouring drafts and dating Frau Blücher on John's behalf.

CHAPTER THIRTY

The next day started with my first public bath. Sure enough, after a few minutes in the tub there was a knock. "Enter," I said before pulling the curtain closed and praying I had not granted toilet access to Norman Bates. The enthusiasm with which my "companion" scrubbed his or her teeth (I did not attempt to ascertain the gender of the intruder) could have taken the chrome off the bumper of a 1959 Buick Electra. No less than three minutes after I regained my privacy, there was another knock. I realized the public patience for baths was about seventy seconds. There would be no luxuriating in a hot tub and hoping Calgon would "Take me away."

With no option after I got dressed other than returning to bed for a nap, I left the boarding house in search of sustenance. I found a fruit stand where I bought an apple and a twenty-minutes-from-being-mushy banana. I snagged a map at a newsstand and searched for hiking opportunities in the area. I might as well have been looking for "Smith" in the New York City phonebook. Using Random Selection Theory, I closed my eyes and jabbed my index finger into the book. It landed on the Dahner Rundwanderweg. The roundtrip was over eleven miles with an elevation gain of a half-mile. Along the way, I was promised a view of three abandoned castles on the mountain. I wasn't up for doing the entire distance, but decided to do half and see one of the castles. The trail was beautiful and well-marked with plenty of vantage points to look down over the town. Birds were everywhere; some I'd never seen before. The cuckoos serenaded me the entire time, but I never saw one. Or maybe I did and didn't know—an expert ornithologist I was not. I saw Singing Rock, a twelfth-century castle lying in ruins.

Around 1700 I was done with the hike and hungry again. I saw an interesting sign, a life-sized rendering of a sheep with a cigar in its mouth. How could I go wrong in a place called The Smoking Sheep?

The cleaning service must have taken a month off. Cigarette butts overflowed ashtrays on almost every flat surface. I estimated the last time anyone had cleared the butts was around the 1972 Olympics. Half-inch cigar stubs littered the floor.

"Bitte setzen Sie sich."[1]

"Servieren Sie Essen?"[2]

"Do you speak English?"

"Yes."

"Vhat kind of beer do you vant, light or dark?"

The fraulein delivered a massive stein of beer along with a menu in the vernacular. I tried not to envision bacteria encrusted taps. Maybe the alcohol would act as a sanitizing agent. Or maybe the mold and grime added flavor to the brew. Either way, the beer was delicious. I ordered a couple of sausages and potato salad. The

---

1. "Please sit down."

2. "Do you serve food?"

server looked haggard. I realized she was waiting on customers *and* cooking.

The sausages, tangy and hearty, tasted great. One bite of potato salad was one too many. It smelled like a fraternity house the night after a kegger. I pushed it to the side of the plate.

A second beer would have been nice, but the ambience did not lend itself to lingering. John—the guy at the bar who was a friend of mine. I could not get the damn song out of my head, but I always lost the words somewhere after "...can you play me a melody; I'm not really sure how it goes..." I'd heard Flightline started hopping about 2100 hours, so I tried a place with the *very* German name: Taco Bill's. About two dozen people stood at the bar with a few more patrons scattered at tables. I could spot the Air Force guys right away. Their flattop, butch waxed haircuts stuck out like the proverbial "working girl" in the Vatican. I spotted a guy wearing the mandatory bar apron. He was hustling out of the kitchen with a tray of food. On his way back from the patrons, I stepped in his way.

"You must be Bill."

"Ain't you the clever one! How'd ya figure that one out genius?"

"Looks like you're the only person working in here," I said. "I'll take a beer."

"That all?"

His glare told me there was only one right answer.

"Bring me a taco."

"*A* taco. Right away, Mr. Getty."

"Well shit, bring me three."

"That's more like it." He made no move to shake my hand.

"Hard to believe you don't have any help—I mean with your sparkling personality and all."

For a moment, I thought I'd made a mistake. I prepared to defend myself.

He burst into laughter. "You are one world-class American, ain't you, buddy?" he said. "Sit your keester over there and I'll be out in a second. A beer and three tacos. That's a Bill's Special: chicken, goat, and cat. Coming right up."

Before I could express my reluctance to dine on Fluffy, he was gone. He was back before I got properly settled in an aging booth.

"Sorry, mister, all out of cat. I substituted beef."

"And the goat?" I asked.

He laughed again—this one genuine and full. "Damn, buddy, you are dumber than a prune pit. You got a chicken, a beef, and a fish—just like everyone else."

I peeked into one of the shells with suspicion, then cut my eyes back to Bill. "Ever wonder why you're having an employment issue?" I asked. "You have all the warmth of Don Rickles with herpes."

"It's not my aura," he said. His tone indicated he thought anyone who bought into the aura concept was an idiot. "Most of the Americans work on the base. And the locals would rather deal with an asshole who speaks their fucked-up language."

"What kind of help do you need?"

"Everything but a nuclear physicist," he said. "I've been here since 0800. Opened two hours later and have been busting my hump ever since. You looking for a job?"

"I am, but to be honest, I want to work on the base."

"Damn place is why I can't get any help. It pays better and the work ain't as hard. I'll tell you what, the kids today don't want to work. I remember growing up in Enid, Oklahoma, my ma and pa had me working on the farm seven days a week by the time I was knee high to a mallard. I got Sundays off, but only after I'd milked three hundred cows."

"By hand?"

"You are a rube, ain't you, buddy," he said. "We had milking machines, but I had to hook 'em up and tote buckets and such. You're a Yankee, I can tell. You know what you call a cow in an earthquake?"

I didn't know they had seismic events in the Sooner State. "No," I said.

"A milkshake! Get it?" Bill roared at his horrible joke. "Whaddya call a cow who can part water?"

I shrugged.

"Moo-ses!" More raucous laughter.

Less than half a minute ago, this guy had been a total horse's ass. Now he thought he was Henny Youngman.

"Where do you get cow medicine?"

"A vet?" I said while I cringed in anticipation of the answer.

"At the farm-acy! Get it?"Uncle," I said, "I surrender. For the love of all things sacred, please stop."

Bill wiped a tear from his eye. "Only if you'll work here. Trust me, I have hundreds more—"

I held up both hands. "Stop...no more. I cow-er in your presence."

Bill cocked his head to one side, then let out another bellowing laugh. "Cow-er...very good. I'll have to use that one. Say, do you know how—"

"Tell another one and I'm leaving," I said. "Tell you what. I can help out for an hour or so if you'd like. All it'll cost you is a couple of beers."

"Employees drink free anyway," Bill said. "We'll work something out."

"Okay, what should I do?"

"Start in the kitchen with the dirty dishes."

I walked into the kitchen. The guy hadn't washed a dish since D-Day. Rancid food was barnacled to plates left over from the Treaty of Versailles. A dead mouse floated in a half-filled cup of beer. I felt the tacos rising in my stomach.

I filled the sink with hot, soapy water and let the science experiments soak. The only thing Bill had remotely resembling twentieth-century technology was a serious (and new) commercial dishwashing machine. Fifteen minutes later, it was churning away while I busied myself with a mountain of soiled glasses (sans rodents).

A little over an hour later, I was done. The sink was free of soiled dishes and cutlery, the glasses were dry and polished, the pots and pans were scrubbed, and I had mopped the floor. When I took off my apron, Bill put a beer in my right hand and a hundred marks in my left.

"Been here twelve years and still can't do the math on the exchange rate," he said. "That should be close to fifty bucks. Not a bad hourly wage."

"It's close enough," I said. "And too generous."

"If you hadn't been here, I'd have to hire some other asshole to do it," he said.

Ever the charmer.

When I got to Flightline, the vibe was different. I could hear music through the outside wall. Two guys who made The Terminator look like Peewee Herman were checking IDs at the door. I wasn't worried. If anyone thought I was under eighteen, they needed their eyes (and head) examined.

I drank beer and bided my time until 2330 hours. Then I made my move—no, not on a woman. Nothing remotely resembling the distaff side had come within ten feet of me. I was job hunting. The band must have been fans of Spinal Tap because their amps were turned to 11. As long as they were playing, conversation was impossible. They took a break and I turned to the guy to my right.

"Band's pretty good, huh?"

No response.

I went to my left.

"Never heard 'House of the Rising Sun' played like that," I said.

The guy remained in a deep meditative study of his beer.

I turned around to the guy who was waiting on a drink. "Been stationed here long?"

"Second week."

Success!

I opened my mouth to continue the witty repartee. He returned to his table with his beer after eying me with the caution of a six year old experiencing "stranger danger."

John at the bar (he was a friend of mine, you know) was going under for the third time. The band's break had resulted in a tsunami of patrons, all demanding immediate attention to their alcohol deficit.

"Looks like you could use some help," I said.

"If you're serious, get your ass back here," he said.

And presto! I was a bartender once again.

CHAPTER THIRTY-ONE

I'd just finished refilling the coolers for the third time when John—remember, he was at the bar and... never mind—unleashed everyone's least favorite announcement. "Last call for alcohol."

I zipped around the place dumping ashtrays and sweeping empties into a trash can. Ten minutes later, John threw on the house lights. It was an obvious ritual, because almost everyone in the bar parroted the words along with him.

"That's right, folks. Here's what she really looks like."

I saw my younger self in more than a few of the folks who staggered out of the door. They would hate themselves in the morning—and have almost no recollection of the night before, even if they awakened next to someone whose foul beer-laced morning breath equaled their own.

When the last victim cleared the door, John locked it.

"You blew me off when I asked you about working here. I watched you tonight. You know your way around a bar. You can make some serious money here," he said.

"How about part-time," I asked. "Weekends and any night I'm not working at the base."

"Got something lined up, do you?"

"Not yet."

"Well, why don't you work here until you actually land a position with the sky pilots. If you need to go in for an interview, I'll give you the time."

"What's the rate?" I asked. "And before you answer, remember the old saying, 'Baby, if you say you love me, let me hear your panties hit the floor.'"

John chuckled. "Never heard that one before." He swiped at the bar with a towel. I doubt he disturbed one dust mite. "The hourly rate is shit, but the tips are through the roof. I sell beer for $1.50 American. Most everyone who isn't a cheap SOB hands me two bucks and tells me to keep the change. Three or four hundred beers a night—probably closer to six on the weekends and holidays—I'm getting two hundy before anyone hits the tip jar."

"What's the split?" I asked.

"Like ole Bing used to sing, 'Straight Down the Middle.'"

"I'm in," I said.

I lay in bed and thought about my plan. Landing a job at the base didn't look as easy as Florian Krug had claimed. He made it sound like they were taking anything with a pulse. I couldn't get arrested. Check that. I was absolutely sure I could get arrested—and hanged—if the wrong people figured out who, what, and where I was. Right now, my best option looked to be working at the bar and hoping for something to break the right way at the base.

Why I cared so much about the job had never crossed my mind. Thinking back, I believe it was the allure of the unattainable—like longing to date the head cheerleader only to discover she slobbers a la a Saint Bernard when she kisses.

§§

I wasn't due at Flightline until 1600. With a free morning, I decided to hike back up Dahner Rundwanderweg. I started at the opposite end this time, so I could see new views. The route was a little more challenging, but I'd done more than my fair share of hiking, so I managed.

I took a break and sat on a boulder overlooking yet another venerable castle. I imagined sieges and swordfights—all sorts of Errol Flynn stuff. Something moved behind me. My first instinct was to raise my hands, but no one said, "Freeze," so I turned very slowly.

It was a wolf...an albino wolf. No, wait, it wasn't. It was the biggest dog I'd ever seen. White, over three feet at the shoulder, and every bit of one hundred and fifty pounds. He looked at me with curiosity as if as surprised to see me as I was to see him. He didn't growl or display. There was no menace in his gaze. His tail beat like a lethargic metronome.

I didn't speak. Neither did he. But his head snapped to his right when he heard a female voice.

"Tank! Tank!"

His responding woof carried a resonance that would have made Howard Keel jealous. Still, he did not move. Whoever I was, he knew he had me trapped and he was not going to let me go until...

...a petite blonde woman broke through the trees. Petite—and very cute. She was fussing. I was pleased I could understand her German. "There you are, bad boy. You should not run like that."

Tank looked penitent for a moment, then looked from her to me as if to say, "Look, Mommy, I found dinner."

She noticed me for the first time. If she was startled, she didn't show it. Her lack of fear probably stemmed from her mammoth canine companion.

"Hello," I said.

"Hello," she said.

"Does Tank bite?" I asked.

"He hasn't yet," she said.

I began to slide off the rock.

"But you never know."

I froze.

Her laughter sounded like a zimbelstern[1] I'd heard in church at Christmas.

"I'm Greta," she said. "You've already met Tank."

"Klaus," I said.

Her Teutonic accent was heavy—and very sexy. "You are not German. American, yes?"

---

1. A "cymbal star" (also spelled Zymbelstern) is a "toy" organ stop. It consists of a metal or wooden star or wheel on which several small are mounted. When engaged, it makes a "tinkling" sound.

"Guilty as charged," I said. She looked confused. "I am American. My family came from Germany, and I am trying to track down my relatives. I hope we're not related."

"Why do you say that?"

"Well, I just meant that if we were related, we couldn't...ah...date."

"You mean your male parts couldn't invade my lady parts."

She must have been able to feel the heat from my cheeks at over twenty feet. I was openmouthed. "Ah...uh...n...no...I wasn't implying...I didn't mean—"

"Shut up," she said. "You Americans are so hung up. I am just, as they say in your country, busting your balls."

I let out a huge breath of relief.

And so it began—the answer to a prayer. I wanted a friend—someone I could hang with, confide in, and maybe some other stuff if it worked out. Greta was quick witted, loved dogs, and was easy on the eyes. By the time we reached the end of the trail, she'd filled me in on all sorts of hiking possibilities and Tank and I were buddies.

"Well, my car is over there," she said. "Bye."

"Wait," I said. I cringed inside because I was sure I sounded desperate. "Uh...can I see you again? And Tank, of course."

If I reminded her of a drowning man, she gave no indication of it. "Sure," she said, "be here next Saturday at 0900. I will pick you up and we'll all participate in the Volksmarching in Dahn."

"I'll be here," I said.

I watched her drive away. Tank navigated from his position with his head out of the passenger side window. Her little sedan belched enough smoke to pollute Pittsburgh, but I didn't care.

I still had it.

§§

I walked into Flightline with a smile on my face.

"Mate, I said 1600. Getting here early won't get ya a bigger split on the tips."

"Just making sure everything is set, boss," I said. "And I don't have anything better to do."

John shook his head. "We need to get ya laid."

You got that right, I thought, but instead of engaging in adolescent flexing about my potential dalliance with Greta, I went about stocking the coolers and straightening the tables and chairs.

Maturity is such a lovely thing...and as fleeting as cottonwood puffs on a summer breeze.

The band was scheduled to start at 2100 hours. We had about four hours of quiet until the masses started coming through the door. I got to know John a little better, along with Sam and Freak at the door. Sam seemed somewhat normal, but I couldn't tell what planet Freak called home. Freak drank the whole time he was on duty. Every so often, he came inside to replenish his dwindling beer supply. Whenever I asked a question, he grunted.

"So, how do you remove an unruly customer from the premises?" I asked.

He grabbed a beer can and smashed it into his forehead. I'd seen a lot of jocks do the same thing, but never with a full, unopened can. Beer ran down the front of his shirt. He sopped it up with a bar rag. When he finished, he looked at me as if awaiting a response.

"Cool," was all I could think of to say.

Thirty minutes before the band's opening number the place was full. We were killing it. By my count, we'd already sold close to two hundred brews. There had been six non-beer orders: three wines, a couple of G&Ts, and a rye and ginger—nothing I couldn't handle. Apparently, no one cared about a Sex on the Beach or a Harvey Wallbanger.

The front man was one of those annoying performers who loved to talk to the audience while he faked like he was tuning his guitar between songs. I recognized the stunt. It meant "limited repertoire." "Bodin" —apparently, he thought the name would catch on like Cher—told stories with limited appeal or talked about why he'd chosen a particular tune. Not a single one of the band's selections had more than four chords. The "why" was readily apparent. These guys were not slated to meet Johnny Carson any time soon. But Bodin's tedious monologues offered an opportunity for some conversation with random people. Somewhere along the line, one of them broke my way.

"Hey man, you don't look familiar, first night behind the bar?"

"Yes sir, I'm living the dream." I said.

"Guess you're not military." He pointed to my haircut. "You must be with the Company?"

"Not sure you'd call this place a company, but I'm working for John if that's what you mean," I said.

His eyes narrowed. "You're messing with me, right? I'm not talking about John."

"What do you mean?" I asked.

"The Agency, dude. You know," he leaned in close, "C...I...A."

I laughed. "You got me. Agent X. Got my decoder ring and everything."

He was still slit-eying me. "Well, what are you doing here in Dahn, man?"

"I was living in Heidelberg. Some folks I knew said there was work here in Dahn. I'm trying to get a job at the base."

"Cool. Maybe I know a guy who knows a guy. If you're willing to play, I could open some doors."

"Willing to play what?" I asked. I was trying to remember how many beers I'd served his guy—or if he was high. "I'm interested. What do I do?"

"You take care of me, and maybe I'll take care of you. You want a job on the base, I can make it happen."

Take care of me. Suddenly I had a disturbing mental image of the two of us in the alley—one of us with his pants down.

"Uh..." Now I was looking for a way out. "Spell it out," I said.

"Normally you'd pay me a hundred dollars, but in this case, I'll make it easy on you and take it out in trade."

Oh shit. Here it comes.

"Won't cost you a cent."

Oh shiiiiiiiiiiiiiiiiiiiiiiiiiit.

"All you gotta do..." He paused and looked around.

Oh shiiiiiiiiiiiiiiiiiiiiiit.

"...is let me drink free every weekend for a month."

I rubbed my face and said a quick "Thank you" to whatever divine interloper had rendered assistance.

"Ah...come back at the break and I'll give you an answer."

I found John and told him the deal.

"Won't cost you a thing," I said. "I tell the guy he's drinking free, and I'll give you two nights of my tips."

"Ya know that's probably over two hundred, right?" John asked.

"Yep."

"Deal," John said. "Yer one lousy businessman."

The band took a break after the worst rendition of "Free Bird" I'd ever heard. The house lights came up and the patrons rushed the bar like Crazy Horse's braves charging Little Bighorn. It was good to be king. Suddenly everybody wanted my attention. Women who would not have given me the time of day before were leaning over the bar to expose their assets. Guys were waving cash. I was the Man Behind the Curtain. No one was getting to Oz without my help.

When "the guy who knew" leaned in, I handed him a beer and waved off his payment. He disappeared into the mob. The lights blinked and the crowd eased back towards the tables. By the time the light dimmed and Bodin started trying to adjust his balky E string, everyone was in place with proper lubrication. I began to clear the bar carnage.

Someone at the far end of the bar waved at me. Chiseled cheekbones, brush cut, about 6'4", good teeth. He was either an airman or a castoff from *The Lawrence Welk Show*. I walked over.

"Can I get you something?"

"No, but I'm told I may be able to get you something. Something on the base perhaps?"

"Wow, that was quick. Yes, I'm looking for a job."

"How would you like to work on jets?"

"Huh?" Ever the cunning conversationalist.

"Jet engines. There's an opening in the flight crew. You mechanical?"

"With things that stay on the ground. I replaced a carburetor on my '72 Ford Torino—"

"Good, the less experience the better. Report to the main entry Monday at 0700. I'll hook you up with the folks who'll arrange your security clearance."

I turned to check the bar to make sure no one was waiting for drinks. When I turned back, he was gone. I didn't even get his name. I went back to cleaning up, then wandered through the tables dumping ashtrays and picking up empties. The band finished with a less-than-stellar attempt at "Layla" and the crush at the bar reassembled.

Ever vigilant, I spotted a cute brunette leaning on the bar three customers removed. I'd seen her earlier and was certain she'd smiled at me before her date whirled and I feigned enraptured attention to the glass I was cleaning. This time, when she looked my way, the smile was undeniable.

"Hi there, what can I get for you?"

"You."

"Excuse me."

"You asked me what you could get for me, and I said I wanted you. Are you married?"

"Me? Hell no. Are you?"

"Not yet, unless we tie the knot tonight."

"Right to the point, aren't you?" I was trying my best to act suave. I was pretty sure she couldn't see my knees buckling behind the bar.

"Not a shy bone in my body. I'm just a cowgirl from West Texas looking for a cowboy to ride tonight. You interested?"

Damn right I'm interested. But the village idiot whose body I inhabit said, "I'm a get-to-know-the-girl kind of guy before we go making babies. That bother you?"

"Disappointing, but not disqualifying. What's your name?"

"Klaus Schneider from New Jersey."

"You can call me Shari, Klaus Schneider. You're kind of cute."

"So are you, Shari. So, what's the plan? You moving on to the next cowboy?"

"Nope, Klaus Schneider. This was a once in a lifetime chance. I'm about three drinks past sober. Got a Dear Jane letter from my boyfriend in Lubbock. Figured I could get over the heartbreak fast if I boffed someone I didn't know. You were it, but you didn't want to dance. Soooo...the gods are telling me to head back to the base. Sayonara, babe."

I was about to launch into a "I respect you so much for your decision, why don't we get together when you're sober" speech, but she was out of the door before I uttered the first word.

I told John.

"Klaus," he said, "yer a nice guy."

"Tha—"

"But yer either brain dead or a world class dunderhead. Ya get a chance like that, ya hang up the apron and come back when yere done, which in yer case would probably be about two and a half minutes."

I ignored the insult and went back to polishing a glass. I knew I would be satisfied with my decision later—much later—but for the moment, all I could hear was Al Green's magnificent voice: "I'm so tired of being alone."

CHAPTER THIRTY-TWO

The next day, for reasons I didn't fully comprehend, I went to church. The majority of my prayers since I left the U.S. had been some form of, "Oh God, get me out of this mess." I guess I felt compelled to put in some due diligence—pay a little respect to my Heavenly Firefighter.

I walked downtown and grabbed a roll at the bakery. The locals were dressed in their Sunday best and parading towards their respective houses of worship. I arrived at a little Catholic church fifteen or so minutes before the festivities commenced. I spent the time saying Hail Mary and testing my memory of the Our Father. I finally got them both right on the fourth attempt.

The service did little to lighten my mood. The mass, homily, and songs were all in German. I spent a lot of time counting the candles and fighting the temptation to look at my watch. When everything was over, I glanced at the time. The *four*-hour service had really only taken fifty-eight minutes.

Greta had told me about a shorter hike called the Zuder Dahner Burgengruppe. I finished the one-mile loop so quickly that I did it a second time. Halfway through, I ran into Greta and Tank. She was with a guy.

"Hi," I said. Mr. Nonchalant.

"Hello, Klaus." Greta gave me a kiss on my cheek. Tank did not rip off my arm, so I figured this was her standard form of greeting. "I'd like you to meet Dieter, my brother."

I knew this church business would pay off!

We chatted for a few minutes. Greta asked, "Have you found a job?"

"Bartending at Flightline," I said.

She wiped her perfectly sculpted brow, one I could envision resting on my shoulder after a night of passion. "What a relief. I was so concerned you would work at the Air Force base."

Against everything in my nature, I decided to be patient...and quiet.

"I know you're American," she said, "and I didn't think you were a soldier, but I had to be sure. I want your American bases moved out of the Rhineland."

"Yeah, I heard some of the military guys aren't the best behaved—"

She cut me off. "No, no. I don't care about their actions. All men are pigs. They are simply fulfilling the imperatives of their biological wiring. No, I want the missiles gone. It's not safe for me to live so close to nuclear weapons."

I hesitated, thought about arguing some finer points of the NATO arrangement (about which I knew next to nothing), then said, "Well, if any generals stumble into my bar, I'll be sure to tell them."

"They won't listen," Greta said. Apparently, sarcasm didn't translate well. "The bases need to go. I am a member of a group dedicated to their removal. Would you like to join?"

My interest in "joining" Greta had nothing to do with a political group.

"Ah...I avoid politics most of the time, but you can tell me whatever you'd like."

"Good," she said. "Don't forget—I am picking you up on Saturday at 0900."

She whistled for Tank, who was probably hunting for a bear to kill, then took her brother's hand and walked along the trail in the opposite direction of my travels.

The walk to the bar went quickly, but the shift dragged on. I figured there would be a lot of family business, but then I considered our three Michelin star cuisine: sausage, chips, and pickles. My surprise evaporated—as did the passage of time.

I mopped the floor and tried to make the bar look less like a petri dish. John had some significant cleanliness issues. I realized I had overdone it when a couple came in, sniffed, and left holding their noses. I went outside to catch them but was unsuccessful. When I reentered, the smell of bleach made my eyes water.

I opened a window.

At 1700, a single woman entered.

"Greetings, what can I get for you?"

"Well, if you come out from behind the bar, maybe a hug." She took off a pair of sunglasses big enough for Wilt Chamberlain and I recognized Shari from West Texas.

I gave her the requested hug but was careful not to do any grinding. She stepped back and looked at the floor.

"My friends told me how drunk I was last night. I came to apologize."

"No apology necessary."

"I also want to say thank you."

"For what?"

"Rumor has it I asked you to...ah..." She pumped her fist back and forth.

"Oh...that," I said. "Not an issue. Happens all the time. I'm the Warren Beatty of bartenders."

"Well, you didn't succumb to my drunken advances, and I appreciate it. Not everyone is so much of a gentleman."

"You're quite welcome. Anything else I can do for you?"

She gave me a hard stare. "The sex thing is off the table, buddy," she said.

"No doubt," I said. "I'm stunned you thought I'd be easier this time."

This time, she laughed. "Touché," she said. "But I need something else. I can't find my base ID." "It's not here," I said. "I've been cleaning for hours; would have found it by now. Sorry. You in trouble?"

"Could be," she said. "If I can't find it, I'll have to report it to my captain. He's a hard ass."

"Want a beer?"

"When I woke up this morning, my head was the size of a regulation basketball," she said. "I swore off drinking forever." She looked at her watch. "It's 1500 hours. What the hell. Eight hours on the wagon is enough. Pour me a Bitburger."

"Coming right up."

John gave me carte blanche on the drinking, so I drew two and sat across from her at one of the tables. She told me she was a first lieutenant assigned to the Security Police (SP). She commanded twenty men and women. Her responsibility was the security of eighteen miles of fencing encircling the base as well as all internal security.

"I get to break up barroom brawls off base as well if they involve military personnel, she said. "Been in here a couple of times when guys starting slinging fists."

John had never mentioned any fights.

Halfway through our beers, John showed up. I was free to go. Shari didn't move.

"Wanna go to dinner?" I asked. "If you prefer, I'll walk you back to the base."

"A little ashamed to go back right now," she said. "There's a nice wine bar down the road: Heidi's. We could go there."

So, we did.

CHAPTER THIRTY-THREE

We agreed to split a bottle of wine, and decided on the dry Riesling. Shari thought it would be appropriate to do a toast in German.

"Prost!"

She treated me to the expanded story of her break-up. Gil, her high school sweetheart in Seminole, Texas, had not been thrilled when Shari announced her intention to follow in her mother's footsteps and join the military. While she was stationed at Lackland in San Antonio, they'd made it work. Young love refused to allow a six-hour (one way) drive to stand in the way. But he was considerably less enthused when she announced her European assignment.

Though they vowed to remain faithful and to pine away for one another, Gil began offering the mattressed bed of his Ford pickup to anything with a skirt before Shari's transport plane was 200 feet in the air. He wrote her for a while. They even talked every Saturday for a little bit, but the letter came...

...she stopped.

"You know the rest of it," she said.

"He's a fool," I said.

"You're sweet," she said, "but the offer is still off the table."

I must have looked hurt because the follow-up came fast.

"Oh, you're a nice guy and you're much better looking than Gil—he was a lineman, a little chunky—but I'm going to watch my heart for a while. We'll be friends. You understand?"

I nodded and tried to look sincere. "Friends it is," I said. "But if you change your mind..."

"You'll be my first call," she said. She saw my eyes brighten. "Don't hold your breath."

I gave her the number at my apartment and the bar's phone number, just in case. We parted ways and I went home for a good night's sleep—alone again.

§§

I was up thirty minutes before my alarm sounded. I cleaned up without interruption and arrived at the security gate well before the appointed time. Corporal Sutphin ran his finger down a list on his clipboard. His lips moved as he scrolled. He was not going to win any speed-reading contests.

"Schneider...Klaus, got it," he said. "Stand to the side while we wait for the others."

Once everyone assembled, we went for temporary ID badges. My photo made me look like your garden variety felon, but no one else's was much better.

The next stop was the classroom. I had a slight advantage over the others in class because all the instructions were in English. The other applicants' English was about as good as my German. A hardnosed looking guy entered the room. He looked a lot like Sergeant Carter from *The Gomer Pyle Show*. I almost said, "Gawllll-ly," but knew I would be out on my ass, so I controlled myself.

When Sutphin snapped to attention, I stood.

"Sit down civilian!" People in Berlin probably sat. "I am Master Chief Sergeant James Papaliosas. I will be overseeing your training. Whatever leverage you slimeballs used to get onto this base, it won't keep you here if I don't like you."

Not one single eye left the chief. "Welcome to the 88th Tactical Fighter Wing of the United States Air Force. There are pads in front of you. Take notes. I do not repeat instructions. If you do not remember something I said, I will personally kick your ass off this base. I don't have time for slow learners. As a TSF we are responsible for 53 TFS NATO Tigers, 22 TFS Stingers, and 525 TFS Bulldogs."

Everyone was writing too fast to ask what the hell he was talking about.

"These jets are all F-15s. The F-15C is a single seat aircraft; the F-15D is a two-seater. If any of you maggots perform exceptionally well, I will give you a joy ride. F-15 pilots are known as Eagle Drivers. Your training will begin with hands-on experience working for the 36th Maintenance Squadron at Aerospace Ground Equipment—the AGE. Do you have any questions?"

"What are our duties, sir?"

Yes, it was me.

Popo Gigo's (or whatever the hell his name was) stonelike expression never changed. "I'm not a 'sir,'" he said. "I work for a living. When you address me, you call me 'Chief.' And no one—I mean *no one*—salutes."

Sounding like the bass section of the Mormon Tabernacle Choir, everyone in the room said, "Yes, Chief."

He smiled—I think. "Good."

I raised my hand. He stared at me until I stood.

"Chief," I said—I was afraid I sounded like a West Point cadet, "is there a job description outlining our duties and the attendant expectations?"

"Jesus H. Christ, son," he said. "You go to Harvard? Just ask what the hell you're supposed to do."

I had resumed my seat. He neither moved nor spoke again. I stood.

"Chief, what are we supposed to do?"

"Glad you asked, son," he said. "Shows you're not as stupid as I suspected." He nodded. "You retards—and I'll assume you are all mentally diminished until proven otherwise by outstanding performance on your part—are going to learn how to maintain portable diesel generators, and gas turbine compressors. Those are the units required to start an F-15. This is not your mommy's Ford station wagon. There are no keys. We have systems to support the jets and mo-rons to support the systems. Do you understand?"

Our response crashed into the walls like the Red Sea descending on Pharoah's army, "Yes, Chief!"

We followed him to the maintenance facility. From behind, he reminded me of a bull mastiff. His square head disappeared into broad, thick shoulders seemingly without benefit of a neck. When he walked, he threw one side out in front, then the other. His stride lacked grace, but it advertised power...and menace. Woe unto any who might get in his way.

The guy next to me—long on humor, short on discretion (a guy whose whisper sounded like a truck passing a pedestrian on an interstate) leaned into me. "Chief walks like he's trying to pass a corn cob."

When baby cobras are learning to strike, they watch movies of Chief Papaliosas. He was nose-to-nose with my neighbor before I had time to blink.

"What's your name, dumbass?"

Dumbass said, "Huh?"

"Your name, retard. What did your mother call you when she wasn't putting out for sailors?"

"Uh...uh...it's Oscar."

"Oscar what, you pimply faced Nazi sympathizer?"

"Uh...I'm not...uh...Oscar von Stimple."

"Von Scrotum what?"

I spoke out of the side of my mouth, "Chief...call him Chief."

Papaliosas glared at me and probably would have killed me if he hadn't already had missile lock on Oscar.

"Oscar von Stimple, Chief."

"Oscar...like the hotdog."

Oscar looked blank.

"Goddamn it, you Teutonic twit. How many times were you dropped on your head? You don't know Oscar Meyer? Well, you will. From now on your name is Weener. Omar von Weener."

"Oscar, Chief."

The guy did not know when to shut up.

"Well, it's Omar now, Von Weener." The Chief had never raised his voice. It was the most terrifying thing I'd ever heard, a low growl from somewhere dark and menacing—the sound everyone hears just before they die. "Let me tell you something von Weener—you want to see somebody walk funny, wait till you see how you perambulate once I stick my size twelve up your hind."

Oscar stared at the floor. His lips moved but nothing came out. I picked up what he was repeating about the time he got to, "Holy Mary, Mother of God, pray for us sinners now and at the hour of our death."

By the time he was finished, Chief was on the move. We followed along, a line of little mute ducklings...a very silent line.

We entered a classroom in the basement. Chief stood at the door while we filed in. I was last. Chief blocked my entrance.

"What's your name and why are you here?" he asked.

My training from Ireland kicked into high gear. "Klaus Schneider from Cranberry New Jersey, Chief. I was living in Heidelberg. Couldn't find work. I heard there might be something here."

Chief stepped aside and walked back up the stairs.

For the next hour, we toured the maintenance facility. I was fascinated by the G-suits. The pressurized get ups prevented blood from pooling in a pilot's lower extremities during acceleration and helped to minimize blackouts. Fainting at Mach 2.5 is hazardous to one's health. I wondered if a G-suit might keep blood in my big brain when I met a good-looking woman. I'd gotten into serious trouble thinking with my small head.

At the end of the tour, our guides showed us a series of 5'x7' boxes. They were on wheels. The engines inside produced high-volume, low-pressure air, which fired up the jet fighters. My four companions seemed fascinated. The longer the instructors talked, the "loster" I got.

An F-15

At 1530, we cleaned up the shop and stowed the tools. When we were finished, Corporal Sutphin appeared. He shook each man's hand and said the same thing, "Report at 0800 tomorrow." He said the same thing...until he shook my hand.

"The Chief wants to see you," he said.

Best case scenario, they have too many people and I didn't make the varsity, I thought. *Worse case, the Brits have found me and I'm going out of here in leg irons.*

Chief was at his desk. He did not stand. He pointed to a chair. I sat.

"How did your first day go, Klaus?

"Not too bad, Chief. Very impressive place. Your mechanics seem top shelf."

"They are, son," he said. "They know what they're doing." His gaze was hard. "They also know a phony when they see one."

Oh shit.

"Chief...ah...let me explain."

I waited. The eyes softened.

"It's alright, son," he said. "They just said that from a mechanical point of view, you can't find your ass in the dark with both hands and a flashlight."

I couldn't stop the little grin when it twitched at the edges of my mouth. "I'm no Big Daddy Don Garlits," I said.

"Son, you're not Big Mama Cass Elliot. They tell me you can't tell a monkey wrench from an orangutan."

I laughed. Then flinched.

The Chief's Clint Eastwood façade broke. He smiled. "It's okay, son. Times are hard. Everybody needs work, but the Air Force can't afford the time to teach you how to hold a screwdriver."

I stood to leave. "Thank you—"

"But something tells me you know how to make one."

CHAPTER THIRTY-FOUR

We walked outside and headed across the base. Aircraft took off and landed. I saw men—and a few women—loading lethal looking ordnance as casually as dads packing the family station wagon for a trip to the shore.

"Don't remember me, do you Schneider?" Chief asked.

"Sorry, sir...I mean, Chief...I don't." I braced for an assault.

"Relax, kid," Chief said. "The gung-ho stuff is for the guys whose every little mistake might cost a life. Where you're going, you're not going to hurt anyone...at least not permanently."

I gave my standard, all-knowing response. "Huh?"

Chief opened a door. Over the portal was a sign: ~~NCO~~ Club. "You serve a few too many drinks, someone'll have a headache the next morning, but nobody dies, right? Can't say the same thing about screwing up a jet's mechanical system."

I was blinking and trying to adjust my eyes to the low light. "Guess not," I said. "Someone vandalized your sign."

"Nope," he said. "The on-base military club system has been struggling since the early seventies. Almost no one has clubs exclusive to NCOs and officers. It's one big happy family."

"Oh," I said with my customary conversational brilliance.

"But when a fight breaks out, you need to be damn sure who you're punching," Chief said. He thought his joke was hysterical. I laughed with him. He looked at me. "Don't know me, do you? Still nothing?"

"Sorry," I said.

"You served me at Flightline—this past Saturday. It was packed. Not surprised."

"Chief, I'm as lost as I was during the jet motor in the box lecture," I said.

"It's an engine," he said, "but that's beside the point." We walked over to the bar, and he held up two fingers. A uniformed airman nodded. Two cans of beer slid along the bar. The Chief popped the top of one and handed it to me before opening his own. "I watched you all night. You interacted with every customer. Even if only for a moment, you made every person you served feel special. That's a gift not everyone has." He pointed to the airman who was staring out the window while polishing a glass mug. "Like McClonkey there. I bet he doesn't know my name."

"Not everyone is good with names," I said.

"Shit, Schneider, he's been here three years."

I laughed. We clinked cans and drank. "So, why are we here?" I asked.

"If you want it, this is your new job," Chief said. "You sling beer and polish glasses. How's that sound?"

Before I could answer, a rail thin man entered the room from behind the bar. Chief shook his hand.

"Klaus Schneider, this is Master Gunnery Sergeant Tyler O'Rourke. He's on loan from the Marines. Rumor is he wanted to see what the real military was like before he retired."

"Up yours, Pap," O'Rourke said.

"You'd like that, wouldn't you, Marine," Chief said.

The two men, obviously good friends, laughed. O'Rourke held out his hand.

"It's nice to meet you, Klaus."

"Nice to meet you Master Gunnery Sergeant."

"Call me Gunny," he said.

"Yes si— yes, Gunny."

O'Rourke looked at Chief, who rolled his eyes. "Civilian," Chief said.

"Rumor has it you know your way around a bar, is that correct?" Gunny asked.

"I think I can hold my own."

"Experience?"

"I presently bartend on the weekends and fill in during the week at Flightline, but I got my start at a bar in Belfast." I heard the words and fought the urge to wince. Something akin to a five-car pile-up rattled in my head.

What in the hell did I just say? Shit!

"What were you doing in Belfast?" Gunny asked. "I wouldn't go there with an entire squad of leathernecks and a grenade launcher."

I lied my ass off. "Belfast, New York," I said.

"I'm from western Pennsylvania," Gunny said, "but I know New York pretty well. Never heard of Belfast."

"Alleghany County," I said. "Rather not talk about it if it's all the same. Bad...uh...bad experience with a girl."

"Roger that," Gunny said. "Just promise me no one's gonna show up here with papers for a paternity suit."

"No chance of that," I said.

He hadn't asked about other little things like terrorism and murder.

By now, Gunny had his own beer. He drained it in about five seconds. He sighed, wiped his mouth, and said, "Bottom line, instead of being a grease monkey, you go home smelling like beer—maybe a little like puke on weekends. But no one gets rowdy too often. You interested?"

I must have hesitated. Chief spoke up.

"No rule against fraternizing with female personnel," he said. "I don't want anyone getting busy with it in the back, but if you hit it off with one of the women, as long as she's not spoken for, it's all good."

"I'd be honored to accept your offer, Gunny," I said. "Can I keep my job at Flightline?"

The two non-coms shared a nod. "We'll work with you on the schedule," Gunny said. "My clerk will call you and hammer out the details."

"Thank you, Gunny."

"Just don't let us down, son," he said. "It's a long drop from an Iroquois." He shook my hand and left.

I must have looked blank. "Iroquois?" I asked Chief.

"Helicopter, Schneider."

"You really think he'd drop me out of a copter if I don't do a good job?"

Chief laughed. "Probably not," he said. "But you never know. Marines are batshit crazy, you know."

CHAPTER THIRTY-FIVE

Wednesday came quickly. I reported to the base at 1300. I picked up my permanent ID at the personnel office, then humped it over to the bar to help set up for the party at 1600. When I finished with the grunt work, Gunny gave me *Mr. Boston's Official Bartender's Guide.*

"Most of the orders will be pretty simple," he said. "But there's always some asshole who'll order a mojito or a Commonwealth. There will be officers tonight. One of the majors likes a gin rickey. Be ready."

The airmen were lined up at the door by 1530. A lot of them had dates. At first, all the uniforms threatened to give me flashbacks. I had visions of arrest, cuffs, musty cells, and rats the size of collies. The night wore on...and the tension eased back down into the dark recesses of my brain.

Dinner came out of the back at 1830 on the button. We used the down time to clean up and refill the bar. When dessert came out, I saw a familiar figure stalking towards me. I had a cold Bitburger ready by the time Chief was within reach.

"How's the new duty station?" he asked.

"Five by five, Chief," I said.

"Just keep your head down and do the best job you can. If you fuck up, Gunny'll never let me hear the end of it."

"Sir, yes sir!"

He started to correct me, but he saw my smile. "You're a smartass, aren't you, Schneider?" he asked.

"That's the rumor," I said,

"Alright, now let's drink some beer," he said.

"No can do, Chief. Rules, you know." I looked at him full on. "That was a test, wasn't it?"

"Roger that," he said. "Keep at it, and you'll have a good time."

The room went blank for a second. I heard Alec's voice. "We'll go to Ireland for two weeks. It'll be epic!"

§§

Fourteen days. We were supposed to be gone fourteen days. Had I known I might never see home again, I would never have gotten on the plane. What did Alec know about what had happened? What did Mom and Dad know? Did anyone in Ireland still care about it? Did Billi think about me in the dark reaches of the night when she was next to her husband in bed? Did Michiko still have feelings for me, or was she seething and scouring through security footage from international airports while harboring thoughts of revenge?

I could hear the sounds of battle, feel the explosion ripping through the guard hut, see the fallen British soldier. And I could see

Gwendolyn's eyes, red from crying—and her asking, "Why do you want to be a cop?"

Day after day in a hospital reeking of antiseptic...week after week of rehab...month after month of living on the run, every one of them regardless of some momentary moment of joy or hope or passion, tinged with a sense of impending doom and unrelenting fear.

"How about a drink, Gringo?"

I shook my head and came back to the moment,

"Sorry. Just thinking about home. What'll it be?"

The guy in front of me did not belong in a military club. His suit was not off-the-rack, and his ponytail was decidedly not standard issue.

"Give me two beers—cans," he said. "It'll save you a trip."

"You with the party?" I asked. I was a little unsure if I should charge the guy.

He flashed an ID long enough for me to read "U.S. Embassy."

I wiped down a brace of cans and handed them across the bar. I looked for Chief—wanted a little intel on the guy. I couldn't find Chief and when I looked back, Antonio Banderas was gone.

About thirty minutes later, Gunny came out from the back. I asked about the guy.

"What'd he look like?"

"Six foot one, long dark hair, mustache, tanned, maybe forty."

"Ponytail, right?"

"Yep," I said.

"Should have led with that. Don't worry about it," Gunny said.

"I didn't see him at the dinner," I said. "But I didn't charge him. I screw up?"

"No," Gunny said. "He gets whatever he wants—always. But watch your six."

The evening wound down. It was a party—and a good one—but everyone there had a job to do the next day. There would be no late-nighters here—by 2130, only about fifteen people remained. I was wiping off the bar when I heard a voice from the far end.

"You're new here. What's your story?"

"Ponytail" was back. I was going to make some smart comment, but I remembered Gunny's warning.

"Bar's closed, sir," I said.

"You know better," he said. "I'll take a beer and the 4-1-1 on you. And don't lie. I know when a man is lying, understand?"

"Of course," I said. I felt tightness in my nether regions—and not the good kind. "I'm an ex-cop. Got tired of writing up speeders and decided to cruise around Europe. Came to Germany to forage through the family tree. Looked for a job in Heidelberg but nothing materialized. I met some people from Dierbach, and they advised me to apply at one of the local bases and here I am."

"You make it sound too easy. No one just shows up in Dierbach and ends up tending bar at an Air Force base."

"I was tending bar at Flightline."

"I know the place. You tend bar there?"

"Yep. Came here to be a mechanic. Got made on the first day. Chief had seen me at Flightline. Thought I might not be quite as big a screw-up here. This is my first night."

He paused for a few beats—a man who was turning my story over in his head and looking for holes.

"That'll do for now," he said. "Get me a beer and grab one for yourself." Before I could protest, he said, "Don't give me any crap about drinking on the job. We're the only ones in here, except for the guys in the back."

I drew the beers. We clicked glasses and took sips.

"I'll see you later," he said.

The minute he was out the door, I went to the back and told Gunny.

"Thought I told you not to drink on the job."

"Didn't know what to do, Gunny," I said. "He sort of ordered me to have a drink with him. I only took a sip...or two...okay, maybe three."

Gunny cocked his head. "He *told* you to drink with him?"

"Affirmative," I said.

Gunny nodded. "If that guy tells you to ride a broomstick around the bar like Roy Rogers on Trigger, just ask him how far you're supposed to go. You copy?"

"That's affirm, Gunny."

CHAPTER THIRTY-SIX

I'd made it through the first night—and it was a piece of cake compared to rush hour back in Ireland. I was confident I'd solidified my status as the new barkeep.

I turned my back on the bar to store some glasses. The voice sounded again.

"Karl, working at the bar tomorrow night?"

Geez, the guy moves like a panther. What's his deal?

"It's...ah...Klaus."

"Who gives a shit," he said. He waited.

"Uh...sure...I'm working tomorrow night here and the weekend at Flightline."

"I'll see you here tomorrow night. If you're interested in a little side hustle, let me know."

I responded before I thought—not altogether an unusual reaction from me. "As long as it's legal, I'm all over it."

"We'll talk tomorrow but everything is on the QT, you get it? You tell anyone what we discuss in private, I'll know about it—and I will not be happy. You understand?"

"Yes sir, I understand."

And he was gone. It took me a moment to realize he had not addressed the "as long as it's legal" issue.

Gunny came up behind me. "You've got people waiting," he said. "Why are you standing here with your thumb up your ass?"

"The dude came back. He asked—"

Gunny cut me off. "Don't want to know. Just do what he says. And you've got people waiting."

"I thought the bar was closed," I said.

Gunny jabbed his head sideways. "Feel free to tell that to *the major* at the other end."

Tall and slender with a face carved from an Italian marble quarry, the officer was about two drinks over his limit—the rosy glow under his hard, but glassy, eyes told me. The blonde on his arm who was overflowing the top of her scanty dress was obviously not his spouse. She ordered some frou-frou drink I'd never heard of before. But she was so hammered, I could have served Cherry Kool-Aid and she wouldn't have known the difference as long as I topped it off with a pink umbrella.

When I was finished and back to wiping down the bar, Gunny came back. "What did he ask, kid?"

"He wanted to know how I got here. It wasn't casual, more like an interrogation. I've seen his type; not someone I want to cross."

Gunny nodded.

"What's his name?" I asked.

"He goes by many. Better you don't ask."

"Jesus, that sounds like a line from a bad western," I said.

"I'm just saying, the last time he chatted up a bartender, the guy disappeared."

"Which guy?" I asked, but I already knew the answer.

"The one behind the bar. Never even picked up his final paycheck."

Pray for us...now and at the hour of our death.

"Anything you *can* tell me?" I asked. No one ever lost a bet by wagering against my intelligence.

"Best you don't know. All I've heard are rumors. If I were you, I'd pray you never see that long-haired spook again."

I cringed. "Ah...Gunny...he wasn't black." I hesitated, then decided I might as well get fired then as later. "And you can't really use that term, you know."

Gunny looked at me like I'd dropped my pants. "Son, you may be the dumbest sumbitch I've ever met," he said. "I said he was a 'spook,' not a brother...a spook—you know—like James Fuckin' Bond."

The dawn broke slowly in my brain. "Ohhhh," I said. "Got it."

Gunny walked away shaking his head. I could hear him muttering. "Dumb sumbitch...spook my ass."

§§

The next night was a bit different: no band, but they did have a DJ spinning records. They had an all you can eat buffet for the airmen, but I didn't dare to go near it because I wanted to keep all my fingers, and the boys resembled a feeding frenzy of tiger sharks I'd seen on television. I served a lot of beer. Not one person asked for a pink umbrella. I saw Chief and called to him using the nickname I'd heard everyone use.

"Pap, you ready for a cold Bitburger?"

"What did you say?"

"Pap. I heard everyone calling you that last night."

"You disrespecting the guy who got you this job? I've been in the Air Force since before Moses hit puberty. Who the fuck do you think you are?"

Heads turned. People at the tables were staring.

"I meant no disrespect, Staff Sergeant."

Chief looked around.

"The balls on this fucking guy? 'Pap' he calls me. 'You want a Bitburger' he says." He looked at me like a sniper zeroing in on a target. "From now on, you see me approaching, you just hand me one without asking!"

One beat...two beats...three beats...and the place erupted in laughter. Pap doubled over.

"You should see your face. You look like you walked in on your parents doing the mattress mambo." He couldn't stop laughing. "Grow a set, kid, I'm just messing with you!"

Something akin to a squeak came out of my mouth. I poured a beer and retreated. The bar returned to its normal decibel level, and I became part of the background again.

Until...

CHAPTER THIRTY-SEVEN

"How about a drink, Gringo?"

I waited until my sphincter relaxed before I turned.

"Two beers, right?"

"Good memory. You'll go far, Kurt."

"It's Klaus."

"Who gives a shit," he said. He took a long pull on his beer. "You still looking to make some cash?"

"Maybe. Who do I have to kill?"

He didn't laugh.

Oh God.

"Easiest money you'll ever make," he said. "Army plays the Air Force Academy back home this weekend."

I must have looked blank.

"Football, son...real football...not that candy ass stuff they play here."

I nodded.

"They had to juggle the schedule," he said. "They usually play later in the year, but they moved the game up to the beginning of the season."

I looked at him like I knew what he was talking about. As Lincoln said, "Better to remain quiet and have people think you are a fool..."

"The NFL starts next week, so the game's on Sunday. You like football?"

"Yes, sir," I said.

"Flightline will be ground zero for the game. You'll have hundreds of airmen and soldiers in there, so expect some fights." I'm sure I resembled a chimp at a typewriter. "I'll get to the point," he said. "I've been watching you; you're good with people. But I need something a little deeper. Can I count on you?"

I had no idea what he was talking about.

"I have no idea what you are talking about, sir," I said.

"You know much about the army base up the road; about its mission?"

"No, sir."

"The place has more nukes than Uncle Ben has rice. It's top secret. So, you can't repeat any part of this conversation. Do you know what happens to you if you blab about our conversation?"

"I think I'd rather not," I said.

"That's a good boy," he said. "Let's just say it would be more than mildly unpleasant."

His grin reminded me of Snidely Whiplash in the old Dudley Do-right cartoons.

"But I knew there were nukes," I said. Then I remembered what Honest Abe had said.

Damn!

"Who told you about the nukes?" he asked. "Give me a name." He sounded like the characters from the old Cheech and Chong's skit, "Sign ze paper, old man."

"Ah...Greta."

"Good looking broad, big ass dog?"

"Yep...his name is Tank."

"Who gives a shit. Tell me about her."

"Tank's a he." I chuckled.

He leaned over the bar, his eyes slits of anger. "Crack wise with me one more time, *Karl,* and you'll spend the rest of your life drinking through a straw and pissing through a tube."

I took a moment to get my heart started again. "I...uh...I went for a hike up the Dahner Rundwanderweg. I stopped for a rest, and they came along. We chatted a little, then they took off. Ran into them again the next time I was hiking. She asked where I worked. I told her I wanted a job at the base. She sorta made a face. When I asked if there was a problem, she said something about the base having nukes and how she didn't like that."

"That all?" he asked. "Nothing about associates."

"Oh yeah." I could hear the cadence of my speech picking up, but fear had me by my short hairs and I couldn't slow down. "She was...uh...is...uh...part of a group. They want the weapons out of Germany. She asked me if I wanted to attend. Ithinkthat'sallshesaid." My speech was careening downhill, and the brake pedal wasn't working.

He smiled. He liked people being afraid of him. "You said yes, right? I mean, you go to a meeting, it makes her happy, you have a little wine, you get a little something on the side."

"Ah...well...I don't think I gave her an answer."

"You did or you didn't," he said. "Which?"

"I didn't."

"Well, that figures."

"How's that?" I asked.

"You look like a dumbass." He tilted his head back and polished off the first beer. He didn't even look at me while he started on the second.

Under other circumstances, I might have taken offense, except for two things. One, he looked like he would enjoy hurting me. Two, everything I'd done over the past couple years indicated that he was right.

"I'm supposed to see her again on Saturday morning."

He put down his beer. "Where? Why? When?"

"She invited me to something called Volksmarching," I said. "I'm not sure what it's all about, but I think it has something to do with hiking."

Something almost like a smile twitched across his face. "Good, this is good. You might be less stupid than you look."

"What do I have to do—and how are the two things related?"

Ponytail rapped his knuckles on the bar. "Looky here. Kasper is making connections." He paused, no doubt waiting for me to correct him about my name so he could garrot me. I chose to keep my throat intact. He continued. "Sunday, you wear a transmitter at the bar. You'll know the soldiers when they come in. They aren't as charming as I am."

"What do I do with the transmitter?" I asked.

"You *transmit*," he said. "Damn, no wonder we're losing to the Russians. They've got rocket scientists; we've got Pauley Shore. You wear it—hide it in a pocket. Everybody'll be drinking and watching the game. As long as you keep them full of suds, no one will care if you set your hair on fire."

"Okay."

"About the time they're on their third brewski, ask a few questions."

"What kind of questions?"

"Height, weight, favorite sexual position. Damn, Karsten, let me finish."

I let him finish.

"Chat them up about what they do at the base. Act real interested. See how much you can get them to tell you about what goes on there. If they get suspicious, give them another beer and knock it off. Copy?"

"Copy," I said. "Am I supposed to remember everything?"

"Your first intelligent question," he said. He reached over the bar and patted my head—a master who's taught his Labrador to fetch.

"I'll be in the bar listening and recording everything."

I made a show of looking around him at his hair. "Disguised, no doubt," I said.

"Now you're a regular Mr. Phelps, aren't you?"

Ah ha! A reference I understood. *Mission Impossible* with Mr. Phelps, Barney, Willy, Rollin, and the ever-delectable Cinnamon.

"Always loved that show," I said. "I assume if I am caught or killed, the Secretary will disavow any knowledge of my actions."

This time the smile was genuine. "Good one," he said. "No, if you're caught, they'll kill you and I'll help."

My jocularity subsided.

"Base personnel are not supposed to talk about what they do," he said. "It's a matter of national security. But someone over there is running his mouth like an old lady in a sewing circle. You're going to help me plug the leak. You understand?"

"Seems pretty easy. I talk to the soldiers and see if they'll tell me anything about the base."

"You're a regular Enrico Fermi," he said.

"How do you know they'll be at Flightline?"

"I sent an operative to the base—local guy. He told the base commander there was a beer special for American servicemen at Flightline in honor of the game: $1 beer. I...uh...made arrangements with John."

"John at the bar—"

He pointed his finger at me. "I swear to Christ if you say he's a friend of yours, I will pull your nads out through your nose."

I didn't finish.

CHAPTER THIRTY-EIGHT

After a slow Friday night, I lay in bed thinking about my new assignment. Ponytail had encouraged (well, commanded) me to keep my date with Greta. I was excited about the possibilities. But the super-secret spy stuff had me a little worried. I could imagine the transmitter splatting onto the table when I bent over to serve a drink and the resulting whuppin' I would receive courtesy of Uncle Sam's finest.

When I awoke on Saturday, I decided to deal with one thing at a time. Once Greta picked me up, I would focus on her and forget about everything else. On Sunday, I would worry about trying to act like Maxwell Smart.

In perfect German style, Greta arrived two minutes early. I asked her about Volksmarching.

"It is a form of non-competitive fitness walking," she said.

We arrived at the staging area and paid twenty-five deutschmarks each to walk a ten-kilometer trail. Because she knew there would be hundreds of people, Greta had left Tank at home. I liked the dog, but was pleased to have some time alone without Greta's fanged bodyguard.

Once the hikers were dispersed along the route, we had a wonderful conversation. Greta asked a lot of questions. I was happy to be spending time with someone who didn't have to devote any thought to the management of their facial hair.

Thirty minutes into the walk—it was not a stroll, we were moving—we rounded a bend to find a big table set with steins of beer. Greta did not hesitate. She grabbed one, took a hefty swig, then handed one to me.

"Go ahead," she said. "The fee includes all the beer you care to drink—as long as it lasts. It's Germany, you know."

Her laugh was hearty. It reminded me of a similar laugh from long ago, one issuing from beneath the sheets in a small apartment on the outer edges of my college campus...a memory that simultaneously warmed and broke my heart. The first time Gwendolyn laughed during sex; I got my feelings hurt. We'd been "doing it" for a while and she'd made what I thought were all the appropriate noises. Then, one night—at college—she let loose a deep, throaty laugh, something almost feral. I was young and inexperienced. For a moment, my feelings were a little bruised. But she pulled me close and assured me if I stopped, she would hurt me. I learned to appreciate (and eagerly await) her laughter as an expression of her joy and rising passion.

"Klaus, are you alright?" Greta asked.

"Fine," I said. I gulped a mouthful of beer to keep from having to talk...then another. "I'm fine. Got a little lightheaded I think."

"Should we slow the pace?"

"I'm okay." I was trying like hell to convince myself. "Let's finish the beer and keep going."

A mile later, we passed a table laden with hotdogs and pretzels. By the time we'd marched and munched, we found more beer.

"They ought to put this event in the Olympics," I said. "Of course, they'd have to disqualify the Germans for professionalism." I was hoping for another nostalgia-inducing laugh. I got a blank stare instead. "Never mind. Weak joke."

Greta smiled and quaffed. Like most Germans, the woman would drink her weight in beer without any effect on her mood, personality, or balance.

We finished the 10k walk in a little over two hours. No one had pushed; very few had passed us.

I had never experienced an Oktoberfest in Munich, but when we completed the course and saw the massive tent along with many vendors, I felt like I was there. In the center of the tent was a quintessential German Oompah band. They were grinding out polkas; people were dancing. The guy on the accordion would have made Myron Floren bow in respect. I could not remember when I'd seen such a genuinely joyous crowd.

By 1300 we were sitting at a picnic table in the sun working on our third...or fifth...stein. I turned; Greta was looking at me with a gentle smile. Her face was radiant. I wondered if she'd ever used makeup. She certainly didn't need it. Her beauty emanated from some deep, natural spring, a place where naked Viking goddesses rode unicorns. Okay, I was getting carried away, but it had been *a while* since my last significant interaction with a woman.

"You're staring at me, Klaus," she said.

This was my chance to kiss her—or to make a fool of myself. I opted for neither and reached for her hand. She did not pull away.

"I'm going to buy you another beer, Klaus Schneider."

"Pretty strong talk for someone getting it for free," I said.

"It's all part of my plan," she said.

"It's working," I said. "Can I kiss you?"

Robert Redford should be so smooth.

"Oh, very direct," she said, but she did not look like she was about to vomit—always an encouraging sign. "I'll think about it while I get your beer."

CHAPTER THIRTY-NINE

I went away again to a time long passed and a past long regretted. Greta nudged me when she returned.

"Where did you go?" she asked. "You were obviously remembering something...or someone."

"Want me to be polite or do you want the truth?" I asked.

"The truth, of course," she said, "however painful."

"I was thinking about how similar you are to my first love, a girl I knew in college. I feel very happy when I'm with you. I know this is only our first date—"

"Our first date?" Her reaction did not fill me with confidence there would be a second. "Where did that come from? This is just Volksmarching, a simple walk. Do you really call this a date?"

"I'm sorry," I said, but I wasn't.

"Perhaps a date in Germany and a date where you're from are two different things. I thought you met a date to get married."

"No, no, no," I said. "In America, we go on dates to get to know people—you know...boys want to meet girls...girls want to meet boys."

"Well," she said, "you may be a boy, but I am certainly not a girl."

I was about to kick myself again when she laughed.

"Busting my balls again?" I asked.

"Ya," she said. She waited for a moment to compose herself. "According to your definition, this is, indeed, *a date*, and I am enjoying myself very much." I felt a little better—and a lot less idiotic. "Come now, they are giving out the awards."

A little round man who could have been a stunt double for Spanky from *The Little Rascals* draped copper medals the size of coasters around our necks. He shook my hand—or tried to wrench my arm from the socket—and then said, "Wir können Ihr foto machen."

Volkswanderung Medal

Even if I hadn't known any German, I would have recognized the cognate for "photo." I put my arm around Greta. Just before the camera clicked, Greta planted her lips on my cheek.

"There's your kiss, Klaus," she said.

"That's it?" I asked.

"You're the only guy I know who would complain about getting a kiss from das fuchste Mädchen Deutschlands," she said.

"No complaints," I said. "It's just when 'the foxiest girl in Germany' kisses me, I want more."

"All in due time," she said. "Let's walk again next Saturday morning. I'll bring Tank. He likes you." She paused. It seemed calculated. "And we need to talk more about the nuclear weapons your country is hiding in my backyard. Would you be open to meeting with some people in my group?"

Jackpot.

"I'm not much into politics Greta," I said. "But I'll come for a chance to see you again."

"Okay, Wednesday at 0900. I will meet you in the parking lot where we first met."

She hugged me, waved goodbye, and walked away. I appreciated her spectacular hindquarters until she disappeared into the boisterous crowd.

§§

When I got to Flightline, the customers were two deep at the bar. John looked up and grinned. "Never been happier to see someone in my life," he said. "Early rush. Grab an apron and start working the tap."

The rest of the night was an uphill battle. John had the wrong date for the Volksmarching on his calendar, but he was always well stocked, so we weren't concerned about running out of product. We were swamped until 2100. I was swabbing the deck when a voice startled me from behind.

"Howdy, cowboy."

Shari, the contrite (and formerly horny) airwoman. I must have flinched a little.

"Never fear," she said. "I'm not looking to jump your bones."

I clutched my chest. "Ouch."

"No offense," she said. "I mean, you're not bad for a guy drenched in sweat and bar stink, but I'm not in the market for another broken heart and I get the feeling you are a short timer here."

I let the comment pass. "How long have you been here?" I asked.

"Long enough to watch you serve about four hundred people. You must be exhausted."

"Nah," I said. "I walked 10k this morning before my six-hour shift." I flexed my tired right arm. "Strong like bull."

"Good, then you wouldn't mind taking me out for a drink when you're done," she said.

"Thought I wasn't your type," I said.

"That was ten seconds ago," she said. "A woman's prerogative, you know."

"Give me thirty minutes to wash this place down and change my shirt. Then, we'll go wet our whistles."

John witnessed the interaction and told me to take off. (He's my friend, you know.) I washed up, sniffed the pits of three shirts I kept in my locker, picked out the least offensive, and was out of the door with Shari in five minutes. We went to The Globe, her "favorite." We ordered sausage and beer.

"I've been thinking about you," she said while we waited for our food. "I was kinda rude last time. I apologize. I was such a snot."

"Yes, you were," I said. "I rescued you in your time of need, but refused to take advantage of your considerable attributes."

She pulled her head back in mock (I hoped) revulsion.

"Hey, you're a snot. I'm a pig."

She raised her stein. "To individualism," she said. We clinked.

"So, where do we go from here?" she asked.

"Well, you made it clear that the sex thing is off the table." I hesitated a moment, to give her a chance to demur. She didn't. "So, how about we be friends? You know, hang out, have dinner. I have every confidence you will eventually succumb to my considerable charms."

"Klaus," she said, "I apologized already. Friends sounds like a winner."

We clinked again; we drank again. When we put down our glasses, she grabbed my hand and squeezed. It felt good—really good. I'd been alone for a while and now there were two lovely women in my life.

I wondered if I should mention Greta. But there wasn't a lot to tell. We'd gone on a walk, and she'd run into my face with her lips. Hardly the stuff of *9½ Weeks*. I let it go and enjoyed the moment.

We ate; I paid; we walked out holding hands. The minute the night air hit my face I started looking for Greta. I expected her to wander past at any moment and blow whatever I might have been hoping for with either woman to shreds.

We got to the end of the block and waited for a car to pass. Shari pivoted and lip-locked me like she was giving me CPR. The kiss was long, deep, and expertly executed. I'd had cavities filled in less time. It was nice. It would have been great if I hadn't been looking out of the side of one eye for a Greta drive-by.

Damn, guilt is a terrible thing. Guilt about what? I hadn't done anything. I hadn't made any promises. I hadn't gotten down on one knee and professed my undying affection and fidelity. The situation was as confusing as shit.

Shari came up for air. Her nose started twitching.

"Do you smell that?" she asked.

"What?"

"Garbage can maybe," she said. She looked left.

She looked right.

She looked *at me.*

"Oh God," I said. "Sorry. I promise, I bathe regularly. I even changed my shirt."

You could have fried an egg on my blushing cheeks.

She giggled. "It makes sense," she said. "You hiked; you worked all night. Not a problem."

But she'd backed up a step.

When I got home, I sat in the tub for twenty minutes and dared anyone to disturb my depressed solitude.

CHAPTER FORTY

Long black hair cascaded across my bed partner's shoulders. I reached out and touched the creamy flesh. A face came into focus.

Ponytail!

I sat straight up—fully awake.

"Damn!"

I hadn't slept well. Between Shari's abrupt, nose-holding departure and dreams about being curb stomped by GI Joe, it had been a long night. The more I thought about the espionage mission I had accepted, the less I wanted to do it. Sure, I was going to make money, but had anyone told me *how much*? Would it be enough to cover my medical bills?

Still, I had some miniscule reserve of patriotic fervor. If the guys at the base were leaking classified information, didn't I have a duty to stick my finger in the dike? I could be like the little Dutch boy who saved his country from a catastrophic drenching. With Ruskies at every turn—I'd seen way too many spy flicks—shouldn't I step up to help the Ol' Red, White, and Blue?

I showed up at Flightline at 1550. John looked at me a little sideways. I was usually thirty minutes early. He gave me a questioning shrug. I responded with a thumbs up; I looked a lot more chipper than I felt. Luckily, he'd filled the coolers the previous night, so all I had to do was bar set-up. I refilled the napkin and straw holders, then cut up enough lemons and limes to fill a Florida orchard.

Ponytail skulked in about 1700. He looked ridiculous, with a wig he must have stolen from some aging Beatles' fan. He was wearing oval sunglasses, which he refused to remove. Everything about him shrieked, "I'm here incognito."

What a maroon.

I gave him the old *Sting* hi sign—Paul Newman running his index finger along the side of his nose. He jerked his head towards the Badezimmer. I hoped no one was paying attention because it looked bad when I followed him through the door of the john.

"Bus from the base will be here soon," he said.

"Could you look more like a cartoon spy?" I asked.

I was about to laugh when he pulled off his shades. "Smart off again and you'll never father a child," he said. I didn't smart off. "Okay, you ready? Any second thoughts?"

"I've got plenty, but I've come this far. Mind telling me your name?"

"MacArthur," he said. "Doug."

"I shall return," I said. If he was Douglas MacArthur, I was Michelle Pfeifer, but I wasn't going to push it.

He looked at me a little sideways, then produced a black box about half the size of a pack of Winstons.

"You sure I can keep that hidden?" I asked.

"Son, you may be a virgin, but I'm not. This is what I do. I'm the guy who fixes stuff before it fucks up. Nobody's going to die here tonight; nothing's going sideways. Just do your job, keep your cool, and don't step on your pecker."

"I'll have to fold it in half," I said.

He hit me in the solar plexus so fast I never saw it coming—and so hard I thought my heart had stopped. Three minutes later I could breathe again.

"Any more smartass remarks?" he asked.

I shook my head. Answering would have required air.

"Okay," he said. He clipped the transmitter inside the back waistband of my slacks and taped the mic to my relatively hairless chest. "Let's do this thing."

The place was half-full of Air Force personnel when I came out of the john. "Mac" waited for a while before he exited. Just before 1800, I heard a raucous rendition of the Army marching song.

"The grunts are here," John said. "Lock up the women and sheep."

In they came. A swarm of 150-pound locusts in combat boots. The men were bigger.

"First to fight for the right, and to build the nation's might, and the Army goes rolling along...Then it's hi! hi! hee! In the field artillery, Shout out your numbers loud and strong. For where e'er you go, You will always know, that those caissons go rolling along."

Pretty impressive. Even the airmen (and women) clapped along. Once the singing stopped, they greeted one another like gladiators on the floor of the Colosseum.

From then on, my role was, "Name's Klaus. Whatdaya want? It's on the house."

When the National Anthem was played, every person in the bar stood and saluted. Then it was butts in seats and beers to lips. The rowdiness meter climbed steadily as the game—and alcohol consumption—progressed.

The score was tied until the last two minutes of the first half. Army scored another TD, then kicked a period-ending field goal after the Falcons' running back handled a pitchout like a porcupine.

I had a nice conversation with a young corporal.

"Name's Klaus. What can I do you for?"

"Scott Miller, nice to meet you."

I think the kid probably shaved with a washrag. Barely looked old enough to drive.

"Where do you hail from, Scott?"

"Aberdeen, Maryland, the home of the best butter and steamed blue crabs in the world. You like seafood?"

"Hell yeah. As long as it's served with a cold beer, I'd be all over it."

He took a long pull on his beer but made no attempt to return to his table.

"So, what brings you to this part of Germany?" I asked.

"Courtesy of the Honorable Cecil Tanner," he said.

"Who the hell is that?"

"Traffic judge in Harford County, Maryland," he said. "I'd been out with the boys. Had a few pops—shouldn't have been driving. Tried to stop at a light but hit the gas instead. Was doing almost fifty when I introduced my GTO to the front desk *inside* the Sheriff's Department. Judge Tanner gave me a choice: nine months in the lock-up or a two-year stint carrying a rifle. Most of the shooting has stopped and I don't think jail is like that old movie, *Women in Cages*, so I chose the Army. They sent me over here after basic. I made corporal last week. Not too bad."

"Not driving tonight, are you?"

"Hell no. Lesson learned."

"How long you been here? What do you do at the base?"

"Going on fifteen months. When my tour is up, I'm headed back stateside. Don't get me wrong, I like it here; it's great. On the weekends, I can travel all over Germany, and France is only a three-wood away. Ever made love to a French woman?"

Danielle's unclothed form came into my mind. Damn, the woman was something else. But I lied. "No, haven't had the pleasure."

"They know their stuff, man," Corporal Miller said. "Take my word for it. Get over there PDQ."

"Roger that," I said.

"I gotta get back to my buddies, but I'll be back to see you." And off he went.

It took about three seconds to spot Inspector Gadget. He was in the far corner. He'd found a slouch hat somewhere. He could not have been more obvious if he'd had a sign over his head reading "This Guy is a Spy," but no one seemed to notice. He stared at me. I knew what he was thinking.

Don't waste my time. Get someone to say something.

I had similar conversations all through halftime. I met soldiers from all over the U.S., but no one opened up about their duties. Army won the game, and the fun began. The victors decided to do shots and the information began to flow.

A tall redhead told me his job was to guard nuclear weapons. He did everything but draw a map. A stumpy looking dude who could have played a stunt double for a fire hydrant slurred his way through an explanation of sitting in a guard tower where, by his own admission, he "drank the night away 'cause there weren't shit to do." A third guy, who might have been yanking my chain, told me he'd once put an M-16 slug through a stag standing next to a missile silo.

"If I'd a missed him, I'd a blowed up half of Germany and all of my ass," he said.

I heard a customer at the other side of the bar, "Couple of beers, Gringo."

I took over a pair of cold ones. He leaned in. "You're getting the hang of it, but we need something more solid. Get a picture with one of those mouthy clowns."

"How am I supposed to get them back over here?"

"Well, either with booze or tail. I don't see any pros and I don't think you go that way, so..."

One by one, I retrieved the blabbermouths and told them they'd won a free bottle of booze. Mac told them to pose and say, "Cheese." I was disappointed he didn't instruct them to, "Say espionage."

The bus pulled away and I was left with several hundred "dead soldiers" to put in the trash and a few dozen tables to clean. When John was not at the bar—but he was still my friend nevertheless—Mac slipped a thick envelope into my back pocket.

"Good job," he said. "Dump the transmitter in the trash somewhere."

"Hope I didn't get those guys in trouble," I said.

"No worries," he said. "They probably won't be in Leavenworth more than five or six years."

Kids at Christmas should look so happy.

"Any way this comes back on me?" I asked. "I imagine they all have guns."

Mac smirked. "Clever deduction, Sherlock. No, those chuckleheads will be on an 0600 flight out of here tomorrow. They'll disappear like Marley's ghost."

I felt something like relief. Might have felt better if Mac weren't so absurdly creepy. His wig was a little askew and somewhere in the middle of the evening, he had "grown" a handlebar mustache.

"Ah, did you have the face lace earlier tonight?" I asked. I scratched my upper lip.

"Hell no, taint bonnet," he said. "Got to stay on my toes. Dumped the hat in the trash. Put the 'stache on. I'm like one of those kaleidoscope lizards."

"A chameleon," I said.

"Not the song, moron," he said, "the lizard."

Somewhere in South London, Boy George shed a tear. I let it go.

"You're not bad, kid," Mac said. "You do good work. I promised you an easy mission. That's what you got."

"I appreciate the money," I said.

"Got another job. You interested?"

"Depends," I said.

"Good, you're in," he said. "Tell your boss on the base you need an hour." He squinted. "Did he tell you anything about me? Don't lie. I'll know."

"He knew who you are, sorta—he said you weren't anyone to fuck with."

"That's all he told you?"

"Yeah,"

"He's a smart man. Okay, I'll find you."

He pulled up the collar of a trench coat he'd conjured from somewhere and eased outside.

That is one weird dude. I patted the envelope in my pocket. *But this spy business pays well.*

After a couple hours of cleaning the place and filling the coolers, John said I could go home. It had been a long night, but no one had thrown leather or broken anything, so it was a win.

I hummed "Karma Chameleon" all the way home.

CHAPTER FORTY-ONE

The next day I was exhausted. Fortunately, I had a short shift at the base. When I got home, I made a mockery of attempting to clean my room, then crashed on the bed. I dreamed about walking through the woods with Greta—we were both naked. It might have been a nice dream, but somewhere along the line Tank showed up and things got weird. When I woke up, I wasn't very well rested.

Tuesday was going to be a long one, so I ate a light dinner and turned in. If I dreamed, I didn't remember anything.

We had a luncheon for the base wives. The annual event featured an after-meal tumbling demonstration by Bavarian gymnasts. They weren't exactly Olga Korbut, but everyone applauded and had a good time. I spent more time serving food and washing dishes than mixing drinks.

By 1630, we were restocked and straightened. I had just finished hauling the last of the trash bags to the dumpster when Mac appeared.

"Got time for a chat?"

"How'd you know I was finished?" I asked.

"Better you don't know," he said.

"Your name really Mac?"

"You really want to know?"

I didn't.

"Okay," he said. "Let's get inside. We can talk in the storeroom."

He locked the door behind him.

Uh oh.

"Klink, you did good last night."

I decided not to correct his grammar.

"You made me proud. I've been looking for a partner for a while, but no one's worked out."

I wondered what happened to his former associates.

"What happened to—"

The hard stare returned. This guy could go from a cartoon character to scary as shit in five seconds. "You don't want to know," he said.

"I'd feel more like a partner if you got my name right," I said.

"You got paid, so shut up."

"Copy," I said.

"Just rest assured I have all the power of the U.S. government behind me. Don't worry about anything else," he said.

I sucked on my lip.

"Good," he said. "Let's get to it...*Klaus*. We got trouble right here in River City—with a capital 'T' as in 'traitor' or 'terrorist.' There are a number of terrorist cells in the area, and I need intel."

"How the hell can I help with that?" I asked.

"Ever heard of the Jaeger-Vogel gang? Named after the leaders Hans Jaeger and Joel Vogel."

Staying on topic had never been my specialty.

"I know about the James Gang." I started playing air guitar and singing the intro to "Funk #49," complete with wah-wah pedal. I'd just gotten through "I sleep all day, out all night...I know where you're goin'" when he slapped me.

"Dammit, Kringle, this is serious shit. I know you think I'm a clown, but I'm not."

I rubbed my cheek. I did not like being hit. I lost my cool and got within three inches of his face. "Then what's with the stupid wig and the fake lip foliage...the Sonny Bono shades and the ridiculous trench coat. You think people didn't see you?"

"*Everybody* saw me, asshole," he said. "That's the whole point. When I want to be seen, everyone *always* sees me. I'm the village idiot—the town weirdo."

"Damn right you are," I said. "Everyone in the bar pointed at you at least once during the night."

"Precisely," he said. "And as long as they think I'm a buffoon, no one thinks I'm a threat—and no one notices anyone else or the questions they ask."

I stepped back. "Shit...that's genius. You're a spook in plain sight."

"Yep," he said. "And my goofy behavior covers your ass." He waited. "By the way, you do a passable Joe Walsh impersonation—but your guitar needs work."

"Point taken," I said. I sat on a case of beer and put my elbows on my knees. "What do you need me to do?"

"The Jaeger-Vogel gang has been spying on these bases for months. They record logistics from the perimeter of the fences. My gut tells me they are planning a breach, but we need to be sure. Best guess is they plan to steal at least one nuke.”

“Damn, that would be bad, right?”

He was going to explode again, but he saw my grin. “Yeah,” he said. “Very, very bad.”

“Mac, you’ve got to have a hundred guys who can get you good intel.”

“We had one,” he said. “German dude. He was giving us good stuff. Three weeks ago he went dark. He turned up late last week.”

“Good,” I said.

“He didn’t think so,” Mac said.

“Why?”

“Because someone had ventilated his head with two behind the ear.”

Mac put two fingers to his head and pantomimed a gunshot.

“Jesus! And you think I’m going to help? That’s way above any pay grade you established, my friend.”

“You sure? It’s for your country,” he said.

“Let me think about it—ah, nein!”

“You don’t even know the details yet.”

“I know everything I need to know. I know I’m not a spy. I know the guy I would be replacing got dead. And I know I can’t fake my way into a terrorist cell.”

“You don’t have to,” he said.

“Huh? Don’t have to what?”

“You don’t have to fake your way into the cell.”

Every cell in my brain screamed at me to shut up and walk away. But what did they know? “Why not?”

"Klepto, if brains were dynamite, you wouldn't have enough to blow your nose. You've already been invited by your friend."

"You are not my friend," I said.

"I know," he said. "But Greta Lewis is."

CHAPTER FORTY-TWO

Mac had not been happy when I turned him down, but my head was about to explode, and I did not want anyone to turn my figurative "mind blown experience" into a literal one.

He'd promised a lot of stuff. I mean...a lot.

Money.

The love of a grateful nation.

The possibility of sexual romps with Greta.

A brand-new house in the States—something of absolutely no use since I could not return without being arrested.

Did I mention the stuff with Greta?

But he wasn't mad, either. He thanked me for the help in the bar, asked if I was happy with the payment from the first gig (I was), shook my hand, and wished me well.

Seemed a little too easy.

Turned out, it was.

§§

The week lumbered along with all the fervor of a giant tree sloth. I rose, showered, worked, and went home. The tedium was exceeded only by boredom. Friday night, I could not get to sleep. When I wasn't tossing and turning, I was opening the window to cool off the room or closing the window to block out some perceived noise. I awoke Saturday morning feeling hungover even though I had nothing to drink the previous day.

Everything changed when Greta and Tank appeared at the appointed time. She smiled and kissed me on the cheek. It wasn't anything passionate, but it was more than a peck—seemed more like a promise of something yet to come.

We walked and talked and looked at another venerable castle. Greta explained the history; I fought the urge to yawn.

At the apex of the trail, we sat on a boulder and ate lunch. We munched on fruit, cheese, and bread and sipped on a nice bottle of Riesling. Tank gnawed on what Greta said was "organic jerky." Looked like a dead squirrel to me. When he finished, he broke wind, rolled on his back, and lay in the sun with his tongue lolling from the side of his considerable mouth.

The day was warm, and I was full. My head bounced off my chest.

"If you fall asleep and start snoring, I'm going to leave you here," Greta said.

"I'll get eaten by a bear," I said. "I have no idea where we are."

She smiled. "Isn't this view beautiful?"

"Not as gorgeous as you," I said.

Dr. Smooth.

"Are you always making the moves?" she asked. (The way she pronounced "making ze moofs" woke me up—at least part of me.)

"Just telling the truth," I said. I was about *this close* to sealing the deal when a strange noise pierced the afternoon's tranquility.

"What the hell was that?" I asked. "Sounds like a steroidal seagull."

"Muntjac," she said.

"Munt-whuh?"

"Muntjac...also known as a barking deer."

"You're putting me on, right?" I asked.

"Nein," she said. "The scientists say they are extinct here and they only live in Asia. But ask any German...they are still very much around. There are probably thousands of them trapped inside the fences of American military bases."

A week ago, the comment about the bases would have slid off. Now, the hair on my arms stood at attention.

"Tell me more about what you do at the base, Klaus," she said. "You work there still, ja?"

"Yep," I said. "I have top security clearance."

Her eyebrows arched. "Seriously?"

"Yep," I said. "I have one of two keys..." —I swear she leaned forward a little— "...to the closet where we keep the expensive, for-officers-only liquor."

"All you do is tend bar?" She sounded skeptical.

"Sling suds and work the shaker," I said.

"Who do you serve?" she asked.

"We get a lot of folks," I said. "Air Force, Marines, Army...some Navy pilots."

"And you talk to them?"

"I'm good with people," I said.

"And they've been drinking?"

"If I do my job," I said. "And I am very good at my job."

She was quiet for a while. I could tell she was turning something over in her mind.

"Klaus, there's so much I'd like to tell you, but you'll have to meet someone first."

"Like I said, I'm good with people. Who is it?"

"One of the leaders of the group I told you about."

"Like a hiking club?"

"Nein," she said. "We are a political action group—a *peaceful* political action group. We mobilize in opposition to the U.S. military's presence in Germany. Would you be willing to meet one of the leaders?"

"Sure," I said.

"Full disclosure, we used to be lovers."

I felt something curdle in my stomach. But she'd said, "used to be."

"Sure, why not? What's his name."

"Jaeger," she said. "Hans Jaeger."

CHAPTER FORTY-THREE

I played it cool the rest of the morning. Greta didn't. On our previous walks, she'd been appropriate and a little distant. The only time we had much physical contact was when we maneuvered around a rock or up a steep incline. She wasn't all over me; she only held my hand. Once when she brought my hand up to her mouth for a kiss, she ran my wrist across her chest.

It was not unintentional. I could see it in her eyes.

When we got to the cars, she kissed me lightly on the mouth. "Think about it," she said. "I think time with the group would be well worth your while."

Did she have to emphasize the last part?

Damn, I do not need this shit.

On the way home, I reconstructed our conversation after the lunch break. Greta's group was concerned about the nukes but also about the possibility of poison gas canisters they suspected were housed in bunkers all over the base. Hans was, in Greta's words, "a target of political persecution." The Bundeszollverwaltung, national security force, routinely took him in for questioning. When he came back, usually after a day or two, it was obvious that Landespolizei goons had tap-danced on his face.

I'd managed to steer the conversation out of the political arena. There was another, altogether different area of Greta's influence in which I was interested. Despite her increased warmth, she pushed back anytime I suggested a romantic interlude.

I let it go. When we got to the end of the trail, she went her way, and I went mine.

CHAPTER FORTY-FOUR

Sunday stretched into Wednesday, by which time I was hopeful that Mac was in my rearview. I was off on Thursday but showed up at Flightline about 2100 in hopes of seeing Shari. She wasn't there, but Holly was. We had not met, but she was friendly, and cute.

"Wanna dance?" she asked.

I was sitting by myself at one of the corner tables. I looked up at a tangle of auburn hair over the bluest eyes I'd ever seen. She was wearing a retro-miniskirt. It was over a foot above her knee with a shiny, four-inch belt that settled on her very nice hips. Medium size, about 5'5", her personality would have overflowed the Astrodome.

"Come on," she said. "You're the only one not dancing.

"I suck," I said.

She giggled then said something that sounded like, "That's supposed to be my line," but the DJ had cranked the music so high I was afraid my skin was going to peel away and I was not about to get slapped. She grabbed my hand and pulled me onto the floor where I proceeded to prove my earlier statement. My abominable footwork was exceeded only by my random, and totally unsynchronized, flailing arms. I consciously fought the urge to bite my upper lip and point—the standard white guy move.

No matter how loudly the Bee Gees claimed they were Staying Alive, I looked like a man in the throes of a life-ending seizure. The music segued into "Super Freak" by Rick James. I watched Holly perform some gyrations I was sure would have gotten her arrested in Des Moines.

I didn't mind at all.

About the time I'd worked up a sufficient sweat to classify as disgusting, Michael Bolton's raspy "How Am I Supposed to Live Without You" took over. I preferred Laura Branigan's version, but I didn't have time to tell Holly because she grabbed me like Robinson Crusoe clinging to a floating ship's mast. Holly's thigh slid between mine with the ease of an experienced urologist with a lubricated glove. We did the grind until the song ended and the DJ announced, "A short pause for a good cause."

Everybody hooted and hollered. Holly kissed me on the cheek and said, "Thanks."

When I sat down, I was glad there was a tablecloth. I needed a few minutes to...ah...get composed.

Shortly after things had returned to their normal dormant state, Holly reappeared. "This is Gina," she said.

If I hadn't known better, I would have sworn I was looking at Jami Gertz—dark brown eyes, a face by Michelangelo, and ringlets of thick black hair cascading below her shoulders. Her stiletto pumps made her about six feet tall.

"My God," I said. I tried to recover. "Did I say that out loud?"

Holly laughed so loudly people started to stare. "No problem," she said. "Everybody reacts the same way."

"Glad I'm not the only one." I stood and offered my hand to Gina. "I'm Klaus."

She smiled a shy smile. "No inglese," she said.

"She doesn't speak English," Holly said. "Russian and Italian."

"How do you guys communicate?"

"I majored in Russian at Vassar," she said. She said something with a lot of hard consonants to Gina, who nodded.

"She likes you," Holly said. She walked away.

Gina and I stood looking at each other. I pointed to my glass, then at her. She nodded. I shrugged my shoulders, obviously the international sign for, "What would you like?"

"Wod-ka," she said.

I looked at John across the room and pointed to the upper right shelf of the bar. He nodded and sent over a bottle of Kleiner Feigling, and a brace of shot glasses.

We sat. I poured. She held up her glass. I did the same.

"Nah zdarovhyeh!" she said.

"Here's mud in your eye," I said.

I sipped. She threw her head back and poured another before I put mine down. Three shots later, she pointed for the door and made a suggestive motion with her fist.

Why the hell not? I thought.

Twenty minutes later, we were in my room and performing maneuvers most gymnasts only dream about. I'd tried to explain about the need for quiet—the other guests and all—but she neither understood nor cared. She was energetic and very talented in the lovemaking.

By the time I awakened in the morning, she was gone. I washed my face and walked downstairs to go to breakfast. The building manager was standing at her door. She scowled at me without blinking.

I did not give a damn.

§§

I'd worked out a day off with Gunny because I was running on fumes. I spent my down time browsing the little shops and reliving every detail of the previous night. It had been a long time, but at that moment, the wait seemed worth it.

I was staring into a shop window and remembering the feel of Gina's skin when someone touched me on the shoulder. I jumped. A voice behind me said. "You wouldn't be so twitchy if you weren't guilty of something."

Greta...shit.

I turned with the same smile a hemorrhoid sufferer plasters on his face halfway through a boring meeting at work.

"Hi," I said.

"What were you thinking about so intently?" she asked. "I called your name from across the street, and you didn't answer."

"My mother," I said.

Oh God, that is so gross.

"Is she ill?" Greta asked.

"No," I said. "I just haven't seen her in a long time."

"You should call her."

"I can't," I said.

"I told you that you are welcome to use the phone in my building," she said.

I noticed she did not say her "flat."

"Ah..." —*think fast, think fast!*— "...Mom had a stroke. She's comatose," I said.

You are such an asshole.

"I'm so sorry," she said. "You should go home and be with her."

"No, no," I said. Now I was trying to dig my way out of a hole. "Happened a few years ago. She's been that way for a long time. You look lovely."

Nice transition, Slick.

If she was startled by my conversational swerve, Greta didn't show it. "Thank you," she said. I realized she almost never used German phrases when we were talking. "Have you been keeping yourself busy?"

"Ah...very," I said. "Very...very busy. Busy every minute of the day...no time for anything."

Stop...talking.

"Have you thought anymore about my proposition?" she asked.

"I didn't realize you'd made an offer of that nature," I said.

She lowered her head and looked at me through her eyebrows. "You are relentless," she said. "But you are funny so I will not punish you...yet. You know what I mean. Would you like to meet Hans?"

I looked at my watch like I needed to be somewhere. "Can we put that on the back burner until our next walk?" I asked. "I still need some time to think."

"Lovely," she said. "Sunday morning—0900."

She kissed me on the cheek the way she probably kissed her granny and walked around the corner.

CHAPTER FORTY-FIVE

Friday night.

I was wiping down a table when someone covered my eyes. Warm lips nibbled at my neck. Greta was not so forward. Shari only got frisky when she was hammered. Had to be...

"Gina!" I said.

Somehow, she had found a shorter skirt and a tighter top. My non-comatose mother would have been appalled. I was not.

"Surprise," Holly said. She was standing behind her scantily clad friend. "We thought we'd come see you. When do you get off?"

"About ten minutes after Gina and I get home," I said.

It was a somewhat less than gallant comment—some would call it tasteless. Holly laughed.

"Good thing Gina doesn't speak English," she said. "She might slap you just to look proper." She nudged her friend and the two of them giggled. "Anyway, we have an idea."

"I'm all ears," I said.

"Gina told me about the great time she had with you." I winced. "Don't be embarrassed," Holly said. "She says you are a dynamo."

"Well...truth be told..."

"So, we were wondering." She paused for intentional dramatic effect. "You think you could handle both of us?"

§§

We were in our third bar in as many hours. I'd given McCloskey $100 to cover the end of my shift. It was 0100 and I was beginning to believe I'd been played for a fool.

"So," Holly said, "one more round of drinks, and then to your place for a little fun."

She mumbled something to Gina, whose response was a lascivious grin followed by significant lip licking.

"Ready when you are," I said. "But I'm trying to watch what I drink. Don't want to disappoint my fan club."

"You won't, big boy," Holly said. "Gina kept calling you an animal."

There wasn't a big enough Stetson in Texas to cover my swollen head. I motioned to the server.

"A beer for me and..." I waved for the girls to order.

"Tequila shots all around," Holly said. "Cancel that candy ass beer."

The server nodded and went to the bar.

"Seriously, Holly," I said. "I'm pretty much at my limit."

"Fiddle-faddle," she said. "It'll be fun."

The drinks arrived. Both girls licked the backs of their hands, sprinkled on salt, downed the shot, and then sucked on a lime.

"Your turn," Holly said.

"Let's just go," I said.

Holly frowned. "Don't be a party pooper," she said. "Tell you what, if you down that shot, I'll..."

She bent over and whispered into my ear. Before she finished, I picked up the glass and drained it.

"Fabulous," she said. "Let's get it on!"

We bolted out of our chairs. The girls were yelling, "Woo-hoo," and I was trying not to let my "enthusiasm" show.

Three feet from the door, my world went black.

CHAPTER FORTY-SIX

It hurt like hell to open my eyes. All I could see was the moon spotlighting through the window. Had it not been for my blurred vision, I might have seen as well as on the clearest of days. The fuzzy focus—a combination of being slightly overserved earlier (that's what the cottonmouth told me) and the Titleist-sized bump on my forehead—slowly cleared. I had a vague recollection of the floor coming at me like a runaway UPS truck. I shook my head and began stumbling through a room I did not recognize towards a door I did not remember.

The little men stationed behind my eyes with a pickaxe and a jackhammer were working vigorously to make my every waking second a living hell. They pounded and jabbed and clobbered away. Each step offered a new understanding of the word "agony," but something—some inbred, primitive, mental self-preservation warning siren—told me I needed to get the hell out of wherever I was as fast as I could stagger.

The beam of light through the window illuminated a doorknob—a celestial Q-light signaling the route of my escape. I squinted and tried to focus past my pain. The way of egress beckoned to me, a shimmering oasis of rescue.

Fifteen feet.

My foot slipped a little and I stumbled. I regained my balance with the agility of an arthritic Tabby, but at least I managed not to fall on my face again.

Got to learn when to quit drinking.

My shoes made a little squishing sound, sort of like I was walking across a freshly painted porch. I started stepping flatfooted, stomping steadily towards the exit—a hungover, very confused fugitive looking for salvation behind a brass knob.

Ten feet.

My right foot stubbed against a piece of furniture...*no, not rigid enough.*

A dog...*no, no snarl or welp.*

I looked down. In my blind, half-drunken, half-concussed state, I'd been so fixated on getting the hell out of Dodge that I had not even noticed the fully dead body on the floor. A trail of blood featuring a magnificently preserved set of my shoeprints oozed along the concrete from the gaping chasm in the deceased's head. Even though I knew the outcome, the former cop in me reached for the carotid on the off chance there was a pulse.

Zip.

Something happened...a cloud moved I guess...the room was suddenly as bright as if someone had hit the light switch. Despite the blood, I recognized the face.

Gina.

Oh shit, not again.

§§

It was Belfast repeated...a dead body—this time a beautiful woman instead of a pimply-faced kid of a soldier—and a readymade suspect: me.

I pulled open the back door and walked out into the night. I had no idea where I was, except I remembered it was Germany. And I was Klaus Simpson...no, Schneider.

There was a wooded area about twenty yards away. Just before I reached the trees, I looked back. Jose Feliciano could have tracked my bloody steps. I walked into the forest for a while, then slumped against a tree and tried to sort out my situation.

Okay, where do I go? Who can help? John—he wouldn't be a friend of mine long if I showed up like this—Chief, Gunny? Olga was out... No...no...her name is Greta. Still not an option.

I exited the thicket onto a dirt road. I heard a car. *Salvation.* I stuck out my thumb and faced the approaching headlights. The car slowed, then accelerated and left me in a cloud of dust. I looked at my hand in the moonlight. My fingers and palm were covered in blood. So was my shirt.

Okay, no more hitchhiking.

I tried to reconstruct the events. I had been working at Flightline. Something...no, someone interrupted. Holly...yes, Holly and Gina. We'd gone to a couple of other places. We were heading to my place...

...and the movie in my head ended.

Nothing made sense. I kept walking. I became vaguely aware of a change in the ambient sounds. I'd been hearing crickets, and nightcrawlers, and cuckoos—the songs of nighttime in the country.

But another sound crept into the audible range...a city sound...a frightening sound...the bi-tone wail of a siren.

I could stand here, look guilty, and get taken in—or run, look worse, and still make the perp walk. I decided to trust my luck and native charm.

A white van emblazoned with the Landespolizei logo pulled to a stop about fifty feet in front of me. Officers slid out behind opened doors, sidearms aimed.

"Hande Erhoben! Hande Erhoben! Hande in die Luft!"[1]

I complied. Two more officers hopped out of the side door. Now I had two pistols and two semi-automatic rifles aimed at various vital organs. The two from the front wore standard issue uniforms; the other two sported green fatigues and were weighed down with an assortment of lethal looking equipment.

When they got closer—I was on my knees by then—I could differentiate their ranks. The driver's green patch read Polizei—Mittlerer Dienst[2] with one small stripe. The older gentleman's patch read Hoherer Dienst[3] with three gold stars. After the obvious SWAT guys searched me, one of them said, "Entferne alle deine kleider schnell!"[4]

---

1. "Hands raised! Hands in the air!"

2. Medium Service

3. Higher Service

4. "Remove all your clothes, quickly."

I didn't move until the one who didn't—or couldn't—speak in complete sentences drew back the butt of his rifle with the intent of splattering my brains along the roadside.

I took off my clothes and lay on my stomach. Mr. Higher Service knelt down, pulled a cigarette from a pack, and lit it. "Willst du eine Zigarette?"

"No thank you. Nein!"

"English, yes?"

"Yes, sir."

"What's your name? Are you an American soldier, yes?"

"No sir, I'm a civilian, but I do work at the Air Force base in Dahn. My name is Klaus Schneider from Cranberry, New Jersey. I am an American citizen."

"Mr. Schneider, my name is Police Councilor Miller. Are you claiming diplomatic immunity?"

"I am not."

"Good. Then perhaps you would be so kind as to explain why you are wandering a country road miles from your base and covered in what experience tells me is blood. You don't look like a hunter, and if you are, you are poaching because nothing is in season."

"I'll try. I was at a bar last night in Dahn—well, I was at more than one. I think someone drugged me. When I woke up, I had a big knot on my forehead and was in a basement about a mile from here. I think it was a basement...it might have been a back room, but it had a cement floor."

"Well, Mr. Schneider, you might have been in a house, and you might have been in a basement, but you were certainly not on a cement floor. Cement is an ingredient in concrete, so you might have been on a concrete floor. What you have just told me is that you are not in construction work. What do you do at the base, Mr. Klaus Schneider?"

"I'm a bartender."

"Are you a good bartender?"

"I am, sir."

"Do you drink in excess, Mr. Schneider?"

"Not so much now that I'm a little older."

"So, it is your contention that a person or persons unknown slipped something in your drink at random. Is that your story, Mr. Schneider?"

"Ah, no...you see, there were these two women."

"Always the frauleins, eh, Mr. Schneider?"

I almost said, "Ain't that the damn truth," but I showed uncharacteristic restraint of my smart-assity and said, "Yes, sir. Two women. They had suggested...well...ah..."

Miller laughed, pinched out his cigarette between his wetted thumb and forefinger, and put the butt in his breast pocket. "We have an idea of what they suggested, Mr. Schneider. And how much had you agreed to pay them?"

"No, it wasn't like that at all. I knew one of them...I mean, I had...ah...well..."

"No need to spell it out," Miller said. "You have enjoyed the carnal company of one of the young ladies. Several nights later, they decided it would be—how do you Americans say it?—a blast to engage in a menage a trois."

He spoke over his shoulder. His German was so rapid I couldn't follow it, but I figured it out when one of the officers pulled my wallet from my pants pocket.

"Nichts," he said—nothing.

"Mr. Klaus Schneider, I believe, again to use your vernacular, that you were 'rolled.' They set you up and robbed you. But a question remains: what is the origin of all the blood on your person?"

His certainty about my being some rube who got mugged by a couple of working girls took a hit when I mentioned the dead body in the house.

"You must show us," he said. "Get in the van."

"I can't find the house in the van," I said. "I'll have to retrace my steps. Shouldn't be hard. I dropped breadcrumbs the whole way."

"Ah, like Hansel and Gretel," Miller said. "A good German tale." He played his torch around the area, and froze on the spot where I'd entered the road. "Only your breadcrumbs are bloody footprints."

I dressed and followed the officers as they picked through the undergrowth. I had not traveled nearly as far as I thought. We were at the house in less than fifteen minutes. The officers looked at Miller. When he nodded, they drew their firearms and crossed the yard. The back door was unlocked. I braced myself for the impending horror.

CHAPTER FORTY-SEVEN

The guys in the body armor went in first, pistols at the ready, flashlights sweeping the area. A few moments passed before a shout came from inside.

"Klar!"[1]

"Stay here, Mr. Klaus Schneider from Cranberry, New Jersey," Miller said.

Thirty minutes later I was in the back of the van with my hands cuffed behind me.

Belfast all over again—a dead body and every finger pointed at me. I'd run then; I wasn't going to run this time even if I managed to get out of police custody. I was done being a fugitive. This time I was going to fight for the truth—and for my freedom.

My zeal for justice and decision not to skedaddle cooled off a bit after I was washed down with a fire hose at the station house jail. Both sentiments disappeared about the time the cavity search commenced.

Someone handed me a pair of boxer shorts with enough starch in them to make Quasimodo walk upright.

---

1. "Clear!"

They've been washed. That means...someone else used them. Gross.

The jumpsuit had apparently last been used by a member of the NY Knicks. I had to roll the cuffs up eight inches to keep from falling on my face—again.

Two grim officers put me in an interrogation room and shut the door. I waited...and waited. I knew better than to drink the bottle of water. I'd seen a lot of cop movies. I wasn't falling for their tricks. They figured once my bladder started to scream, I would confess to the Lindbergh kidnapping.

An hour later, I drained the entire bottle.

I had a lot of time to think—to consider every fork in the road I'd faced and how I'd gone the wrong way *every frickin' time.*

Gwendolyn begged me not to be a cop. She said she would be happy if I decided to be a plumber. She didn't care; I just couldn't work for The Man.

I became a cop.

Got the hell beat out of me.

Alec invited me to go to Ireland. Seemed like a lark, and it was at first. We had some adventures, played a soggy round of golf, drank a lot of Guinness. He went home; I stayed because of Billi.

She smuggled me into Northern Ireland in the boot of her car. Did I pick up on the clue that she might be involved in something nefarious? Nope.

I could have tended bar in a nice little pub and minded my own business. Nope, first I had an affair with a married women (okay, in fairness, I didn't know Billi had a husband). Then I started palling around with a bunch of freedom fighters—the Green Liberation Front. When they pulled a bunch of weapons out of a hidey hole in the wall and went to blow up a guard station, what did I do? Skipped along with them like we were on our way to a garden party.

Boom went the bridge—*Eeeerg* went the dead soldier.

After bullets whizzed past my head, did I turn myself in and go all Serpico on the GLF? Hell no! I wore a ridiculous disguise to get into France, hiked a gazillion mile walk through the Pyrenees, played hide the sausage with a hot French woman who nursed me back to health (a situation brought about because I got lost in the dark and fell on my head—apparently my go-to move), fell in love with a gorgeous Asian woman who turned out to be an agent of Her Majesty's government sent to arrest me—had to be rescued by an Arkansas pig farmer who really wasn't one... *Goddamn it!*

I was still thumping my head on the table when the door opened. I looked up.

Mac!

"What the hell are you doing here?" I asked.

"Came to get your sorry ass out of jail," I said.

"How are you going to do that?" I asked.

Mac shrugged. "Didn't you know? I'm a magician. I can make things disappear." He put his hand on my shoulder. "Come on, let's go. You've got work to do."

"What kind of work?"

"What do you think?" He looked at me with something akin to disappointment. "You know what you have to do."

"I'm not infiltrating a terrorist cell," I said.

"Yes, you are," he said. "Unless you'd like to stand trial for murder."

I decided to make one last stand. "I'm not working with you until I know your real name."

"I told you my name," he said.

What little self-control I had evaporated. I jumped to my feet. The chair skittered across the floor. I pushed Mac against the wall.

"That's not your name," I said. "If you're Douglas MacArthur, I'm—"

"Who?" he said. He got close enough for me to count his pores. "Conor Caldemeyer?"

Shit. I had been about to say, "Santa Claus."

CHAPTER FORTY-EIGHT

We drove in silence for a while. Finally...

"Okay," I said, "I can't take it anymore. What happened to Gina?"

"Who?"

"Gina, the girl I...uh...dated," I said.

"Nice euphemism," he said. "What about her?"

"Where is she?"

"Hard to keep track of her," he said. "Here one day; gone the next. It's a tough business."

"Business?" I thought about it for a while. The light inched into my brain like sunbeams breaking through the fog at dawn.

"She was a pro?"

"Yep."

"But she...and I...I mean...we had a good time...she..."

Mac's laugh was loud and harsh. "You are a piece of work, Caldemeyer," he said. "You're not bad looking but you ain't Richard Gere. You really think those two girls walked into Flightline, scanned the room, picked you out of *everyone else*, and decided they had to have some of that?"

"She spoke fluent Russian. Holly went to Vassar."

The laughter stopped. "Did you ever hear Holly speak Russian?"

"Well, it sounded like Russian, all garbled and the like. It was loud in there. But...Vassar..."

"Holly is from a little place called Carthage. Not the one in Africa—it's in North Carolina. Gina hailed from a trailer park in Hermitage, Arkansas. They started working military bars about four years ago."

"But we...I mean, she and I...I mean...Damn, Mac, I never paid her!"

Mac looked away from the road and regarded me with pity. "No, *you* didn't."

No one spoke for a while. There were things I wanted to know but didn't want to ask. But I had to. "She drugged me?"

"Technically, I did," he said. "Put something in the tequila shot."

"I didn't see you.""Of course you didn't," he said. "I'm a master of disguise. I don't always act like Inspector Clouseau. I followed you guys all night and waited for the right time."

"She didn't know?"

"All she knew was that she was supposed to show you a good time. If it makes you feel any better, the three-way that never happened was her idea. She said you were fun."

It didn't make me feel any better.

"What happened to Holly?"

"She collected her money and split right after she helped load you in the car."

"She wasn't worried about Gina?"

"They weren't a team. They hadn't met until I put them with you at Flightline." Mac stopped outside my apartment. "Go ahead," he said. "You want to know, but I'm not volunteering anything."

I swallowed hard. "Who killed her?"

"Does it matter?" Mac said.

"Was it you?"

"Same answer, Slick. Now...you get one more question and then we put you to work. And before you protest, remember, I am a magician. Dead bodies go away...dead bodies come back. Same thing with murder charges—here and in England."

There it was. The ultimate threat.

"Okay," I said. "Last question. Why did Gina have to die?"

Mac shook his head, a father disappointed in his son. "The choice was national security or the life of one hooker," he said. "Not much of a decision, if you ask me."

§§

I dreamed about Gina all night. Sometimes she was laughing; other times her head was back screaming in satisfaction. I saw her smile, her body, her lips, her eyes.

And in every single moment, her head was split like a bleeding melon.

When the sun hit my window, I awakened to sweat-soaked sheets and pounding depression.

I couldn't remember the taste of my morning coffee and Nußschnecken.[1] I bought a newspaper, which I stared at without absorbing a single word. I spent my waking hours doing something but could not have recalled any of my movements if someone had held a gun to my head.

In many ways, that was what was happening. Mac, whose name I still did not know, had his itchy finger on the hair trigger of multiple homicide charges and would gladly squeeze away if I didn't cooperate in an enterprise almost surely guaranteed to get me killed.

§§

"You okay, Klaus?" It was John.

"Ah, sure boss. Why?"

"That's the fifth time ya have screwed up a drink order and ya ain't been here but fifty minutes." His eyes reflected concern, not anger. "Tell ya what. Ye're beat. Take the rest of the night off—tomorrow too. Get some rest. Deal?"

I didn't ask if he meant it. I nodded, put my towel on the bar, hung up my apron, and walked out into the evening.

I'd never been drugged before. Michiko was drugged. Oisin had slipped her a mickey to save my sorry ass back in Santiago. I wonder if she felt as lousy as I did. Probably not. She woke up to an escaped

---

1. A spiraled pastry filled with almonds or hazelnuts – often with marzipan and raisins as well.

felon; I came to next to a bludgeoned women I'd boinked the night before.

I got home at 2005 hours. Funny how important time becomes when you associate with military types. I had a free day coming. I needed to clear my head and sweat whatever vile substance I had ingested out of my body. I called Greta and we agreed to walk in the morning.

She showed up sans Tank.

"Where's the pooch?" I asked.

"Pouch?"

"Dog...hund," I said.

"He was tired. Long walk yesterday. He's not getting any younger," she said.

The way things are going, I might not get any older, I thought.

We tried a trail in the Palatinate Forest called the Felsenland Sagenweg Etappe.[2] It was about a ten-mile trek with significant climbs and descents, and spectacular views of a bunch of ruins. We were looking at what was left of Altdahn Castle when she put her arms around my waist. I reciprocated.

"Stunning, isn't it?" she asked.

"Not as stunning as you."

Okay, not my best line, but I was traumatized.

"Do you ever stop striking me?"

I pulled back a little. "No, no...you mean 'hitting' on you."

"Ja," she said. "That's what I said."

"Guy's gotta do what a guy's gotta do," I said.

---

2. Rocky Land of Legends

I didn't care anymore. My life was in the toilet. I knew I'd be dead in a matter of days, if not hours. Why not go down swinging?

"Well." She took a deep breath. "I think this guy..." —she nudged me with her shoulder— "...needs to meet Hans and Joel."

And there it was. She served up the invitation like a weak lob at Wimbledon. All I had to do was put it away. I thought about whiffing it, running one more time, but I was tired.

"Sure," I said. "That'd be great."

Then, as the old song says, "The way she did when she did what she did to me made me think of you."[3]

I guess the way to a girl's...ah...heart is through her politics.

I'd waited for the moment. I'd nearly begged for it. When it came, I felt absolutely nothing.

---

3. Delbert McClinton, "B-Movie."

CHAPTER FORTY-NINE

Good thing I got home before dark. On the way back, I remembered Mac had told me to meet him at The Independent. I got there with two minutes to spare, grabbed a beer, and sat in the same corner booth where I'd last seen Gina alive.

Mac slid in across from me. He had a notebook and his signature dual beers.

"Now that you have finally decided to work with me, let's say we bury the hatchet," he said.

"With all due respect, Mac, get bent. I didn't agree to anything. You're holding all the cards. Let's get this meeting over with without the phony slap and tickle."

"You're feisty," Mac said. "I like that. We'll make a good team."

"Who the fuck are you?" I asked. "No answer? You can go ahead and call Buckingham Palace."

"You are a persistent booger," he said. "Gotta be honest, I've used so many aliases, I ain't sure if I remember my real name. I think I've had it legally changed a half-dozen times or so. Anyway, name aside, I work for the Company."

I remembered the annoying singer—Bodin. He'd asked me if I worked for "the Company."

"You're CIA?" I said.

"Wanna speak a little louder?" he said. "I don't think they heard you in Lebanon." I made no attempt at an apology. "You tell anybody, I'll kill you. I do goofy disguises. I do not joke about offing people. Got it?"

"Got it."

"Despite what I know, going forward, you're Klaus. We've got two objectives. One: take down the JV Gang. Two: if we can—though I could give a damn about PR and the like—we try to repair the 'steadily fracturing relationship between the German people and the United States military.'"

"You sound like you're reading a memo."

"Roger that," he said. "So...prime objective—stop the bad guys." His eyes gleamed with conspiratorial delight.

"You like this stuff, don't you?" I asked.

"Live for it. Set a goal, achieve the goal, move on. Speaking of which," he said, "congrats on knocking down your own Berlin Wall this afternoon."

I didn't understand until he cocked his head and grinned in the creepiest way I could imagine.

"Holy Mother of God! How do you know about that?"

He tapped his fingernails on the tabletop. "Klaus, Klaus, Klaus. Have I taught you nothing? I am the Great and Powerful Oz. I see all, hear all, know all."

"Sure you do," I replied, sarcastic only because I was a little freaked out.

"Okay, let's review," he said. "I know you wear a 15½ x 34 shirt. I know you have a 31-inch inseam. You wear whitey-tighties. You use Burma Shave—very American, but cheap as hell. There was a young lady long ago who left you and broke your heart. You used to be a cop. I know what brand of condom you use—you're a double bagger. Wise choice. Other clandestine observers and I have calculated that your personal best...how should I put this?...from sequence initiation to lift off is seven minutes. Not Hall of Fame caliber, but most women aren't interested in much more than a pleasant encounter that will leave them happy and with enough time to catch up on their book club reading. You are charming, adept—although routinely clumsy—at survival, and utterly helpless in the presence of available women, even if they intend to do you harm. The most recent one of which I'm aware was the Asian chick in Spain who was going to get you hanged after she led you around by the crotch."

"Okay," I said. "You've made your point. Please stop."

I realized I had my hand over a fork, which I would have gladly shoved in his eye if he'd kept talking about Gwendolyn—well, I would have tried. Then he probably would have killed me before I got the flatware off the table.

But then, the long, winding, torturous joke of my life would at least have been over.

CHAPTER FIFTY

The plan was simple. I would join the JV Gang and get involved in as many things as they would allow.

"Something's up," he said. "Something big. No one will trust you enough to outline the plan, but these amateur types tend to blather on a lot. Keep your ears open." He looked at me. "And for the love of God, keep your big mouth shut."

I kept my mouth shut.

"Questions?"

"You recruit a lot of civilians?" I asked.

"Been known to," he said.

"What happened to the last guy?"

"Don't know," he said. "No one's seen him in six months. On the positive side, none of his body parts have shown up, so there's still hope."

"Really?"

"Shit, you are stupid," he said. "Of course not. He's at the bottom of a lake somewhere with his face shot off and his balls missing."

I put down my beer.

"There's one hard and fast rule," he said.

"Watch my ass?" I asked.

"Watch your ass."

He finished his second beer and reached across the table. "Doesn't look like you're thirsty. You mind?"

§§

"You've met Hans Jaeger before, you know."

Mac's eyes were onyx and opaque...dull, flat, lifeless. I'd always heard sharks looked the same way. He was looking right at me. I was sure he hadn't blinked a single time in the last three minutes, but it seemed like he was focusing on something behind me...no...something *through* me.

"When?"

"On one of your walkabouts," he said. "She introduced Jaeger as her brother."

I clicked my tongue. "The hand holding should have been a clue."

"Ya think?" Mac's stare was beginning to get to me. I looked away.

He launched into a monologue. "He not the All-Aryan boy—just the opposite. He was born outside Berlin in March thirty-five years ago. No one knows who his father was, not the Company, not Interpol, not Scotland Yard, the Sûreté, the KGB—nobody. Best we can tell, his mother was a former East German female athlete selected as a breeder."

He noticed my widening eyes. "Exactly what you think. She was assigned to have sex with suitable men in the hope of producing uber-kids. She disappeared early in Jaeger's life. Attempts to locate her have proven pointless. About the time Hans was five he went into the old Soviet training system and disappeared until he showed up on our radar about five years ago. But we had an idea someone was on the way—or rather, something."

"Meaning?"

"There was a time when bodies began to appear all over Germany and other selected parts of Europe. There was never more than one stiff per city and there was no discernable pattern to the locales. A stabbed hooker would show up in Paris, then a garroted businessman in Prague. The murders—excuse me—the executions appeared all over Germany with the same lack of repetition in either the method of death or victim characteristics. Young, old, fit, frail, it didn't matter. They didn't all have the same hair color or work in the same industries. None of them had any connection to government intelligence or diplomatic services."

"But someone in your agency was convinced they were related?"

"Someone still is. There were too many."

"Could still be totally random," I said. "There must be dozens of murders in Europe, in Germany, every year."

"About eight hundred—one per every hundred thousand in a population of nearly eighty million."

"I would think that proves my point," I said. "And you just told me there were killings in most of the major European cities."

"True," Mac said, "but each of the killings I was talking about shared one distinct characteristic."

I waited.

"What are the odds there would be one committed on the fourteenth day of every month for exactly eighteen years?"

He wasn't telling me everything.

"You're not telling me everything," I said.

"There are only two more things we absolutely know about Jaeger," Mac said. "First, the killings stopped the moment he appeared in public."

"What's the other one?" I asked.

"We know the day of the month when he was born."

"The fourteenth," I said. "It was the fourteenth."

Mac touched his index finger to the tip of his nose.

"You win a cookie," he said.

He quit talking. I stared at the beer glasses I had not emptied. My stomach did the cha-cha while I tried to figure out exactly how many hours I had left to live.

"You know something else about Jaeger," I said.

"What's that?" Mac asked.

"No one kills that much..." My throat went dry. I gulped and tried to keep my voice from cracking. "...unless he likes it."

CHAPTER FIFTY-ONE

For the next few days, I flinched every time I saw a cop. I almost wished someone would haul me back in for Gina's murder—at least I would avoid death by Hans—but no one hassled me. Whatever acts of prestidigitation Mac had performed were working. I started attending meetings of the JV Gang with Greta. The "official name" was "Germans For Germany." The group got together every other week.

Everyone there looked like a castoff from a 1968 Vietnam War protest—a lot of long hair, bellbottom jeans, fringed jackets, tie-dyed tee shirts, sandals, and body odor. I officially met Hans Jaeger after three months. This time Greta did not bother to feign like they were related.

"Impressive physical specimen, huh," Mac said. "Still can't figure out why he and that Teutonic babe used to engage in amorous congress."

I blew bubbles in my beer.

"You still tapping that?" he asked.

I ignored the lewd question. "I was expecting Thor, the God of Thunder," I said. "He's short, stout, stringy black hair, and the worst mustache I've seen this side of one of your disguises."

"Except his is real and he's damn proud of it."

"Looks like he has an immature caterpillar sewn onto his lip," I said.

"Notice anything unusual about him?" Mac asked.

"You know I did," I said. "His feet are too large for his body and his hands belong to a cartoon character. I saw him pick up a soccer ball one time; it looked like a baseball in his hand."

"That ought to help you figure out what blondie saw in him."

I went into the classic movie scene.

Me: He would have to have an enormous schwanzstucker.

Mac: That goes without saying.

Together: He's going to be very popular.[1]

It was the first time I'd ever heard Mac laugh. Didn't last long, but it was genuine. A little bonding moment...tiny...more like microscopic.

"I've got something big," I said.

"We'll see," Mac said.

"No seriously," I said. "From what I've overheard, they're going to hit the Army base's payroll shipment."

"Line it out," he said.

"Money to pay the civilian employees comes into the air base and gets trucked over to the Army base. There's a sharp turn on the L478 where a bridge flows over the Brumbach River. They're going to have a car broken down by the side of the road. They'll flag down the

---

1. From the brilliant mind of Mel Brooks and rendered with comedic excellence by Gene Wilder, Terri Garr, and Marty Feldman in Young Frankenstein, 1974.

transport truck, then rush it and overpower the transport team when it stops to help."

"You a betting man?" Mac asked.

"Been known to place the occasional wager on the Yankees back in the day."

"Two beers says they're setting you up."

"How so?"

"Some time in the next few days, someone—probably Mr. Hung Like an Elephant—will ask if you'd like to make your bones. Since your squeeze is easy on the eyes, he'll ask you to take her along. You'll be in the car needing assistance. She'll sit on the hood, flash a little thigh, and get the transport truck to stop."

"That's perfect," I said. "I was thinking about volunteering."

"You do, and someone'll put a nine-millimeter slug in your head. You didn't 'overhear' anything. They made sure you heard. This is a test."

"Say more." This spy stuff was fascinating, even though I realized my arms had broken out in goosebumps.

Mac noticed the horripilation. "It's good for you to be a little shook," he said. "Shows you know this ain't no joke." He sipped his beer. "Let them come to you. I'm guessing it'll be a day or so before the heist. They'll say something like, 'Gunter was going to be the driver, but he has the clap, so we need a substitute. You're new and enthusiastic. We like the way you carry yourself. Would you do it?'"

"I say yes, right?"

Mac rolled his eyes. "I'm surprised you didn't get pregnant in high school," he said. "You'll drop your drawers for anyone. Hell no—you say 'Hell no.' You don't want any part of it. You're not cut out for stuff like that. You just attend the meetings because it makes Brunhilda hot—something like that. Play hard to get, son. You think you can do that?"

"Yeah," I said. I polished off my beer. "How did you know it was a test?"

"First, as I said, they made it too easy for you. No one's going to discuss an operation of any kind where some newbie can hear it. Infiltrators show up all the time. Second, and more important, it's small potatoes."

"I don't think so," I said. Now I was an expert. "They said the shipment was a hundred grand. That's a lot of money."

I could tell Mac wanted to hit me, but there were too many people in the place, and we had to keep things low-key.

"Not to these guys," he said. "They've got backers...international bankers...governments. Best intel says the Ruskies finance most of the operations and supply all the armaments. There's some Middle East oil money there too. The JV Gang wouldn't bend over to pick up 100k if they passed it on the street."

"Damn," I said. "You're pretty good at this stuff. Ever thought about being in the movies?"

I swear he smiled...a little. "Thanks," he said. "And no. This shit is more important. You understand how to play it?"

"Yep," I said.

"Hard to get."

"Yep."

"Don't be too eager."

"Yep."

"Let them tell you about the plan. You don't know anything about it. You haven't heard a damn thing."

"Yep."

And that's exactly how, two nights later, I ended up sitting in a "disabled" car by the side of L478.

CHAPTER FIFTY-TWO

Two narrow lanes merged into a single lane bridge. Our car was stationed close enough to the road to make the route across the bridge unpassable, but not far enough into the road to look like a barricade. We didn't need Army guys falling out of the truck "locked and loaded."

It was 1127. Hans chose midday. Anything after sundown would have screamed, "Ambush." I shut off the engine, raised the hood, and loosened the distributor cap. I knew how to disable a vehicle but couldn't have fixed one if my life depended on it. We could hear the truck's gears grinding from around the bend.

I had suggested that Greta wear something low-cut and short. After hoots of derision, Hans said, "Why doesn't she just hold a sign that says, 'This is a stick-up.'"

We sat inside the car as the truck rolled to a stop. I waved the driver around. The passenger side door opened and a young soldier wearing a helmet emblazoned with an MP logo jumped to the ground and approached. He had his hand on the butt of the Beretta. He spoke with the flat accent of someone from a flyover state.

"Problem, buddy?"

"Car died," I said.

He looked at me and cocked his head. "I know you. You're the bartender."

"Depends on where you're drinking."

"Air base," he said. "And Flightline." He looked a little sheepish. "I like beer."

"Don't we all?" I said.

"Who's with you?"

"This is my girlfriend," I said.

"Mind if I take a look?" he asked. "I know my way around an engine."

"That'd be great," I said.

He took a step towards the front of the car, then stopped. "Do me a favor, pal. Stay in the car and keep your hands where Private Barnhardt can see 'em, okay?"

He jerked his head towards the truck. The aforementioned Barnhardt was standing next to it, his M-16 at the ready.

"No problem," I said.

I was suddenly aware I would be the first "man down" if Mac had been wrong and this was not a test.

Twenty seconds later, the kid said, "Try it now."

I did. The car started. I scanned the tree line. There was no activity.

"Your distributor cap was loose," he said. "Funny, they don't usually shake loose when you're driving."Was he looking at me with suspicion, or was I being paranoid?

"Lucky for me you came along. All I knew how to do was open the hood. Thanks."

"Sure thing," he said. "I'd appreciate it if you'd head on out. Once you're clear of the bridge, we'll get going. That'll make sure everyone is well on their way."

The message was clear. If we stopped, all hell was going to break loose. I looked at Barnhardt. He looked very eager to shoot someone. "Next time you're in Flightline, first one's on me," I said. I hooked a thumb at "Buffalo Bill" Barnhardt. "You too."

"Thanks."

We drove over the bridge and headed home.

§§

When we got back to the group, I acted pissed.

"Where the hell were you guys?" I asked. "Some pock-marked kid was ready to blow us away."

Hans came forward with his arms outstretched. "It's okay, my friend. Everything is okay."

"Fuck you and your okay! It wasn't your butt out there flapping in the breeze."

Hans turned to the room. "Dramatic American with his flapping butt."

Everyone roared their approval. I moved close to him and lowered my voice to a perfect growl. "You shouldn't screw around like that. There were very real soldiers out there with very real guns loaded with very real bullets. I don't know what kind of sick game you're

299

playing here, pal, but you can damn well play it without me. I'm out."

I had my hand on the knob when Hans called to me. "Klaus, my friend, I am sorry." I kept my back to him. He kept talking. "At the last minute we learned there might be extra security with the shipment. We could not take the chance of trying to get a message to you. I'm sorry for the danger you were in, but everything turned out okay. Please forgive me. I think you can be very valuable to us."

I opened the door and called over my shoulder. "Anything like this happens again, I'm gone for good."

Greta held my hand on the way to the car.

"He was lying, you know," she said. "He fools everyone else, but I could always tell. That's why we broke up."

She had never bothered to explain why she lied to me about his being her "brother."

"So, what was that all about?"

"It was a loyalty test."

"Oh," I said—I hoped I sounded surprised. "Did I pass?"

"With flying colors," she said. She pulled me close to her and kissed me with significant intent. "Let's go to my apartment to celebrate."

My interest in things carnal had cooled considerably. Making whoopie with a terrorist sort of kills the mood. But Mac had told me to act like everything was copacetic.

"It would be rude to keep a lady waiting," I said.

Just before I shut her car door, she looked at me. "Just so you know, yours is bigger."

I shut the door and walked around the front of the car. I didn't care if it was the truth.

It's the thought that counts.

CHAPTER FIFTY-THREE

I continued meeting with Mac. He hadn't been kidding. He knew how to camouflage himself. Most of the time, he was on me before I knew anyone was close.

"Something big is coming," he said.

"What have you heard?"

"It's got something to do with poison gas. Find out."

The bell on the front door of the shop where'd he'd found me rang. I looked over to see who was coming in. Mac left. I never saw him go.

Damn.

Hans let the other shoe drop two nights later. Five of us were in the back room of a pub.

"We need to get our hands on the gas," he said.

"Regular or unleaded?" I asked.

Hans looked at me and chuckled. "Verruckter Amerikaner."[1]

Once everyone stopping chortling, Hans said the most frightening word I'd ever heard: "Sarin."

---

1. "Crazy American."

The planning took several weeks. Meantime, I was working the club at the base, filling orders at Flightline, and seeing Greta at least once a week—purely for appearances sake, at least that's how I soothed my conscience. I felt a little guilty. This wasn't Michiko. I had no feelings for Greta. And she certainly wasn't Gwendolyn. But, in for a penny...

Greta was working on the same project—she was more fanatical than I had originally surmised. She was assigned to the same mission but met on a different schedule. I huddled with nine guys, none of whom had bathed since the Carter presidency.

Apparently, in the early days of the Cold War, the U.S. had stored gas canisters in bunkers across the Rhineland. After a leak killed a couple of hundred sheep and the herdsmen, the German government demanded removal of all toxic substances. The U.S. nodded, promised, and promptly transferred everything to secret, underground storage facilities—still in Germany. If the Germans knew about the subterfuge, they ignored it. Better to remain friendly with a prevaricating NATO ally than to stand vulnerable to the Soviet wolf.

Recently, in a spasm of conscience, the U.S. had decided to remove all the offending articles but couldn't make a big deal out of it because all the gas was supposedly already gone. Hans had learned there was to be a secret transfer of all the gas to Poland.

"Klaus, your job is to obtain a canister and deliver it to us," Hans said.

I looked at him like he'd lost his mind. "I'm a bartender," I said. "I have less than no security clearance."

"I know, my friend," he said. "But as of now, you have up to $400,000 American dollars to...ah...incentivize someone to help you."

After the meeting, Hans took me into another room. Greta was waiting.

Hans dropped the "old buddy, old pal" routine. His voice was sharp; his words clipped. "You have had many chances to walk away," he said. "Now, you are one of us. There is only one way out."

Greta's eyes were flat as if we'd never met. "You try to leave, you die."

Talk about a buzzkill. She was, and always had been, one of them. I noticed Hans's hand on her backside.

No wonder she can only see me a few times a month.

Hans saw my look of dismay. "A simple diversion, my friend," he said. "Lovers will tell things in the heat of passion. You've never divulged anything to Greta. We know we can trust you."

I felt my stomach churn and hoped I wouldn't puke. I was tired of being played for a fool. But Hans was still talking.

"Your target should be married, have a wandering eye, and perhaps financial issues. You hear things at the bar. You will know who to approach."

I had to focus. Shit was getting real. "I've got a few ideas," I said. "But they aren't going to let me waltz out with a tank of gas."

"All you have to do is point out the candidate. We will do the rest," Hans said. "That is all."

I left the room. Behind me I heard the rustle of clothing...and Greta groaning.

§§

I spent most of the night sharpening the big picture. Rumors abounded about sarin gas. Story was it had been used by the U.S. to cover rescue operations in Vietnam. The Pentagon would not confirm. It was highly toxic—even a drop on the skin caused sweating and muscle twitching. Whatever Hans planned to do with it would not have a happy ending.

I'd briefly considered Chief as my target. He loved to chat up the ladies, but Mrs. Papaliosas was a force of nature. Stepping out on her would be worse than inhaling the sarin. No, he wasn't my guy. Besides, he was too gung-ho. He would take a corkscrew in the eye before he betrayed Uncle Sam.

Mac had a slightly different take on my situation.

"The gas is a feint," he said. "They'd like to get their hands on some, but what they really want is a nuke."

"Hans never mentioned one," I said. "Trust me. I've been studying these clowns for a long time."

I told him about the $400,000 sweepstakes.

"They give you a timeframe?"

"Not really," I said. "They want the mark, then they will do the rest."

"Perfect," Mac said. "I know who we can use."

"They were pretty specific about what they wanted. They've got someone on the inside," I said.

"No doubt," Mac said. "But so do we. We've got you."

I was not happy about it, particularly after my discovery of Greta's bed-hopping duplicity.

My turmoil must have been evident. "You found out, didn't you, kid?" he asked.

"About?"

"You know damn well what. You found out she's still schtupping the terrorist."

I knew better than to express surprise. Of course he already knew. "You could have told me," I said.

"What, and ruin your good time? Relax, kid. You got played but you had a little fun."

He had a point.

Five days later Mac was sitting on my bed when I opened my door.

"Jesus!"

"No, the name is Mac," he said, "but I get that a lot—especially from the ladies."

"Screw you," I said.

"Not if you were the last person left after the Apocalypse," he said. He gave me a sheet of paper. Here's your guy: Colonel Farrelly Higgins, drinks like a fish, always complaining about how much his wife spends on their three kids back in Alabama, and can't keep his hands off a firm, tight ass once he's gotten a snoot full."

"I hate doing this to the guy," I said.

"Don't worry about it," Mac said. "He's a disgrace to the service, to the country, and to humanity."

After the next meeting, Hans took me aside.

"Got anyone?"

I told him.

"You raised no suspicions in your search?"

"People talk to bartenders," I said. "More importantly, they talk *in front* of bartenders. They forget we're there. They don't realize we're listening. This was the first guy I thought of. I paid a little more attention to verify everything. He's our guy."

"I'll be in touch."

CHAPTER FIFTY-FOUR

In a complete change of protocol, Mac came into the base club two days later. I slipped him a note with his brace of beers: *Men's Room.*

"Do this a lot, do you?" he asked. "Solicit guys to meet you in the head?"

I was in no mood. "For once, shut up and listen."

He did.

"I think Hans has eyes on the personnel files at the base. Any way he can trace what I told him about the colonel back to you?"

"Negatory," he said. "We know Hans has someone on the inside. Just not sure who. But the day after you gave Hans the 4-1-1, two different people accessed the records."

Sweat trickled down my back.

"You didn't arrest them, did you?" I asked.

His laugh was caustic. "I ain't Chuck Barris and this ain't *The Gong Show*," he said. "Breathe. There won't be any premature arrestication. We'll bust everybody at the same time."

Great case.

"Who is this Higgins guy?" I asked. "Sounds like a burnout."

"Just the opposite," Mac said. "Top shelf operative. We were roommates in Langley. I haven't seen him in a while, but when I called, he was all in."

"He's not here?"

Mac looked at his watch. "Should have landed twenty minutes ago. No one here knows him, so we can't get fouled up."

"Hans won't buy it."

"Yes, he will," Mac said. "Higgins has been stationed in Athens on an *Eyes-Only* mission, but his file says he's been drying out in Geneva. There are fake clinical notes, the whole shebang." He put his hand on my shoulder. "I know this is scary, kid. You gotta trust me. I know what I'm doing. I will not needlessly put you at risk."

"But there is risk, right?"

"Oh, hell yes," he said like I had asked him if he liked puppies. "You already know Hans is a stone cold killer. He might put a bullet in your head for shits and giggles. Maybe he's not wild about you putting it to his girl. Who knows. But I will control what I can."

"Thanks...I guess."

§§

Greta rolled over.

"Again?" I asked. I kept telling myself I was keeping up appearances, but to tell the truth, I was terrified. Human contact, even with someone I knew was playing me like a Stradivarius, was the only thing between me and a total breakdown.

"You are an animal," she said. She looked past me to the clock on the nightstand. "We've got to go. We have another Volksmarch."

"I've got a better idea," I said. I kissed her neck. I had become the master of compartmentalization.

"We've got to go to Ludwigswinkel. Quit fooling around and get ready."

"Well," I said, "I was getting ready to fool around."

We dressed—I with more reluctance—then made the short drive to the town close to the French border.

It was a beautiful little place with about seven hundred residents, all of whom turned out for the event. Once again, we had lots of beer and walked away with a trash can lid of a medal.

I was sipping on a victory beer when someone bumped into me from behind.

"Entschuldigen Sie mich, bitte."[1]

I didn't recognize the guy, but I felt him slip something into my jacket before he stumbled off.

"You don't see very many drunk Germans," I said. "They usually hold their beer a little better."

Greta seemed amused.

"What?" I asked.

"That man was not inebriated. That was Hans. A good disguise, no?"

I was reluctantly impressed and heard myself getting ready to compare him to Mac. Fortunately, I kept my thoughts to myself.

I pulled an envelope from inside my jacket.

---

1. "Excuse me, please."

"What's this?"

"I don't know. Hans told me you are the only one who is to see it."

I waited until I got home to open it. Damn thing was in German, but I got the gist of it. I was to approach Higgins (Hans referred to him as "our friend") to "see if he might cooperate." Hans had a "cute fraulein" who wanted an introduction at 2100 hours. I was to do the honors. Enclosed was a picture of the young woman. At the end, Hans referenced the code name for our operation: Swimming Pool.

CHAPTER FIFTY-FIVE

Higgins was all in, especially after he saw the picture.

"Looks like rough duty, Mac," he said.

We were in the stock room of a storage closet of a local sex shop. Devices of all descriptions hung on the wall. I didn't know what half of them did—and I was not going to ask.

"Don't get carried away, Higgins," Mac said. "I don't have to tell you how dangerous these guys are."

Higgins looked a little hurt. "I'm no rookie," he said. "Not going to lose my scalp because of a filly in a short skirt."

"Sorry, pal," Mac said.

"No problem," Higgins said. "I know you're watching out for me."

"Always, my man."

"You guys wanna get a room or should we get on with this?" I asked.

When they looked at me, I was pretty sure I was going to get hurt. Apparently, spies don't like it when people are smartasses.

Mac was suddenly all business. "Make the intro and get the fuck out of the way," he said. "That direct enough, kid?"

I nodded. When I didn't leave the room, Higgins piled on. "You leaving, or are you gonna stay and look for some toy to play with?"

I left.

§§

A funk fell on me like a crashing Russian satellite. I even turned down an invitation for some sweat-soaked indoor recreation with Greta on the phony excuse of a cold. I was growing tired of plowing another man's field. I wanted a girlfriend. I wanted a life. This wasn't it. Not even close.

Friday night approached. I was nervous in the extreme.

How hard can this be? I introduce; I walk away.

But I had visions of feeling gunmetal against my head. I wondered if the adage was true, about never hearing the bullet. Would I realize I was about to die? Would I care? Would Greta?

Flightline, Friday night, 2058. The woman from the picture perched on a stool at the far end of the bar. I put on my best friendly barman face and wandered down to her.

"Good evening, what can I get you?"

"Good evening. I'm Julia. Do you know how to make a swimming pool?"

"No, but I'm all ears."

"Equal parts vodka and white rum, pineapple juice, heavy cream, coconut cream, and blue curacao."

"Coming right up, except we only have dark rum and no heavy cream, coconut cream, or curacao."

"Give me a glass of Riesling then."

"That I can do."

I got her a drink. On my way back to her, I saw Higgins come through the door.

"He's here," I said sotto voce. "He thinks he's meeting his commanding officer."

She nodded, then focused on her wine.

Higgins looked a little hammered. He sat at the bar; four seats removed. I slid a coaster in front of him. "What can I get you?"

He looked to his left. "I'll have what she's having."

"Riesling?" I asked.

"Fuck no, asshat. Do I look like a wine drinker? Bring me four fingers of bourbon."

I'd made up a special bottle at home, Maker's Mark, but most of the bottle was tea. I kept the bottle tucked away under the bar and hoped none of the other bartenders found it.

Higgins took a sip. He looked at me and winced a little, but he braved the hideous concoction like a pro. He waited about ten minutes before he made his move. Just before 2130, he and Julia left hand in hand.

I watched them walk out. All other considerations aside—national security, terrorist activity, poison gas plots—it was a hook-up, same as what I had going on with Greta. And for the first time in what had become the aimlessness of my life, I caught a glimpse of the light at the end of a tunnel full of horrors, close calls, and frantic self-preservation.

Understanding crept through my mind like the rising sun poking through on a foggy morning over a cranberry farm in New Jersey no one in my family had ever so much as seen.

My time with Gwendolyn represented the pearl of great value. Its incomparable luster could not be diminished by the passage of time. Its place in my heart would never surrender either to randiness or to my startlingly stubborn immaturity. It was the lighthouse of my soul, the beacon of hope towards which I would always stumble—even if I more than occasionally wandered off the path.

What I had with Greta—and perhaps all the others—might as well have been a knock-off Ming vase. It had a certain surface appeal.

But it was worthless.

CHAPTER FIFTY-SIX

"And a job well done to our good American friend, Klaus Schneider!"

Hans sounded genuinely appreciative. I came to the front of the small assemblage while everyone clapped. Greta jumped up and down and whistled. Hans handed me a thick envelope.

"A little gift of appreciation," he said.

I played baseball in high school. I won MVP of our team. We were 5-25. I also won the team batting title. I hit .267. Once again, I was winning awards on a team of losers. Except this time, they were dangerous.

"We are substantively closer to our goal," Hans said. "Once Klaus completes the second phase of his assignment, no one will be able to stop us!"

For no more than a dozen and a half people, these folks made a hell of a racket. They clapped and pounded on the walls. I'd seen a similar expression on Greta's face—but only when we were naked.

My God, she is a fanatic.

I leaned into Hans. "Thought I was done?"

"You must deliver the colonel."

"That's what I did," I said. "They left together. Done deal, right?"

Greta wrapped her arm around my waist. *Did Hans just flinch?*

"German girls are wonderful lovers, as you know," she said. *Yep, he flinched this time.* "But we are not tramps. The good colonel tried to make a move, but Julia asked him to get a cab for her. She was afraid he would sense a trap if they went to bed the first time."

Like some other American idiot who ended up next to a dead hooker.

"So, what do I do?"

"It can't happen on the base," Hans said. "It must be at Flightline. Next time he is there, we will arrange for Julia to appear. Put this in his beer."

He handed me a small vial.

"I'm not poisoning a U.S. Army colonel," I said.

"Relax," Greta said. "It's only a little sleepy time juice. He will wake up with a headache and think he's hungover. From what we've read, he should be used to those."

So, she's seen the fake file on Higgins. She's closer to the inner circle than she lets on.

I had to play it cool. They knew I wasn't a skilled operative. "Promise this won't hurt him," I said.

"I promise, lover," she said.

The look Hans gave me was not loving in the least.

"Are you going to do it or act like a homosexuell?"[1] he asked.

"I'll do it," I said.

§§

---

1. Not hard to figure out.

I did as I was told. Higgins came in. He must have used Cutty Sark for his aftershave. Julia "appeared" about twenty minutes later and homed in on him with the focus of a heat seeking missile.

"Hello," she said. She looked at me. I gave her a Riesling. "And one more of whatever this handsome soldier is drinking."

I pulled the handle on the tap. While I was pouring, Julia lip-locked the colonel.

Nice diversion.

She side-eyed me during the smooch. I put the beer below bar level and looked down as if in deep concentration. I'd already dumped the contents of the vial on the floor but made sure she saw me toss the "empty" into the trash. When my hand came up with the still-untainted beer, she let Higgins breathe.

"What was that for?" he asked.

"A preview," she said. "I've been thinking about you for days and days."

He looked at me. "Check please!"

She laughed. "Not so fast," she said. "There is no hurry. Finish your beer. You will need your strength."

He raised his eyebrows and drained the stein in four gulps, and they were out.

§§

I got the report the next evening. Mac, Higgins, and I huddled in a basement room where I was sure the rats were the size of St. Bernards.

"What happened?" I asked. "Did you—"

"Hell no, kid," he said. "She's like the stray cat your mother didn't want you to pick up."

"Never know where she's been, right?" Mac asked.

"Exactly."

I was about to ask my question again, but Higgins glared at me.

"If you'll shut up, I'm only too happy to kiss and tell." I didn't say anything. Higgins took a deep breath. "When we got to the room, she was all over me—wouldn't kiss me on the mouth. Must've thought you'd given me curare or some such. Anyway, we got naked pretty fast. Let me tell you, that was worth the price of an E-ticket ride at Disney. Girl's body looked like it'd been designed by Kraut engineers. You could bounce a quarter off her ass. And her—"

"Get to the point," Mac said.

Chastened, Higgins continued his saga. About the time she got me on the bed, I pretended to pass out. She slapped me across the face—twice. Pretty good punch. When I didn't react, she let a guy into the room. No, I did not open my eyes. I could hear them talking. She acted like she was doing all sorts of stuff to me, only she didn't do diddly. Probably couldn't have even if she wanted. I took a couple of ketoconazoles on the way to the room. I was limp as a dishrag."

"That stuff works, huh?" Mac asked.

"The boys in the lab said it would, about eighty percent of the time. If I'd been on the other side of the curve, I'm afraid I might have given into my baser instincts."

"Good thinking with the pills," Mac said.

"Hey man, I know what I'm doing." He spit a stream of tobacco juice into the floor drain. "I could hear a camera clicking—probably three dozen shots while she tried to go all Vanessa del Rio on me. Then they were gone. I waited twenty minutes to make sure they were gone, then vamoosed.""Nice work," Mac said. "A surprising display of self-control."

"Hey, man, I've always been in control."

Mac laughed. "Says the man who screwed my date one night after I passed out from too much PJ."

Higgins shrugged. "You snooze, you lose."

CHAPTER FIFTY-SEVEN

When I got back to my building, the owner handed me a message. It was from Greta.

Surprise birthday party tomorrow night at the clubhouse. 1900. Don't be late.

"Birthday party" —code for "emergency."

When I walked into the room, I was sure someone was going to stick eight inches of Prussian steel into my back. Instead, Hans handed me an 8"x11" manilla envelope.

"Get these to the colonel," he said.

They were as we expected, Colonel Higgins and the lovely Julia, in various stages of undress and posed to convey the concept of in flagrante delicto. Julia, obvious a graduate of one of the Ivy League Porn Academies, snarled, lolled her prodigious tongue, howled, and generally looked animalistic while the allegedly snockered colonel did his best "dead dog" impression. All in all, while Higgins did not appear totally engaged in the coital shenanigans, but if shown—as was threatened—to military overlords, publishing companies, and spousal units, the photos' impact could leave a considerable emotional and upward mobility bruise. There was a handwritten note:

Be at The Independent tomorrow at 2200—corner booth. Come alone.

"Game on, assholes!" Higgins was pumped.

I had mixed emotions. The good guys were going to trap the baddies—a win. But what would happen to Greta, who, despite her entanglement with an international terrorist, was nice enough—and looked really good without her clothes. All in all, I was glad to be done with the whole sordid business.

And then Greta called.

§§

Never knew anyone to have so many frickin' birthday parties in my life.

Of course, I knew it wasn't a soiree and boy, was I right. The look in Hans's eyes would have terrified Clyde Beatty.[1] Once again, Greta was nearly orgasmic.

"Within three days, we will have the sarin gas," Hans said. "How many of you have been trained in its use?"

Hands went up. A voice called from the back.

"How are you getting it?""We have compromising photos of an American colonel who cannot keep his pants on. We pay him

---

1. Legendary "wild animal trainer" with The Ringling Bros. & Barnum and Bailey Circus. He regularly used a particularly dangerous combination of lions, tigers, hyenas, leopards, pumas, and bears and was fearless in the face of all of them.

a pittance—$200,000—and the negatives in exchange for several cannisters of the gas. The substance is illegal, so the Americans will be too embarrassed to admit it is missing."

"What are you going to do with it?"

Hans settled the crowd. "Let me outline the plan. I think I can answer most of your questions."

The scheme was simple—and terrifying. The Army base employed a local pest control service, the owner of which was a member of the gang. Someone had not been thorough with a security check. Once in possession of the gas, the pest company would, during a routine quarterly treatment, frolic across the base dousing everything with sarin.

"What about the guards?" someone asked.

Hans pinched the bridge of his nose between his thumb and forefinger as if staving off a migraine. "Are you not paying attention?" he asked. "We are not talking about a stink bomb. Sarin is debilitating and deadly. It's a neurotoxin twenty-six times more deadly than cyanide. Loss of muscle control, bodily functions—seizures, paralysis, difficulty breathing affects anyone who breathes or touches it."

I guess I'd watched too much television. I knew about sarin—discovered by accident in the late 1930s by a German scientist trying to develop a more powerful pesticide. Once again, something intended for a peaceful application bastardized for nefarious purposes.

"Won't the distribution team get hurt?"

Hans exploded. His face turned purple. He clenched his fists. His voice banged off the walls. "I have planned everything—*everything!*

There are no loose ends. I will be one of the people spraying the gas. Do you think I would endanger myself? I ask nothing of anyone in this group I am not willing to do." He fixed the questioner with a withering gaze. "I...know...my...business."

§§

After everyone was gone, Hans, Greta, and I relaxed with a beer. Well, they relaxed. I was pretty sure Hans couldn't wait to remove offending body parts from my anatomy. But something else was bothering me.

"So, what's the plan, Stan?" I asked.

"Pardon?"

I shook my head. "Never mind—a silly American expression," I said.

"Like, 'Keep on truckin','" he said.

"Sure," I said. "No, seriously. You aren't going to all this trouble for a little poison gas."

"There's nothing little about sarin," Greta said.

"I know," I said, "but something's not right. You steal the sarin, then use it right away. There's no leverage. You're after something else."

Hans chuckled...deep...ominous. "You are not as inept as I initially surmised, my friend," he said.

"Thanks...I think," I said. "So, what is it?"

Greta and Hans exchanged a knowing glance.

"You want access to the base," I said. "You're neutralizing everyone there because there's something you wa—oh, shit!"

"Precisely," Hans said.

"What kind?" I asked.

"They're going for something called a B-83—a nuke."

I thought I might puke. I tried to act nonchalant.

"Radical," I said, "but you won't be able to kill every soldier on the base."

"We will destabilize the personnel sufficiently. My associates have a group of well-trained combat veterans who will be poised in the woods at the perimeter. On my signal, they will crash through the front gates and mow down any resistance."

I thought of Shari. She might not be on an Army base, but there would be scores of other soldiers in harm's way.

"Tell me about the device."

"Weighs about 1100 kilos."

"How you getting it out?"

"Once the base is neutralized, we'll come in with a truck-mounted wench. It's all been carefully planned," he said—a father telling the world about his newborn.

"They call it an RNEP—Robust Nuclear Earth Penetrator."

"Powerful?" I asked.

"Is water wet?" Hans laughed at his own joke. I faked a chuckle and wondered what color my vomit would be. "Max yield is 1.2 megatons. The Hiroshima bomb was 15 *kilotons.*"

"Good Christ," I said. "What the fuck are you going to do with that?"

Hans looked at me with a mixture of pity and amusement. "You are such a child," he said. "Do you really think we would take the extreme step of ruining our country to make the Americans leave?"

"Not that it matters," Greta said.

Han's head snapped in her direction. "Sei verdammt noch mal still!"[2]

I looked at Hans. "No." I looked at Greta. "What?"

"Tell him, Hans," Greta said. "After all," she ran her tongue across her lips, "you've shared everything else."

Hans did not look happy. "Well, I don't really give a damn about the American occupation; they have already ruined our beloved homeland. History shows that, once they arrive, they never leave. All they do is take, and take, and take. It's easier to get rid of cockroaches."

The light in my usually foggy brain flickered. "So...you're not ransoming the nuke—you don't care if the soldiers leave or if America takes the nuclear weapons home."

"Nein."

A little more mental illumination. "You're going to sell the nuke to the highest bidder."

His smile was as broad as a Montana plain. "Ja."

The full plan blossomed in my head. "And you already have a winner."

"Sehr gut,"[3] he said.

---

2. "Shut the hell up!"

3. "Very good."

"Who is it?" I asked.

I imagined Casey Stengel had the same self-satisfied smile when reporters doubted his decision to replace the retiring Joe DiMaggio in centerfield with a rawboned kid from Oklahoma named Mickey Mantle.

"A private group—very mysterious," he said. "Might be Russian separatists...might be somebody else. I really do not care about their politics. My only concern is the gold they have promised. A total of half a billion dollars."

"And you will fly away to some remote island well outside the blast radius of any likely target with enough precious metal to live like a king."

"With his queen," Greta said.

"Well, it's a good plan. I'd appreciate knowing once the target is selected, so I can get the hell out of the way—you know, for old time's sake."

I zipped my jacket and made for the door. I had to let Mac in on the scheme.

Hans stepped in my way. "Not so fast, my friend," he said.

CHAPTER FIFTY-EIGHT

I was sitting in a van somewhere in the German woods. Had I been paying attention I might have had a general idea about our location, but my head was swimming. I was Adam's apple deep in a plot to murder hundreds of military personnel with the deadliest neurotoxin on the planet, and then to assist in stealing a nuclear bomb to be detonated in a location to be named later but undoubtedly one about which I would give a damn.

"These are the coordinates," Hans said. "Get the equipment and let's go."

"The equipment" consisted of two canteens, two flashlights, and a shovel. They were Eric Clapton on guitar and Ginger Baker on water and lights. I got to be the Cream bass player no one can remember—on shovel.

Hans studied the map and checked his compass. "I think fifty yards that way," he said.

He paced it off. Sure enough, we walked right up on a 6'x4' rectangle of freshly turned black German soil.

"This used to be someone's cattle farm," Greta said.

"Probably still is," I said.

"Nein," Hans said. "All the noise—the jets, the strafing and bombing practice, the howitzers—made the cattle skittish. Made the bulls impotent and the cows barren. No, the Americans ruined this too."

Better than turning it into a pile of radioactive ash.

Hans pointed. "Dort graben."[1]

I stabbed my spade into the ground and tossed away the first of many shovelfuls of soil. I didn't bother to ask if anyone else wanted a turn. No one was going to fall for a Tom Sawyer routine here. The dirt wasn't packed, but after some quick mental math, I figured if I was going six feet down, I was going to be shoveling a little over 450 cubic feet.

Once I was down to five feet, Hans spoke in a sharp whisper, "No more stabbing, Klaus. Gentle now. We don't want to puncture the canisters. Use your hands."

I got on my knees and began pulling. Pretty soon...

"Got something here. Cold...metal. This is it."

I dug and swept...swept and dug. By the time I'd uncovered four cannisters, I looked like I'd spent all night at a Grateful Dead concert. Each of the quartet lay in sort of a rope sling with a long rope at the top.

"Toss one up," Hans said.

I did.

He pulled the canister to the top with the care of a surgeon exploring a brain. We performed the ritual three more times.

"Check everywhere," Hans said, "Just in case there is a bonus."

---

1. "Dig there."

There wasn't. I jumped a little, got my hands over the top of the hole and began to hoist myself out. I had one foot out when I felt the unmistakable presence of a gun barrel against my temple.

"Get back in," Hans said.

I laughed. "Nothing else down there, dude," I said.

"I don't care," Hans said. "The other thing we promised the good colonel was a Südenboch."

"Huh?"

"You know, someone to take the blame for the theft of the gas."

I did the translation. "A patsy."

"Yes. And guess what?" Hans said, even though there was not a lot of guessing to be done. "You are it. It's perfect. You are a fugitive from Ireland hiding in plain sight as a bartender at a military base who decided to make a quick buck by conspiring with a rogue gang of thugs to blackmail the U.S. by stealing poison gas."

"God Almighty, does everyone know who I am?"

"Our organization cooperates with similar groups all over the world. You don't think we have contacts in the GLF? Greta knew who you were the first day you met."

I am not good at this.

Hans aimed the pistol. "You were double-crossed by the gang who did not trust you. The police will surmise they used you for your contacts...and *brains.*" He did the Bond villain laugh, I swear to the Holy Mother. "Bwahahahahah!"

I looked at Greta. "Greta...help...please.""No can do, Liebchen," she said.

"But what we had..." I knew it was a weak appeal, but it was all I had.

"What we had was strictly business," she said. She twitched, as if to turn away, but looked back. "And, so you know, you are nowhere near as big as Hans."

Hans cocked the revolver.

Greta threw her head back to cackle just before her throat exploded.

CHAPTER FIFTY-NINE

I never heard the spit from the barrel, but I heard the thud in Hans's chest just before the one through his left eye.

Except for the bullet holes, I might have suspected that I'd disturbed an unground hornet's nest. Stuff zipped past my chin and buzzed just beyond my nose. But I knew these insects carried a 7.62mm sting because they came from a very angry, very expertly wielded sniper rifle.

A stentorian voice came from the darkness behind me. "Statspolizei! Sie sind unzingelt!"[1]

But we weren't. The fire was coming from one direction—two at the most. I dove onto the ground and low crawled towards the woods with Hans's revolver in my hand. I rolled onto my back and fired the gun through my jacket to help cover the muzzle flash. I aimed so high I would have missed Chuck Nevitt.[2] I didn't want to hit

---

1. "State Police! You are surrounded!"

2. Never a great player, Chuck Nevitt played for 11 professional basketball teams in 11 years. He was 7'5".

anyone, but I had to make them think someone would fight back so they wouldn't rush me.

I reached the trees and took off. Bark spit at me as bullets struck the trees. I could hear crashing boots behind me.

How did the police get here? Think. You didn't tell Mac. You...didn't...tell...Mac. He knows something went sideways and ratted out the gang to the Staties. They've been trying to get these assholes for years.

I stopped for a second. I'd been saved. Or had I? Mac could have told the State Police where they could find the leaders, the members, and the gas. But he might have consulted with his old CIA roomie and decided the best course of action in this operation was to burn the asset.

Three more bullets whizzed past my head.

Shit the police think I'm one of the gang!

I was back in cop training. One of my instructors had been in combat in Korea. He told us if we were ever under attack and looking for escape not to run directly away "like a frightened bunny," but to *run around them.*

I sprinted off at a 45-degree angle. When I estimated I'd gone about 100 yards, I made as close to a 90-degree turn as I could. After another hundred, I did it again. I was encircling my pursuers. I could hear them. They were "inside" the box I was describing.

I ran wide again and found a boulder behind which to hide. I figured I'd be okay as long as the cops didn't have dogs. I stayed up most of the night listening for the baying of a dobie, or worse, a rottweiler. I was on the move before dawn and got back about 0500 to where the van had been. I stayed low and concealed until I was sure no one was around.

The van was gone...the cops were gone. The cannisters were gone. The bodies were gone. I was glad I didn't have to see them again.

I sat for a moment to catch my breath and to sort through a few things. I liked Greta in a weird sort of way. We might have been a good couple—well, before I found out about the "being used by the terrorist boyfriend to gain access to poison gas" thing. That put another dent in my already pockmarked heart. I wasn't sure how many more emotional punches it could take.

I walked along the road while the night resisted the morning's intrusion. The darkness gave ground begrudgingly until it retreated, determined to fight another time. It was not a joyful stroll. There were wolves and other critters I had no zeal to meet. There might also have been a contingent of heavily armed, more than pissed off Germans who would gleefully shoot me without the benefit of questioning.

I had to find Mac...assuming he hadn't set me up.

I headed for the base, having no other choice. Chief or Gunny could help me figure out what to do—if they didn't shoot me on sight as a traitor.

It was a chance I was willing to take. I was done.

The guard booth came into view a little after dawn. I'd like to claim my advanced survival skills brought me back. It was dumb luck.

"ID, please." The corporal on duty looked tired. He hadn't been relieved yet. Might be a break.

When he wandered over, I launched a fatigued charm offensive. "Eckhart—right, Corporal Eckhart—shot and a beer? One a night and a game of darts, right?"

"Yeah, right. You're the bartender...ah...Klaus. Sorry, it took a while. Been out here eight fricking hours. Got the shit assignment for losing the dart tournament to Charlie Company. Next time, no shot with the beer."

"Copy that," I said.

"ID, please."

"About that," I said. "Had a little encounter last evening..."

"You get mugged? What the hell happened to your jacket? Looks burned. I need to call the lieutenant and fill out a report."

"Not really," I said. "Let's call it the kind of encounter I'd rather my mother never know about. There was a girl involved, you know—not the kind you take home for Sunday dinner with the folks."

"Oh shit, man. Those working girls are tough. Which one was it?"

"Can't remember man—too much booze—too much..."

I shrugged and let the corporal's imagination finish the sentence.

"I get it," he said. "Okay, sign in and go sleep it off in the back room of the club."

"Roger that," I said.

McClonkey was wiping the bar.

"What the hell are you doing here?" I asked. "It's 0700."

"Never left," he said. "Fell asleep in the back. Woke up. Decided I'd get things cleaned up for you. Didn't want to be a dick."

"Thanks," I said, "but I don't feel like working tonight."

"Hell you don't. I'm off for the next two days and Gunny's on leave with his old lady. If you ain't pouring, the club ain't openin'—and there'll be a fuckin' riot."

He was gone in twenty minutes. I locked the door, went into the back, and slept for five hours.

Dreams—no, more like hallucinations—haunted me. I remembered everything...

...the escapee leaping from the trunk of the car at the roadblock and beating me senseless...only this time he had horns and razorblades for fingertips...

...Billi leering at me in bed and convincing me to stay with the GLF just before she morphed into a naked Hans...

...Greta's throat splitting like a bloody pinata...except when I looked at her body, it was Gwendolyn's.

I only awakened because someone was pounding on the bar's back door.

CHAPTER SIXTY

I unlocked the door. Before it was halfway open, Mac had barged in and had me pinned against the wall.

"Where the fuck have you been?" he asked.

Something snapped—something primal, something prehistoric. Must have been adrenaline because I grabbed Mac by the front of his shirt and slung him up against the wall. His feet were about ten inches off the floor.

"You set me up, you son of a bitch." I was almost frothing at the mouth. "Fuckin' police everywhere. Bullets screaming past my head. I ran for my life." I took a breath. Mac's feet reacquired the floor. I started to sob. "And I ruined my best jacket."

Even though I was hunched over and weeping, I braced for a punch. It never came.

Mac put his hand on my shoulder and guided me to a chair. "I get it, kid," he said. "Scary as hell when people are shooting at you. Damn thing went sideways. Let me tell you what happened?"

I nodded, unable to get enough air to speak.

"Higgins and I expected you back. You never showed. Frankly, I thought you were probably dead—that you'd been made, but I didn't want to take a chance."

"I...appre...appreciate...y...y...your confidence." I wiped my nose on my sleeve. The deluge from my eyes had stopped. My eyelids felt like they weighed 100 pounds each. I looked at the little cot in the corner of the room with longing.

"Stay with me long enough to hear this, kid, then you can sleep. I'll even cover your shift if you want."

"You can tend bar?"

"Kid, I can tend bar, fly a helicopter, work with C-4, and translate Dostoyevsky from the original. And those aren't even my strong points."

He made me laugh. It felt good. "No shit?" I asked.

"Every bit of it is true, but my Russian is a little rusty," he said.

I motioned for him to continue.

"About 2000 hours, Higgins and I made the decision to get the locals in on the deal. They know all about the gang's existence, but none of the fine print—like where they meet and the people involved. But there have been enough bank robberies and stuff that the cops knew it all had to be connected. So, Higgins told them about the gas and the pick-up and stuff. They were waiting while you guys dug."

"You forget to tell them about me?"

"Well." Mac winced. "The cops got so excited about everything; they hung up before we could."

"There're these things called radios," I said. "Maybe you've heard about them?"

"Couldn't risk it," Mac said. "Hans is sharp enough to monitor police band. We took a big chance calling the station, but we had to. Anyway, the unit commander reported back that they had taken down two of the perps and said one got away. When they said it was the guy doing the digging, we figured it was you and told them to pull back. Apparently, a few of the officers didn't get the message."

"Lucky for me it was the ones who flunked their small arms accuracy test," I said. "But the guy on the sniper rifle was dead on."

"I saw the bodies," Mac said. "Glad I didn't have to ID Hans. Not a lot left. The slug took the girl's head clean off."

I did not need that. "Too much information," I said.

"Sorry," he said, "but war is hell—and make no mistake, this is war."

He got up and left the room. I was asleep again in less than two minutes. This time, the angels kept the dreams at bay.

I awoke to the sounds of Wild Cherry's one-hit-wonder, "Play That Funky Music, White Boy." I splashed some water on my face, gargled, and walked out to behind the bar. It was dark outside. The clock over the bar read 2225.

Despite his boasts, Mac tended bar with all the grace of an NFL lineman dancing *Swan Lake*. Patrons were three deep and screaming for service. I took care of the backlog in about five minutes and the hubbub reduced to a mild rumble.

"Nice work," he said.

"You do spy shit—I tend bar," I said.

"Should stay in my lane, huh?"

"Yep."

He smiled. For the first time I could remember, he didn't look like a mongoose getting ready to outsmart a cobra. He handed me an envelope.

"This my pay?" I asked.

"Does it feel like your pay?"

"A little light," I said.

"Then it ain't your pay," he said.

"What is it."

He told me and I collapsed to the floor.

"Say it again," I said.

"You're going home, kid."

§§

My hangover was mostly over by the time my military flight landed in Lisbon. From there, it would be commercial to the U.S. Mac had whisked me out of town on the first available. No time to find Shari—though it mattered little. Mac promised he would say goodbye to Chief and Gunny for me.

No one else in Germany mattered.

But I had a little business left in Portugal. I had to have a farewell Guinness with Oisin.

And I had to retrieve Lucky.

I got him safely stowed away in the plane, took my seat, and waited until we were at cruising altitude before I read the letter Mac had given me again.

Mr. Caldemeyer,

Well done. Your work on the Jaeger-Vogel case was first-rate, especially considering your lack of training in counterterrorism. You obviously have a gift for this sort of work. In my opinion, shared by many in my command, you should not waste your time writing traffic tickets and flagging down motorists with broken taillights.

To that end, I have spoken with Bill Casey. You would know him as the Director of the Central Intelligence Agency. On my recommendation, he has agreed to accept you as a provisional candidate in his next class at the Farm, the CIA's training facility in Langley, VA. (Technically it is the Armed Forces Experimental Training Activity run by the Department of Defense.)

Under separate cover, you will receive contact information. Use the time before the class commences to reconnect with your friends and family. It would behoove you to get into the best physical shape you can achieve. Work on your German; it needs help. Training is rigorous. My recommendation only goes so far. If you cannot "cut the mustard," they will dismiss you from the program and you will be back to crossing-guard duty in Upstate New York.

You have earned the thanks of a grateful nation. Most citizens will never know of your exploits. Such is the nature of our calling—to serve in anonymity. I hope we will meet again.

With respect,
Colonel Brendan Hughes

EPILOGUE

Seven hours later we touched down at Newark Airport. I walked down the stairway and waited by the cargo bay while the ground crew unloaded Lucky. He jumped from his crate, put his front paws on my shoulders, licked my face, then stared at me with a look that said, "Do not ever do that to me again."

I looked at a member of the crew. "Baggage claim?"

"Military or civilian?"

I had to think a minute. "Military," I said.

"Terminal C," he said. "Right over there. Carousel number four. Your stuff will be mixed up with the civilian baggage. Sorry."

I didn't care. I grabbed Lucky's leash, and we headed in the direction he'd indicated. When we got close to the door, I put on my sunglasses. A kid in an Army uniform stood at attention. He looked three years shy of military service eligibility.

ROTC. He's getting his high school service hours.

"Sorry, sir," he said. "No pets allowed."

"Munitions specialist," I said. "He saves lives.""Got some ID, sir?" he said.

I faked going for my wallet, then pulled my shades down the bridge of my nose and gave him my best Mac-the-Spy hard stare.

"I can show you, but I'd have to kill you," I said. I unleashed the ol' "this isn't really a grin" grin, so he would know I meant business.

"Roger that, sir," he said.

I wasn't sure why we were picking up my bag. I was probably going to burn everything anyway. Mom and Dad knew I was flying in, but they weren't coming to get me. Dad's back was acting up and Mom didn't feel comfortable making the long drive by herself. I'd either rent a car or hitch a ride.

The air inside was thick with cigar smoke and fetid New Jersey air. Everyone was in a hurry. People bumped into one another, then glared. Everyone was loud. Frantic mothers shouted for their children to "Quit playing with that and come back here!" All the kids were named "Joey."

Damn, it was good to be home.

The carousel started singing its metallic melody and arriving passengers rushed forward en masse with the certainty theirs would be the first bag. I waited. Mine was the fifth. I had just reached for the handle when someone—or something—hit me from behind. I pitched forward but managed not to fall.

Oh Christ, I made it all the way back and some gung-ho Brit had decided to fulfill a personal vendetta.

Instinct drove my hand under my jacket for the pistol I wasn't carrying. I righted myself and turned with my palms raised.

A little boy looked up at me like I'd caught him stealing candy at the local Wa-Wa.

"Thorry, mith-ter," he said. He pointed behind me.

I turned and grabbed his bag. It wasn't hard to deduce his suitcase was the one with Alvin and the Chipmunks. "Here you go, buddy," I said.

"Thanksth." He looked around.

"Where are your parents?" I asked.

His eyes scanned the crowd. The sea of kneecaps parted long enough for him to spot a woman's back. She was bending over a stroller.

"Mama," he said—and pointed.

I took his hand and walked him over.

"I believe this belongs to you," I said.

The woman bolted upright so fast, I took a step back. Survival instincts die slowly. Her back was still to me, but I could see the tension in her shoulders. When she spun around, I knew why.

Gwendolyn!

THE END

A Glimpse into Book Three...

O'Malley never saw it coming. He was tired with a belly full of Tullamore Dew. Worst of all, he wasn't minding his six.

I was in trouble because I was sloppy. I had forgotten the first rule of working undercover: Trust no one. Clive Byrne owned the bar where I was staked out. Brennan's Pub. It was so Irish, it was almost corny: dark, smelling of grease from the kitchen and Guinness from the oak floors. There were so many dart boards I had to be careful when I served a table lest I catch a nail in the ear. Whenever the band took a break, some joker would take to bellowing "The Fields of Athenry" or, if it was a poser, "Danny Boy."

I was tending bar at Brennan's, my first posting since graduating from eighteen months of training at The Farm in Langley. It had been tough. I was the oldest member in the class by at least ten years. Sure, I had more real-world experience, but my classmates were working with twenty-two year old bodies and something else I didn't have.

Hope.

They figured saving the world was still possible. They had visions of Utopia, where all the boys and girls would frolic with unicorns and watch cartoons while angel food cake floated to earth like manna, and we all lived in harmony. I knew better. I knew the world was a savage and perhaps irredeemable place where humans feasted on one another like wolves over a moose carcass. I'd survived imprisonment, false charges, life as a fugitive, mayhem, bombings, and a round of golf in Ireland. I'd been loved and abandoned, loved and rejected, loved and betrayed. Life was not a bowl of cherries; it was an unending, heaping serving of relentless disillusionment.

O'Malley was Clive's friend. I thought O'Malley was a good guy, so I figured Clive was too. I forgot Rule #1.

CIA training teaches a lot of worthless stuff. And it leaves out a few things – like which type of pliers works best when pulling out someone's fingernails. I would have used a pair of Vise-Grips. Ol' William S. Peterson of DeWitt, Nebraska, knew what he was doing when he invented those suckers. They *never* let go. But Hooper, some guy O'Malley used for "body and fender work," was a little old school. He went with your standard, garden variety carpenter's pincers. I guess he figured he could get closer to my finger before he yanked.

Hurt like a sumbitch. But my training had taught me something about psychological toughness – mind over matter – that sort of stuff. "If you don't mind, it won't matter." That's what my training officer always said. So, I tried to step out of my body and find somewhere the pain didn't exist. Not completely successful because just about the time I found my Happy Place, O'Malley yanked out two more. Then he used a Barlow knife to etch a nice "1″ in all three denuded fingers.

"Need to help da fishes fin' ya when we toss ya overboard."

The nail removal took place after Hooper and O'Malley had used my face for a speed bag with a precision that would have made Sugar Ray Leonard jealous. They didn't just flail away. They focused on areas they knew would hurt. Almost anyone can take a punch on the jaw. They never hit me there a single time.

"Don't wanna knock ya out, lad," Hooper said. "Wantcha here t' enjoy ever moment."

He flayed the skin on my cheekbones with his bare knuckles. Michael DeBakey would have been jealous of his surgical precision. Hooper was a master. He did not telegraph his punches. I never knew when he would hit me again even though I was wide awake and not blindfolded. Every punch introduced a new level of pain. But waiting for the next one was almost worse because I knew how much it was going to hurt.

I don't know how they figured out about me. The Company had put me in Brennan's as a "listener." All I was supposed to do was pay attention to conversations about the IRA. Someone somewhere in D.C. thought Brennan's was serving as a conduit for money going to "Freedom Fighters" in Belfast. In Langley's assessment, I was too green to be an active field operative despite my experiences in Ireland, Spain, and Germany. I'd successfully evaded law enforcement in about a half-dozen countries and almost single-handedly brought down a terrorist cell in Germany, but Uncle Sam did not give me any credit for my extracurricular activities.

A lot of the spy-craft classes were bunk, at least in my experience, but with my hand merrily throbbing away, I remembered one tidbit an instructor had shared. "Blood is your friend."

I'd been in a fetal position since Hooper and O'Malley had gone topside. Now, I sat up and forced my hand over my head. Every nerve in my body protested but I kept my hand aloft until I could feel a warm trickle oozing across my wrists. I began working my left hand out of the cuff. The blood worked better than WD-40. I ignored the rising discomfort. The wrist got rawer with every twist. And then...

My hand was free. I pushed the ratchet all the way through the cheek plate. I gripped the cuff in my right hand with the pointy end extended between my index and third fingers like a giant, stainless-steel claw. Wolverine would have been proud.

I crept up the stairway and cracked the door. O'Malley was shouting to Hooper, who was walking along the pier.

"Bring back some decent stout. I won't drink that Yankee shite."

Hooper held up his hand with the middle finger extended and walked out of sight. O'Malley shook his head, mumbled something, then sat in a deck chair with his back to me.

Thirty seconds later, I'd buried the toothed barb of the handcuff into his carotid.

He should have watched his six.

§§

Sign up to find out where Conor's adventures will take him next!

linktr.ee/authorpatrickdevaney

ABOUT THE AUTHOR

Patrick DeVaney published his first book, *Two Million Steps*, in 2017, a recounting of the author's challenges, achievements, and life-changing experience while walking the five-hundred-mile Camino de Santiago from southwest France to northwest Spain. His most recent achievement is his High Crimes Series, a foray into fiction entitled *High Crimes Against the Crown,* and Book II entitled *The Flight Across Europe*, draws loosely on his early career as a police officer and many of the destinations he has visited.

Born in Ticonderoga, NY, in the Adirondack Mountains, Pat has lived most of his life in the Albany area. His day job is in the residential real estate industry. He spends his leisure time writing, traveling, long-distance walking, reading, and enjoying his family and grand-dog, Lucky. He enjoys assisting other pilgrims with their forthcoming ventures along the Camino.

Pat's future plans include the third and final installment of the High Crimes Series to be released in 2024. He will soon return to Europe for his eighth sojourn on the Camino where he hopes to feed his imagination and to help bring more books to life.

www.ingramcontent.com/pod-product-compliance
Lightning Source LLC
Chambersburg PA
CBHW071227300726
48975CB00002B/321